WHISPERS OF THE HEART

K.A. MOLL

JOHNSTON PUBLIC LIBRARY
6700 MERLE HAY RD
JOHNSTON IA 50131-1269

WITHDRAWN

DEDICATION

For Dana—a dear friend who in the blink of an eye became family.

AUTHOR'S NOTE

Thanks to my wife for being the best wife ever and to my fantastic beta reader team—Kay, Dana, Kathy, Maureen, Paula, Shiela, and Laure.

PUBLICATION INFORMATION

Whispers of the Heart © 2018 K.A. Moll

All rights reserved. No part of this publication may be reproduced, distributed, or transmitted in any form or by any means, including photocopying, recording, or other electronic or mechanical methods, without the prior written permission of the publisher, except in the case of brief quotations embodied in reviews.

- First Edition 2018, Triplicity Publishing
- Second Edition: 2019, KAM Books, LLC
- Cover/Interior Design: KAM Books, LLC

WHISPERS OF THE HEART

SYNOPSIS

Days after completing her fellowship in pediatric ophthalmology, thirty-five-year-old Aki Williams travels from her home in Los Angeles to a small town in Illinois, interviewing for a job that she doesn't want. What she does want is to meet her biological sister, Jack Camdon, a sister whom she didn't know existed until she dreamt of her. Upon their meeting, many things surprise her—that Jack's a lesbian with a wife and children, that she's a dreamer who dreams in spirit animals, and that she's a medicine woman, deeply rooted in the Ojibwe culture.

Three years ago on Sunday, forty-three-year-old professor of archaeology, Carsyn Lyndon, lost her parents and her wife in a tragic accident. Since she's suffered from PTSD and loneliness. She's kind-hearted and handsome but dates no one. When she meets Aki at her four-year-old Godson's birthday party, they're incredibly attracted to one another, and those feelings intensify during a family camping trip —a particularly interesting development for Aki since prior to that she'd never considered that she might be a lesbian.

As Aki comes to terms with her sexuality, Carsyn renews a vow not to make the same mistake twice—a mistake that had devastating consequences. With seemingly no middle ground, an accident will bring them together, forcing them to re-examine their priorities. But will love, even love at first sight, be enough for them to move forward as a couple?

PROLOGUE

ABOUT THIRTY-FIVE YEARS AGO

It was her daily routine; to get up, dress, and comb her hair before making her way to the playground. Before that, it was the park bench, the one across from the daycare. And before that, albeit for a short time, it was the neonatal unit. Routines. Her psychiatrist had said they were good for her. He'd said they were the key to getting better. And she wanted to get better. She had to get better. So, she did as he suggested. She got up each morning by ten o'clock, dressed in a floral-print cotton dress, and combed her long black hair. Thirteen strokes. No more, no less. She did everything that he suggested. Except one thing, staying away from her. Even the court orders, barring her from the house, the neonatal unit, the daycare, and the playground, couldn't make her do that.

"Good morning," the teacher said, dust wafting as he dropped home plate. "Can I help you with something?"

"No," Wabun responded, remembering to smile and make eye contact, "I played softball as a girl. I was just admiring your diamond."

"Thanks," he said. "Pitcher's mound needs some work. I guess that'll be tonight's project."

"Looks good the way it is," Wabun said, remembering to smile, but not too broadly. "I'll bet you're setting up for your next class," she added. "Care if I sit on the bench?"

"Not at all," he responded. "Fourth graders. A couple of the girls are decent. They're fun to watch." He smiled, stepping off to position bases one, two, and three as his students emerged single-file from the red brick, two-story building.

Wabun leaned forward, her gaze fixed on the tallest girl in the class. *Shame on them,* she thought, *cutting her beautiful black locks so that she looks like a boy.* She touched her stomach in response to a healthy kick. Carrying high, she was expecting a girl, her second daughter. Her heart pounded against her chest wall as the group of children began counting off.

"One"

"Two"

"One"

"Two"

"One," the tall masculine-looking girl called out.

Wabun's eyes teemed with tears, her breath catching in her throat. It was the first time in all these years that she'd gotten close enough to hear her voice.

CHAPTER 1

*A*ki's gaze shifted from the road to the water, and back to the road. *Pay attention to your driving,* she told herself. *There's little to no chance that you're related to anyone on that pontoon boat.* But there it was, right behind the house, puttering along with its bright red canopy, six seats, and three people on board—a man, a woman, and a teenage girl. *He could be her husband,* she thought, squinting, her head touching the driver's window. *And the girl could be their daughter.* She bit her lower lip reflecting on the things she'd learned about Jackie Lynn Camdon these past few months—her name, her birthdate, her address, and her place of employment. She'd even read articles about her involvement in a widely publicized dispute over the use of pesticides. But with all of that, she didn't know anything of importance—not if her hair was long and black; not if she was healthy; not if she was married; and not if she had a child or children. As her tires rumbled from the bridge to the blacktop, she stole a glance over her shoulder. The boat was still there, still moseying along the shoreline. A horn blared in the distance. She blinked, and the clangor was on top of her. She jerked her wheel, the wide-eyed driver swerving around. He glared, giving her the finger as he passed by her window. She took a deep breath, her heart pounding against her chest wall. Her blood pressure felt high, she was sweating, and her thoughts were jumbled. In a fight or flight situation, the hypothalamus signals the release of adrenaline and other stress hormones. She blew air between her lips, pulled over, and willed her body to wind down. Minutes passed before she made her way through the beautiful red brick columns.

"Your destination is on your left," the female voice announced in a matter of fact tone, a tone unworthy of what was about to transpire.

Aki slowed, her tongue seeking out moisture as if it were a defining rod. She activated her signal, navigating the driveway. Beautifully rustic, the house had stacked stone, handsome wooden shakes, and a porch surrounding its front and sides. It was the kind of house that one day when her student loans were paid off, she'd build for herself. She took a long drink of water. *You still have time,* she thought, *time to back out and drive off. Go in, and this gets far more complicated.* She pursed her lips, knowing that driving off wasn't an option. She couldn't just go back to her hotel, not after the dreams, not after all she'd gone through to find her. And God knows how long it would be before she'd be able to get back to this part of the country. As a newly hired physician, time-off would be hard to come by. *You could always accept a position here,* she told herself. She had no guarantee of an offer but felt it highly probable. To date, ninety percent of her interviews had resulted in one. She took a breath, exited her car, and walked the cobblestone sidewalk. *You don't know that she'll want you in her life,* she reminded herself, stepping onto the porch. *And if she doesn't, do you really want to set up your practice in Illinois, a state known for cornfields and soybeans?* She shook her head, responding, "No." Given her druthers, she'd practice near Los Angeles, a sprawling metropolis known for its diversity and Mediterranean climate. She'd gone to high school in Torrance, just eighteen miles south, a couple of miles from the ocean. It would be hard to settle for another part of the country, especially one known for cornfields and soybeans. Her shoulders tightened, lifting her finger to the doorbell. She swallowed at the sound of footsteps skidding to a halt.

"You're not my grandma," the little girl blurted out, opening the door. "She was supposed to be here by now." Like Aki, the child had long black hair, dark eyes, and high cheekbones.

"No," Aki responded, smiling, "I'm definitely not your grandma." She lowered to her eye level. "I'm here to see your mommy if she's home."

"She is," the child answered. "She's in the basement feeding our dogs." She pressed her lips together, frowning. "She said I have to leave you on the porch until she gets up here." She tilted her head, making seriously cute eye contact. "But you don't have to worry," she added, "she said it wouldn't be very long."

"I'm not worried," Aki chuckled. "The longer she takes, the longer you and I get to talk." She held her gaze warmly. "My name's Aki," she added, "what's yours?"

"Lizzy," the little girl responded, her eyes twinkling in her smile.

"What a pretty name," Aki commented. "I'll bet it's short for Elizabeth."

"It is," Lizzy giggled. "That's what my grandma goes by."

"Elizabeth is a wonderful name," Aki said, seeing her five-year-old self in her eyes, "but I think I like Lizzy better."

"Me too," Lizzy said, smiling. "My mama says Elizabeth is too formal a name for someone with as charming a personality as mine."

"I'd say your mama's right," Aki responded, chuckling. *What a cutie*, she thought, her mind still absorbing the likelihood that they were related to one another. "So," she teased, "I'll bet you're in high school, right?"

Lizzy giggled again. "No," she said, "Kindergarten. I just started." She furrowed her brow. "My mommy says she's gonna blink and I'll be in college."

"Seems like your mommy's a pretty smart woman," Aki commented, her eyes widening with her nod.

"Uh-huh, she is," Lizzy responded.

"So, Kindergarten," Aki continued pensively, "it's a fantastic grade, you'll like it."

"I already do," Lizzy answered, clearly bored with the topic. "You like my dress?" she asked, swaying so that the lower ruffles lifted-up.

"I do," Aki answered, adding, "and your pink sequined leotards."

Lizzy twirled saying she picked out the outfit.

"You did a good job," Aki responded, "I really like it." She looked up when a woman in her mid-forties stepped into the foyer. She had shoulder-length auburn hair, curled under, and green eyes. A red-haired boy, maybe as much as a year younger than Lizzy came up beside her. Like Lizzy, he was adorable; sporting pleated navy shorts, a pinstriped blue shirt, and a bow tie. He blushed when she caught his eye. Lizzy was probably going to a party with him and his mother.

"Hello," the woman greeted, her eyes narrowing as she studied her. "May I help you?"

"Hello," Aki answered, never as much a loss for words as she was right now. "My name is Aki Williams."

"Courtney," the woman said, extending her hand.

"Pleased to meet you," Aki responded, sucking in a breath. "You don't know me," she continued, "but—."

Courtney lifted her hand, saying, "Hold on a minute." She placed her palm on each child's shoulder with eye contact. "I want you to go into the living room while I talk with our visitor," she said softly. She cocked her head, lifting an eyebrow. "If you'd like," she continued, pausing for both to become attentive, "you may choose one small gift from your pile and open it."

"Now?" the little boy asked, his green eyes enlarging to the size of saucers. "Before everybody gets here for cake and ice cream?"

"Yes, Charlie," Courtney responded, kissing the top of his head. "Unless you're concerned that I've made a poor decision in allowing it."

"Come on," Lizzy urged, taking the boy by his hand, "before she changes her mind." She called out, "Nice to meet you," as they rounded the corner.

"You too," Aki called back. "Cute kids," she commented, meeting Courtney's eye with a smile.

"Thanks," Courtney responded. "And sorry for the interruption," she added, "you were saying?"

"I was explaining that you don't know me," Aki answered, "and preparing to apologize for showing up without calling." She took a soft breath and exhaled. "I assure you that under normal circumstances, that's not how I operate."

Courtney cocked her head, studying her.

"I'm looking for a woman by the name of Jackie Lynn Camdon," Aki continued. "Native American, several years older than I am. I hope I'm at the right house."

"You are," Courtney responded, adding, "Jack's my wife." She increased the width of the opening in the doorway. "She'll be home shortly. Come in."

"Thanks," Aki responded, reminding herself to breathe as she stepped into the foyer.

CHAPTER 2

*I*nteresting, Courtney thought, reading her guest with the skill of an accomplished trial lawyer. *She knows Jack well enough to know her middle name, a name she hasn't used since high school, and yet she was surprised that she had a wife.* She smiled kindly, glancing into the living room to check on her children.

"They play well together," Aki commented, stepping beside her.

"Yes, they do," Courtney said quietly, "but not always this well." She looked over her glasses to meet Aki's eye. "Pure luck that they both opened a toy on their wish list. Had one opened a package containing clothing, well, it'd be a different story."

Aki laughed, nodding. "I'm sure it would," she responded. "Nothing worse than ripping open a beautifully wrapped package to find cotton underwear."

Courtney chuckled. "No, I guess not," she responded, feeling lighter. "You have kids?" she asked, smiling.

Aki pressed her lips together, looking off. "No," she said quietly, "but someday I hope to." She took a breath, changing the subject. "So, what's the occasion?" she asked. "I assume it's someone's birthday."

"Charlie's," Courtney responded, winking when she caught his eye. "He'll be four at eight-sixteen tonight."

"At eight-sixteen?" Aki responded.

"Alright, alright," Courtney answered with a quiet chuckle, "I admit it, I'm clinging to the time I have left being the mother of a three-year-old." She shook her head, her tone taking on a nostalgic quality. "It seems like just yesterday that Jack buckled him into his car seat for his first trip home from the hospital."

"They grow up fast," Aki replied kindly.

"Yes, they do," Courtney responded with a shallow sigh.

Aki nodded toward the coffee table. "Two piles," she commented, "one wrapped for a girl and the other for a boy. You got them both something."

"Always have," Courtney responded.

"That's nice," Aki said, her voice softening, and her eyes sparkling in her smile. "It makes your celebration of a birthday a celebration of family."

"It does," Courtney responded, warmth radiating through her body. "Lizzy made out like a bandit this year, two gifts from Charlie and one from us. He got her a Chewing Gum Lab." She shook her head, looking over her glasses. "Thank goodness she didn't open that one while we were talking," she added, "or I'd have had gum all over my new white carpet."

"The goddess, Fortuna, looked kindly upon you," Aki responded, smiling.

"Yes, she did," Courtney chuckled, stepping over to her peacock green granite countertop. "Care for a cup of coffee?" she asked. "I've got lots of flavors, regular and decaf."

"I'd love one," Aki responded, sliding a high back chair from underneath the kitchen table, and sitting down. "Anything with chocolate."

Courtney looked over, lifting the top on her Keurig coffee maker. "So, how do you know my wife?" she asked, popping in a Mocha K-cup.

"I don't," Aki responded, sucking a breath to the bottom of her lungs. "I've just wanted to for the longest time."

* * *

Jack moved across the lecture hall, sitting momentarily on the edge of the windowsill. "Raise your hand," she said, "if you remember the flurry of headlines several years back telling us that if we didn't take immediate action, the bees were going to die." She scanned, noting that many students had their hand held high. "Well, let me tell you," she went on, "that situation was far worse than was ever reported. I know because my work was at the center of the controversy." She walked to the large desk situated near the podium, returning with a stack of documents stapled in the upper left-hand corner. "As the crisis was heating up," she went on, "I authored several articles against the directive of my superiors, all published in leading scientific journals." She counted off enough for each row, handing them to the student on the aisle. "In those articles, I summarized my research findings, findings that once made public, sounded an alarm that reverberated from one end of the country to the other." She swallowed, adding, "My actions nearly got me fired."

A young woman wearing a t-shirt and shorts raised her hand.

Jack glanced at her seating chart, calling on her.

"Why, Dr. Camdon?" she asked. "Why'd you do it if it meant maybe losing your job?"

Jack removed her glasses, trying not to re-live the pain of the times. "The short answer? Because it was the right thing to do," she responded. "Because bee colonies were collapsing all over the world." Her voice quieted, so much so that the shuffling of feet and book bags on the wooden floor fell silent. "It wasn't something I wanted to do," she added. "I'm not usually one to cause trouble. But I had to because no one else was stepping up to confront our government's dishonesty. The people had a right to know what was at stake— apples, lemons, limes, melons, zucchini, onions, carrots—the list goes on and on." She looked up. "I was afraid that the world's food supply would disappear before my eyes." She took a breath and exhaled. "I stepped up because I was terrified that if I didn't, there'd be no pollinators."

"So, if it was that bad," another student asked, "why did your boss say you couldn't talk about it?"

Jack took a breath, trying to push her wife's role in the situation out of mind. "Because high-ranking officials, many of whom were under the enticement of powerful companies and lobbyists in the pesticide industry, decided that withholding the information was better for business." She exhaled, checking her notes, and decided to wrap up fifteen minutes early. "Can anyone tell me what was causing the colonies to collapse?" she asked. As she scanned for a volunteer, she caught sight of her old friend stepping through the rear door of her classroom. "Come in, Dr. Lyndon," she said, smiling warmly. "We're just finishing up."

Carsyn nodded, raking through her short crop of brown hair as she made her way to take a seat near the podium.

"So, who can tell me?" Jack continued. "Who can tell me why the bee colonies were collapsing?" She nodded to a brown-haired woman in the second row. "Ms. Ash?"

"Because they were using neonicotinoids on crops like crazy back then," she responded.

"Yes, they were," Jack said, nodding. "Agriculture's use of neonicotinoids, neonics, was without a doubt responsible for the problem." She switched off her PowerPoint. "Read the articles and chapter two in your supplemental textbook," she said, exhaling as her students filed out.

"I told you that you were meant to teach," Carsyn greeted, adjusting her lightweight jacket. "And judging from your packed lecture hall, I'd say the students are excited about your new pollinator curriculum."

"So far, so good," Jack responded.

"You're a natural," Carsyn said, sitting on the desk with one foot on the floor and the other dangling.

Jack shook her head. "I'm not so sure about that," she responded, "but I'm trying."

"You are," Carsyn insisted. "Never seen you tackle anything that you didn't end up doing well."

"A month in, and still there's a steep learning curve," Jack responded. "Developing a curriculum, teaching, grading, midterms, and finals are all new to me. At least in my old job, I felt like I knew what I was doing."

"First semester jitters," Carsyn responded, patting her back, "You'll get over them. Next semester, you'll be an old pro."

"Hope so," Jack said, shaking her head with a smile. "Still plan on working us in for cake and ice cream tonight?"

"Wouldn't miss it for the world," Carsyn answered, "but I won't be able to stay too long. I want to get the campsite set up tonight. Students aren't due until three, but experience says they'll start arriving by nine." She looked up. "You guys still coming?"

"You bet we are," Jack answered, "but we're not leaving until late tomorrow morning. Charlie's so excited," she added, "you know, getting to go on a dig with a real archeologist."

"Yeah, right," Carsyn responded, rolling her eyes. "An archaeologist who just happens to be his Godmother. A dig with me and a bunch of freshmen, oh yeah, that's gonna be exciting." She exhaled, meeting Jack's eye. "I'm sure if you'd have asked him, he'd have said he preferred his usual trip to Disney World."

"Don't be so sure," Jack responded, "he's pretty into old bones. Plus, last year he seemed kind of bored. This'll be something different. I think he'll have fun."

"Maybe so," Carsyn said, "but I doubt his mother will. I'll bet she's never, not once in her life, slept in a tent or used an outhouse."

"No," Jack chuckled, "but the experience will be good for her. I must admit it did take a bit of talking though. That, and I had to agree to make lunches and feed the dogs for all of November."

"I figured you'd pay a price," Carsyn said. "Thanks for being a good pal." She crinkled her brow, adding, "I'm surprised she didn't bargain a little harder."

"Oh, she bargained hard alright," Jack said, raising an eyebrow. "It's just that she had a gigantic debt to pay off." She made a face. "Remember when, out of the goodness of my heart, I escorted Elizabeth to the spring gala at the Country Club?"

"Yep, that looked painful," Carsyn responded.

"Oh, for the good old days when she'd have sooner died than have people know that I was her daughter-in-law," Jack added, her eyes widening.

"Gertrude and I, we never had problems," she responded, her gaze becoming unfocused. "Always did enjoy one another's company."

"Yeah, I remember that year she spent Christmas with you guys," Jack said, smiling. "It was easy to tell she was crazy about you."

"She was," Carsyn said, pressing her lips together, and nodding. "Still is. I should get up to see her one of these days." She lifted her eyes. "It's just hard, you know? I mean, it's like we don't have anything to talk about anymore." She shook her head, adding, "Just the accident, what flowers we have on the graves, and that's about all."

"It takes time," Jack responded with a gentle touch on her shoulder.

"It'll be three years on Sunday," Carsyn said, swallowing.

"I know," Jack responded. "And that's why you'll be entertaining company."

"I'm okay," Carsyn answered, meeting her eye, "Really, I am. You don't have to go."

"I know," Jack said, touching her arm, "but I want to. It'll be fun and Charlie will love it." She took a soft breath, holding her gaze gently. "You're still not dating, pal...And the accident, well, it's always on your mind."

"I date," Carsyn countered.

"Yeah, sure," Jack responded.

"I date," Carsyn repeated, "I date when it feels right." She shook her head slowly. "And with regard to the accident, the funerals, and all that followed, I'm not sure that'll ever completely leave my mind." She shook her head, looking off. "I mean, I lost my wife and my parents that day. I don't think that's something you ever totally get over."

"No," Jack said softly, "probably not."

CHAPTER 3

"I'm home," Jack announced, the front door clicking shut behind her.

"Mama's home," Lizzy called out, running toward her.

"Mama," Charlie squealed, zooming around his sister for the first hug.

"Well, there's my birthday boy," Jack greeted, wrapping her arms around him.

"Mommy let us open a package," Lizzy announced.

"She did, huh," Jack responded, grinning. "Well, aren't you the lucky ones?"

"Uh-huh," Charlie said, adding, "and guess what I opened."

"I'm sure I don't know," Jack said, tilting her head. "I guess you're gonna have to tell me."

"Matchbook cars," Charlie answered, "from you and mommy."

"Cool," Jack answered. "Did you get the ones you wanted?"

"Uh-huh," Charlie said, adding, "the Dune Chaser, the Garbage Gulper, and the Swamp Raider."

"I'm glad you like them," Jack responded, setting her briefcase next to the roll top.

"Will you help me put my track together in the living room?"

Charlie asked. "I want to see how fast my Dune Chaser goes over the jump ramp."

"It'll go super-fast," Jack assured. "After dinner, okay?" she asked. "That way your grandpas can get in on the fun."

"Yeah, sure," Charlie answered. "That'll give me time to check the tire pressure and oil before the race."

"Good idea," Jack responded, smiling. "Always good to do maintenance on your vehicles."

"He was gonna open a big gift," Lizzy chimed in, "but mommy said we could only have a small one. I helped him pick out the one he opened."

"Charlie's lucky to have such a good big sister," Jack said, meeting her eye. "I like how you're always looking out for him."

"Vroom...vroom, vroom, vroom," Charlie roared, navigating his Dune Chaser across Jack's soft leather loafers.

"Uh-huh," Lizzy answered, having already lost interest in the topic. "See what I got?" she blurted out. "DC Super Hero Girls Dolls. They're from Charlie." She held up two from the collection, one and then the other. "This is Star fire, and this is Blackfire."

"Nice to meet you, Starfire and Blackfire," Jack responded, lowering down to take each doll by her hand. "I'm sure you'll have a grand time playing with my daughter."

"They already know that," Lizzy giggled.

"They do, huh," Jack said, glancing toward the kitchen at the sound of voices. "I think I need to go say hello to your mommy."

"She has company," Charlie responded, rolling his Garbage Gulper up the coat rack with a rumble.

"So, I gathered," Jack responded, having noticed the unfamiliar economy car in the driveway.

* * *

"In here," Courtney called out.

"I know," Jack responded softly, smiling.

Courtney shook her head, briefly glancing at Aki. "She's so quiet," she said. "She can be right on top of me before I know she's around." She tipped her head back, meeting Jack's eye. "Did you have a good day, honey?" she asked softly.

"I did," Jack responded, kissing her forehead. When she rose up, she smiled warmly to Aki. "Hello," she greeted, extending her hand. "Jack, Jack Camdon."

Aki touched her lips, struck by the similarities in their appearance—the coal black hair, the almond-shaped brown eyes, and the deep coppery skin tone. *Her teeth, dear God, we have the same teeth,* she thought, biting her lower lip.

Jack tilted her head, her eyes narrowing.

"I'm sorry," Aki responded, taking her hand. "My thought processes got scrambled there for a moment." She smiled. "Aki, Aki Williams. You don't know me," she continued, "and to be honest, I have no idea what possessed me to land on your doorstep without calling, but…"

"Walking with the spirit," Jack interjected. "At least that's what some call it."

Aki lifted an eyebrow, saying, "I'm sorry?"

"Walking with the spirit," Jack repeated, "it's when a person is compelled, almost by an unknown force, to do something."

"I'm not sure that a spirit was involved," Aki responded. "If anything, it was more like following a dream." She took a breath, allowing it to slip away gently. "I had this dream that you existed, that I'd meet you, and so I came."

Jack cocked her head. "You dreamt you'd meet me?" she clarified. "Me, personally?" She'd assumed that Aki had come seeking her services as a medicine woman. It happened from time to time, strangers showing up on their porch, asking her to heal them. Her kids saw it as normal. Courtney, although she'd never admit it, viewed each intrusion as a nuisance.

"I need to give you some background," Aki said, "and then I'll explain." She pursed her lips and squared her shoulders. "I was adopted," she continued, adding that she was raised as an only child. "My dad died during my second semester of medical school, and my mom passed the week after I finished my residency. She'll be gone two years tomorrow."

Jack touched her hand, saying, "I'm sorry."

"Thanks," Aki said softly. "They were older, so it wasn't unexpected, but still..."

"It's hard," Jack responded, "losing people, especially those who've always been around." Like Aki, her adoptive parents were older, her mom seventy-two and her dad eighty-one. She'd carried the dread of their eventual loss in her heart since she was a small child.

"The night after my mom's burial was the first time that I dreamt of you," Aki said, looking off, and shaking her head slowly. "The last time was just over a month ago." She met her gaze directly. "You need to know that I'm not someone who believes in things unverified by science—not God, not the supernatural, and certainly not dreams that are based in reality. And yet, I knew you existed. I knew I had a sister, Jackie Lynn. I knew it with such certainty that the morning after the first dream, over a cup of coffee and a piece of toast, I decided to search for you, to search until I found you." She shook her head, pressing her lips together. "If you knew me," she added, "you'd know just how unlike me that was."

"So, you believe we're sisters," Jack responded, furrowing her brow.

"I don't just believe," Aki continued, "I know that we are."

"And how is that," Jack asked, "how is it that you can know for sure?" She'd never thought much about her bio-family until that moment. Her adoptive parents, her wife, and her kids had always been enough.

Courtney crossed her arms, prepared to weigh the evidence.

"How can you know with that level of certainty?" Jack continued. "How, when you've only just met me?" She furrowed her brow. "How, when as far as I know, you've not asked a single question about me, not whether I was adopted, and assuming I was, not what I know of my background." She glanced at Courtney, adding, "Unless you two talked before I got home?"

Courtney shook her head. "We didn't, not about that," she

responded. "And she wouldn't have had access to your information, not an agency record or a legal document, without your knowledge and express consent." She glanced at Aki, adding, "Assuming that such information existed."

"Look," Aki responded, "I understand that you're suspicious. In the same situation, I would be too." She shook her head, exhaling quietly, "In fact, if I opened the door to someone, who once they were inside my house, insisted that they were related to me, not extended, but immediate family..." She smirked, her head shaking slowly. "Well, I'd figure I was being scammed and move them along in short order. My first inclination would certainly not be to pour them a second cup of coffee." She met Courtney's gaze with gentleness. "I wouldn't be as kind to that person as you've been to me. So, thank you for that. I'm not sure with the afternoon that I've had, I'd have dealt well with the way I'd have treated me. But you must think I'm crazy," she continued, "showing up out of the blue, telling you that we're sisters, and then adding that a dream led me to you."

"I don't think you're crazy," Jack said softly. "And the fact that a dream led you here doesn't trouble me in the least. To be honest, I feel better about you, knowing that you paid attention to it. I would, however, like to hear more about how you concluded that we were sisters." She smiled kindly, adding, "And of course, how you managed to find me."

"Sorry, I should've led with that," Aki responded. "I kept meticulous notes," she added, reaching into her purse for her journal. "You can read them if you'd like."

"I would," Jack responded, swallowing, and taking the notebook.

"So," Aki continued, looking off for a moment to gather her thoughts, "it was a lengthy process, a process that started with a request for my original birth certificate." She explained the recent change in the law that allowed adoptees to obtain an unredacted copy of the document.

"Not something that I ever planned to request," Jack commented.

"Me either," Aki said, "until the dreams, that is."

Jack's eyes darted to Courtney and back.

"It wasn't easy," Aki went on, "finding you." She swallowed, meeting Jack's gaze with a thin smile. "The search itself took more than a year and utilized the services of two private investigators, one based in Danville. He has an office near the courthouse."

"Sandusky?" Courtney inquired, removing her glasses.

"Yes," Aki answered. "Do you know him?"

"Just professionally," Courtney responded. "He has an office just down from my law practice." She shook her head, adding, "I'll bet it took no time at all for him to locate us, and then charge you top dollar."

"Right on both counts," Aki responded, shaking her head as well. "So anyway," she continued, "once I got the birth certificate, I was off and running. It took a while for the first guy to find anything on our mother, but once he did, finding you was just a matter of time."

"What was your birth name?" Jack asked, doubt nipping at the bottom of her stomach. In her dreams, she'd always been Ojibwe, but was she? She touched the bear claw on her choker, drawing strength from her spirit animal, sucked in a breath, and held it. When she looked over, she noted that her wife was holding hers as well.

"Songetay," Aki said, "but I'm not sure that my pronunciation's correct."

"It is," Jack responded, feeling tension leave her shoulders. "It's Ojibwe," she added with a thin smile. "And our biological mother's name?" she inquired. "I'm just curious. I don't really have any interest in meeting her."

"Wabun Ahnung," Aki responded, her head shaking slowly, "and I know I didn't get that pronunciation right.

"No, but you were close," Jack answered, enjoying the sparkle in her eyes. "So, did you find her?" she asked.

"No," Aki responded, "just you so far."

"I hate to break this up," Courtney interjected, laying her palm on Jack's thigh, "but our company will be here at any moment."

"Crap," Jack responded, her eyes widening, "and the pizza's not ordered yet."

"Not the end of the world," Courtney answered. "They'll survive."

"I should be going," Aki said, setting her mug on the counter. "It's been wonderful," she added, holding Jack's eye. "Maybe we can get together again sometime."

"Yeah, it's been great," Jack responded, glancing at Courtney, who in turn gave an inconspicuous nod.

Jack shifted her gaze to Aki. "Would you like to join us for dinner?" she invited. "It's the unhealthiest menu on the planet: pizza, cake, and ice cream. But if you think you can stand it, it will give us a little more time to get to know one another."

"I'd love to," Aki responded, smiling warmly.

CHAPTER 4

"You think we did the right thing?" Jack asked quietly. "I mean, inviting her to stay for dinner?"

Courtney looked up, the last of the ice cubes clinking into glass number twelve. "Don't you?" she asked softly. "She's nice and the kids are crazy about her." She lifted a pitcher of tea from the top shelf of the refrigerator, setting it on the counter. "As you said," she added, "this evening will give you more time to get to know one another."

"I know," Jack responded, her voice fading off as she slid her hands into her pockets.

Courtney wrinkled her brow. "What's going on?" she asked, stepping toward her. "You were fine about it and now you're not."

"I don't know," Jack answered, looking off. "I guess I'm having second thoughts about her staying for Charlie's birthday dinner." She bit her lower lip, her head shaking slowly. "I mean, we're going to have a house full of company."

"You're worried about your parents, how they'll react," Courtney responded, putting her arms around her neck, and kissing her softly.

"Yeah, a little," Jack responded, taking a breath, and adding, "and your mother."

"My mother?" Courtney clarified, frowning. "I can't imagine what problem she'd have. I mean, Aki's an ophthalmologist, a surgeon." Her eyes widened. "That's all she'll need to know to like her." She tilted her head, peering over her glasses. "But if she has a problem..." She shrugged her shoulders, "Oh, well." Her gaze softened. "And regarding your parents, oh honey, you mark my words, they're going to love her. Trust me on this one, I know."

Jack took a breath, saying, "I hope so."

* * *

"Anything I can do to help?" Aki asked, noticing dining room decor as she made her way to the kitchen. Spacious and warm, it was accented with autumn colors and had traditional furnishings—a long rectangular table, matching chairs, and a buffet with tapered legs and spade feet. It wasn't the kind of room a person would expect to be served pizza, cake, and ice cream.

"No, but thank you," Courtney responded, smiling. "I think we're all set." She set a glass at the corner of each placemat, adding, "Not much to it really," and then looked over. "Jack should be back with the pizzas in fifteen minutes or so, but in the meantime, would you care for another cup of coffee?"

"I would," Aki said, chuckling, and adding, "I'm on break while Charlie does maintenance on the cars and Lizzy takes the dolls to get their hair done."

"You have a good way with them," Courtney responded softly. "I can't remember them ever having such a good time with someone they were just getting to know."

"Thanks," Aki said. "I hope we didn't get too loud."

"You didn't," Courtney responded. "I love hearing them giggle."

"Relating to kids," Aki said, smiling with a slow shake of her head, "well, it's always come easily."

"Let me guess," Courtney said, meeting her eye directly, "Pediatric Ophthalmology."

Aki smiled, nodding. "I just finished my fellowship."

"Where?" Courtney asked, her pouring halted.

"UCLA," Aki responded, crinkling her brow. "Why do you ask?"

"I was just curious," Courtney answered. "I'm a surgeon's kid," she added with a smile.

"Oh yeah?" Aki said. "Your mom or your dad?"

"My dad," Courtney responded. "He's the chief, at least until December thirty-one." She shook her head. "I can't believe he's really planning to step down."

"Fatigue, forgetfulness, reduced eyesight," Aki commented, "they're not a surgeon's friend." She met her gaze kindly. "Unfortunately, all are part of the aging process." She pressed her lips together with a gentle nod. "He probably feels like it's time."

"He does," Courtney responded, raising an eyebrow, "but he'll be ready to take that scalpel to his neck after he has a chance to be around my mom twenty-four-seven for a while."

Aki chuckled, saying, "That bad, huh?"

Courtney nodded, responding, "Oh, yeah."

* * *

THEY GATHERED around the dining room table, those that had arrived on schedule. Missing were Courtney's parents and Carsyn. They'd be there shortly.

"Took advantage of the good weather to do a bit of harvesting this afternoon," Mo announced. She met Jack's gaze with a nod, leaning back in her chair, her long limbs reaching to the opposite side of the table with no effort. Having consumed more than half of the pepperoni and mushroom pizza, she looked ready for a nap. Jack's friend since high school, Mo prized their friendship as she might a hard-won athletic trophy.

Jenny pursed her lips, her eyes widening, locking gazes with her wife. "Couldn't believe what I was seeing," she interjected. "Less than an hour before we needed to leave for your house, and there she was with a frame pulled out, all covered in propolis." She glanced across the table, catching Courtney's eye as she tucked a strand of dark brown hair behind her ear. "I almost called to tell you we'd be late for Charlie's party."

"We weren't going to be late," Mo countered, fingering through her crop of hair, short, blonde, and erect. "I was watching the time," she added, "like my life depended on it."

"Sure, you were," Jenny retorted, looking at the others at the table. "My wife gets out there with those bees and loses all track of time."

"Whenever would've been fine," Courtney responded softly.

"Just once," Jenny continued, "I'd like to be able to go somewhere without her either being sticky or having to take a second shower."

"It was the same for Mick," Francisca responded, glancing at Jack's adoptive father, "wasn't it, honey?"

"Sure was," Mick responded, catching Mo's eye with a nod. "When a hive's brimming with capped honey, you just have to harvest it. That's all there is to it. Mo knows what I'm talking about."

"Yessiree," Mo answered in a steady, low voice. "And I do it just like Mick taught me." Her gaze softened, shifting to her old boss. "Come out sometime and we'll harvest one together. Be like old times."

"Doctor doesn't think he should be around the hives anymore," Francisca said, sweeping crumbs from her husband's lap into her palm, "but we would love to come out and see what you've done with the farm." She looked at her husband. "What do you think, honey, maybe sometime later in the season after the bees have tucked themselves in for the winter?"

"What I think," Mick responded, pinching his brow, "is that my new doctor is certifiably nuts." His eyes narrowed to slits and he pressed his lips together. "Worked around those bees for all those years without a problem," he added, "and I'm not gonna have one now."

"Those bees," Francisca chimed in with a tisking sound, "I never understood what made them so enthralling." Her eyes widened, shaking her head. "And it's not just my husband who's under their spell," she continued, "it's my daughter as well."

Jack looked up at her mention. Having slipped off to the kitchen, she'd been about the business of inserting candles into Charlie's cake.

"It's the same for Mo," Jenny responded. "She talks about those girls like they're part of our family."

"They are," Mo answered, "and you just watch, Jackie's gonna love 'em just like I do." She brushed her three-year-old's cheek with her thumb, saying, "Aren't ya, boy?"

Jackie dropped his pizza to the floor, giggling to his mother. When he looked over, Aki noticed a misalignment of his eyes. She'd check with his parents to assure that they were aware of his condition tonight.

"You're a doctor," Mick blurted out, meeting Aki's gaze when she looked back, "maybe you can explain to me, why all the sudden I'm not supposed to go around my bees. Can't get a straight answer out of the nutcase I go to." He shook his head slowly, twirling the saltshaker, and frowning. "And Lord knows," he added, "I've tried."

"She's not a cardiologist, Dad," Jack said, setting a triple-layer chocolate cake in the center of the table. "She doesn't know why."

"Well, she might," Aki responded, her eyes sparkling in her smile. She met Mick's gaze with an extra dose of kindness. "He's probably worried that you'll be stung more than once," she said softly. "Although few in number, there have been studies where multiple stings have led to a heart attack."

"So, if I get all suited up so that I won't get stung," Mick said, a lift slipping into his voice, "I'll be able to go around my hives."

"Now, I didn't say that," Aki responded, lifting an eyebrow. "But..." She smiled. "I suppose it would be worth offering up as an option."

"I'll do just that," Mick responded. "In fact," he added with a nod, "I think I'll just tell him I already talked to you about it." He shook his head, muttering, "Don't know why the guy can't just give a straight answer like she did."

Aki took a soft breath, suppressing a smile as she caught Jack's eye.

"I like her," Mick whispered, leaning over. "If you ask me, she's a good addition to our family." He'd been pleased, but not surprised, when Jack introduced Aki, and explained how she'd come to find her.

"She certainly is," Francisca whispered back. "It's wonderful that she found our daughter."

Aki stood at the sound of the doorbell. "I'll get it," she said, moving toward the foyer.

"That'll be Carsyn," Jack called out. "You gotta watch out, she's trouble, don't let her in the door." When Aki looked back, she laughed. "Just kidding," she added. "Have her put her packages on the larger pile."

"Will do," Aki called back, her hand on the doorknob.

CHAPTER 5

Leafy shadows danced across the driveway as Carsyn climbed up, down, and up again, positioning her load. With a groan, she lugged on the last item, a wheelbarrow, situating it so that it wouldn't blow. No matter how many times she did this, it always took longer than she expected to get ready to go. She checked her watch as she straddled the tailgate, dropped down to the gravel, and reached for her cell. "I'm sure you guys have already figured out that I'm not making it for pizza," she said, "but come hell or high water, I'll be there for cake and ice cream. Tell Charlie, I promise." She nodded, listening to Jack going on about not worrying about it, that it wasn't a problem. "Yeah okay," she responded, "well, it is for me...Oh, and remember I'll have the horses in the trailer so I won't be able to stay more than fifteen minutes or so...Yeah, okay...We'll see you in about an hour." She returned her phone to her pocket, taking inventory.

Trowels—check.
Hoes—check.
Shovels—coal, normal, and spades—check.
Mattocks—check.
Buckets—twenty-five of them—check.
Hay—three bales strapped to the top of the trailer—check.

Sweet feed—the kind that smells of warm molasses—check.

Blankets, saddles, and bridles—check.

"Crap!" she growled, running to the barn for her picket line, a critical piece of equine equipment that she'd almost left behind.

Camp stove, campstools, and whatnots—check, check, and recheck.

She tossed over the web cargo cover and buckled it down.

"Okay," she mumbled, making her way back to the lodging quarters, "almost done." There was a time—a simpler time—when she'd pitch a tent alongside her students, sleeping in a down-filled bag on the nylon floor—but no more. When her wife demanded the comforts of home, her forty-year-old bones agreed, and she had the flashy trailer designed and built. A deluxe model, it had all the creature comforts a person could want—a king size bed, outfitted with a plush mattress, a seventy-inch flat screen on the bedroom wall, a copper sink in the kitchen, solid maple cabinets, and hardwood floors. In the rear, was a two-horse straight-load. She'd made big plans to break it in with a trip to San Antonio. That would've been spring, two-and-a-half years ago. But her wife was gone by that time and she never took the trip. Since then, with the exception of her annual dig with the freshmen, she left the beautiful red trailer in the barn. She stepped inside, checked the refrigerator, and put her clothes in the dresser drawers.

Cabinet latches—check.

Bathroom and closet doors—check.

Generator off—check.

She poked two flakes into each hay bag and poured a scoop of sweet feed into each trough. "It's your turn to go first," she told the tall, brown and white spotted horse, leading him out of the barn, and up the ramp. An impatient, strong-willed gelding, he jerked a bite of hay from the bag as she attached his trailer tie. She secured his stall guard and closed his rear door, saying, "Settle down." As she approached the barn, her deceased wife's bay called to her. "I wouldn't leave you behind," she whispered, slipping on her halter. A mild-mannered mare, she waited patiently until the rear door of the trailer clicked shut behind her before daintily taking her first bite. Carsyn smiled, lifting the tailgate, and remembering the day they brought her home as a one-year-old.

* * *

"Sorry, but I can't let you in," Aki greeted, her feet planted firmly in the doorway.

The visitor's mouth fell open. "I beg your pardon," she responded, frowning. She was older than Aki would've expected, old enough that she wondered how she'd have the stamina to teach a full load.

"Can't let you in," Aki repeated, suppressing a smile, "because Jack says you're trouble."

"I beg your pardon," the woman repeated, crossing her arms in a huff. Her face tightened, stretching to see over Aki's shoulder.

Aki's eyes widened, tilting her head. "Sorry, but I can't," she responded, raising an eyebrow.

The woman's eyes narrowed, clearly garnering steam to plow her down.

Aki shrugged. "Sorry," she said, holding her ground, "just doing what I was told." She'd probably carried the joke far enough. Jack's friend didn't seem to be amused, not at all.

"Thank goodness," the woman exclaimed, her gaze fixed on a point just above Aki's left shoulder. "Good grief, Courtney Ann," she continued, "what in the world were you thinking, allowing someone completely unschooled in proper etiquette to answer your door?" She pushed by Aki, stepping inside. "No doubt your wife's responsible," she added, "but still." She took a breath, pausing to exhale, before moving toward the dining room. "Looking for the little birthday man," she chirped in a high pitched tone. "Where's my little guy?"

"Grandma Lizabeth," Charlie squealed, jumping from his chair, and running toward her.

"Sorry," Aki said, dropping her eyes. "I should've known that was your mother."

"Don't worry about it," Courtney answered, winking as she

touched her arm. "She had her sense of humor surgically removed when I was about four. How could you possibly know?" She stepped by and onto the doormat, saying, "Here, let me take some of those."

"Why, thank you, Pumpkin," the balding man responded. "This small one's about to take a tumble." He wore a tie, a suit jacket, and smooth leather brogues.

Courtney collected the package and three others.

"It's a Ground Grabber," the gentleman continued. "I hope it's the one he wanted."

"It is," Courtney responded, her eyes twinkling as her tone softened. "You guys do too much."

"That's impossible," the man said, kissing her cheek, and stepping onto the porch, "not when it comes to our grandchildren." He glanced over. "I don't believe we've met," he said warmly. "I'm Charles Holloman, Courtney's father."

"Pleased to meet you," Aki responded, smiling, "Aki, Aki Williams."

"That's a beautiful name," Charles commented, "unusual. Interesting that I should run across it twice in the same hour." He smiled, lifting an eyebrow. "You wouldn't happen to be the candidate that our Director of Ophthalmology was just raving about, would you?"

"I'm not sure about the raving part," Aki answered, smiling, "but I did interview with her this morning." With that, both children came around the corner, squealing for their grandfather.

"I'm afraid we'll have to talk later," Charles said, catching her eye as he lifted his grandson onto his shoulders.

"I'd like that," Aki responded, smiling.

* * *

"Seriously," Jack said, "I tell you, you won't be imposing. You said you didn't have anything scheduled until your next interview. So, that means you'll just be sitting in your hotel room until you fly to Chicago. Come on," she begged, locking gazes, "come with us. It'll be fun, camping as a family."

"I don't think so," Aki answered, shaking her head, and slipping her hands into her pockets. "You'll be back before I have to leave, how about we just plan to get together that night?"

"I tell you," Jack pressed on, "you won't be imposing." She looked at Courtney. "She won't be, will she, honey?"

"No," Courtney responded, "she won't. We'd love to have her join us." She took a breath, pressing her lips together. "But I don't think that's the problem." She turned, meeting Aki's gaze. "It's not, right?" she asked softly. "It's that you don't want to rough it—sleeping on the floor of a dome tent—in the wilderness with ticks, mosquitos, and snakes—without makeup and indoor plumbing—for an entire week. If that's the case, you just have to tell her." Her eyes widened, tilting her head. "Trust me on this," she added, "I have a lot of experience. If you're not honest, so she can see how miserable she'll be making you, she'll stay on you until you eventually cave."

Aki held her gaze, pursing her lips, and nodding.

"I'm not sure you'd actually have any ticks or mosquitoes to deal with this late in October," Jack responded. "And if you did see a snake, he'd be moving pretty slow." She shook her head, smiling thinly. "But okay, okay, I get it, neither of you want to go." She took a soft breath. "So, how about we do this," she suggested, "how about we come back a couple of days early and then maybe take a trip to see Aki, wherever it is that she ends up, at Christmastime?"

Courtney smiled, nodding.

"That'd be perfect," Aki responded, "no roughing it and I get a visit over the holidays. Definitely a win-win as far as I'm concerned." She met Jack's gaze. "I'll most likely accept the position in LA," she added, "so I hope you won't miss trading snow-covered branches and sub-zero temperatures for seventies and sunny."

"Not at all," Courtney said, smiling.

"Ditto," Jack responded.

* * *

"Sorry," Carsyn said, the moment Jack opened her front door, "I was almost here, just ticking through what I needed to bring one more time in my mind..." She exhaled, her head shaking slowly. "And wouldn't you know it? I forgot something, not just something, mind you, but something important." With a blank stare, she added, "Damn shaker screens, I left them stacked at the edge of my driveway, and had to go back."

"Don't worry about it," Jack said kindly. "Nothing personal, but I'm not sure Charlie even noticed."

"I'm crushed," Carsyn responded, lifting her palm to her heart in an exaggerated motion.

"Don't be," Jack answered with a soft chuckle. "You had a lot to compete with," she added, "both sets of grandparents, his Great Uncle Ben, and an aunt, who until this afternoon, we didn't know existed." She stepped off toward the living room.

"Hey, wait," Carsyn responded, not moving an inch. "He has an aunt that you didn't know existed?" She lifted both eyebrows. "As in one of you just found out you have a sibling?"

"You got it," Jack said, shaking her head with a smile. "Me," she added. "Come on; I'll introduce you to her."

CHAPTER 6

With her palm on Carsyn's shoulder, Jack nodded them around the room. "And you know my mom and dad," she said, straightening Mick's collar.

"Of course, I do," Carsyn answered, taking hold of one and then the other's hand. "Good to see you again, Mr. and Mrs. Camdon."

"It's Francisca and Mick," Francisca corrected, squeezing gently.

"Francisca and Mick," Carsyn echoed, smiling with a slow shake of her head. "I didn't forget," she added, "I was just raised to show respect to those who have a couple of years on me."

"More than a couple, I'd say," Francisca chuckled, "but nevertheless, it's Francisca and Mick to you."

"Yes, ma'am," Carsyn responded with a polite nod.

"Oh, and before I forget," Francisca added, "I brought a container of persimmon cookies for you. Baked them this morning."

"They're on the counter by her purse," Jack interjected.

"Old-fashioned autumn treats from my childhood," Carsyn said, her tone softening with nostalgia. She flashed back, remembering Sunday afternoon drives in the country with her mom and dad—crunchy leaves, orange delicacies, and the old tree just beyond the Danville city limits. There was something about fall that intensified her yearning for simpler days, baked goods fresh from the oven, and family. "I'll pick them up on my way out," she added, smiling thinly. "Thank you for remembering that I liked them."

"You're quite welcome, dear," Francisca responded with another squeeze.

"And Courtney's parents," Jack said, moving them along.

"Good to see you again, Dr. Lyndon," Charles responded, standing to shake her hand.

"Yes, a pleasure," Elizabeth said, lackluster from the love seat.

"And last, but certainly not least," Jack said, coming to a halt in front of the couch between the book cases, "my sister, Dr. Aki Williams, an up-and-coming pediatric ophthalmologist." She glanced at Carsyn. "Dr. Carsyn Lyndon," she continued, her gaze shifting to Aki. "She's the friend I told you about, the one we'll be camping with this week."

"Ahhh, I see," Aki responded, her smile twinkling as she tucked a beautiful lock of jet-black hair behind her ear. "It's a pleasure to make your acquaintance, Dr. Lyndon."

"Yeah, you too," Carsyn answered, noticing Aki's tongue dart out to moisten her lips.

"Archaeology," Aki continued, licking again, "an interesting discipline. I always wished I'd had the opportunity to take a course or two as electives."

"There's still time," Carsyn said, swallowing. If only she could focus on the conversation. She took a breath, painfully preoccupied with the gorgeous woman's insanely firm eye contact and sensuously spicy scent. "I have an extra text in the truck," she added. "I could lend it to you if you want to read up on it." *Dear God, was that ever stupid,* she thought. Time slowed as she caught her breath.

"Sounds good," Aki responded, smiling, and licking again. In the next instant, she looked around as if desperate for an exit.

"It won't stay together," Charlie blurted out, his Ground Grabber rolling across the carpet as a section of his recently assembled track tumbled down around his feet. He kicked, collapsing the rest.

"That's enough," Jack snapped, making uncomfortably direct eye contact.

"Play nicely or not at all," Courtney added, coming in with refills on drinks.

Charlie quieted, his lower lip extended, and a frown on his face.

"Here, honey," Aki said, leaping from her chair as if it were spring-loaded, "I'll fix it for you. We'll have it up and running in no time. Come on, sweetie, we can pick up the pieces together."

Carsyn sucked in a breath, appreciating the rounded backside of Aki's mid-rise jeans and the swell of her pink cashmere sweater. *Whatever this is,* she told herself, *you need to shake it off.* It wasn't that she thought appreciating beautiful women inappropriate, it was that she wasn't in the habit of doing so in public. When the phenomena did occur, it was usually in the privacy of her home, watching television or perusing a magazine, or something. And even then, it didn't occur that often. *I doubt she's a day over thirty-two,* she thought, wondering if being thirty-two would've given her enough time to become a pediatric ophthalmologist? *So, maybe she's a little older,* she told herself, calculating the number of years it would've taken for her to get through medical school, internship, residency, and fellowship—*eight for the bachelors and medical school; five for the internship and residency; one or two for the pediatric fellowship—for a grand total of fifteen years. So, she has to be at least thirty-three,* she tallied, *still ten years younger than you are. She's too young, not to mention she's Jack's sister. Don't even think about it.* She cocked her head, this time appreciating Aki's bottom as she crawled across the carpet. A heat wave went through as she considered that Jack could be watching her watch her sister's butt. She stole a quick glance to see if she was, moving toward the door. "Well, I'd better get going," she blurted out. "Good to see everyone. Catch you next time."

Aki looked up, their gazes lingering for the longest moment.

Carsyn took a breath, swallowing, and sprinting forward.

"If you wait just a minute," Jack said, moving briskly to catch up, "I'll send a piece of cake with you."

"How about you just bring it in the morning?" Carsyn responded, stepping to the porch.

"Yeah, sure, that'll work," Jack said, following her out. "Is everything okay?"

"Absolutely," Carsyn answered. "It's just late, you know?"

"Yeah, okay," Jack responded, her eyes narrowing. "Take it easy on the curves," she called out. It wasn't so much that Carsyn would be driving that far, only twenty miles or so, it was that she'd be traveling on minimally maintained roads—twisty, two-lane blacktops after dark with an extra-long horse trailer in tow.

"I will," Carsyn said, clicking her driver's door shut.

* * *

"She forgot her persimmon cookies," Jack said, setting the colorful tin on a pile to be loaded in the morning. She shook her head. "And man was she ever acting weird just before she left. Not sure what that was all about."

"I know," Courtney responded, looking up from wiping down the counter, "she shot out of here like her pants were on fire." She shrugged, adding, "Maybe she was just nervous about the dig tomorrow."

"She's done it for years," Jack said, "I don't think so."

"Anything else I can do before I take off?" Aki asked, stepping into the room. As she set her glass in the dishwasher, Lizzy and Charlie came in too. She smiled to them and continued, "So, we picked up all the toys, didn't we, kiddos?"

"Uh-huh," Charlie responded, "and we put 'em in the corner of my bedroom."

"I wasn't sure where you'd want them," Aki added. "Charlie suggested his toy box, but I was fairly certain that they wouldn't all fit."

"The corner's fine," Courtney said. "We can sort out where they'll be stored when we get back." She smiled, holding her gaze. "Thank you for all your help," she added. "You can't imagine how much I appreciate you spearheading the living room cleanup." She stifled a yawn. "For some reason, I'm totally exhausted."

"Understandable," Aki responded. "You threw a party, had a houseload of company, and you've been on your feet since I got here."

"You sure we can't talk you into joining us tomorrow?" Jack asked, washing down one of Carsyn's persimmon cookies with a swig of milk.

"No," Aki answered, "I'd better not. I have some reading to do." Her stomach fluttered, thinking that if she said yes, she'd see Carsyn again —and if not, she wouldn't. Her mind raced, processing her strange physiological reaction to the handsome woman.

"Bring it along," Jack responded, holding her gaze. "I promise to fight off all the ticks, mosquitoes, and snakes."

"It's a scholarly article on pediatric neuro-ophthalmology," Aki answered, her head shaking slowly, "I don't think I'd be able to concentrate."

"Pleeease," Lizzy begged, her eyes widening with her plea.

"Yeah, pleeease, Aunt Aki," Charlie echoed.

"Sorry, sweeties," Aki answered, lowering down for a hug and eye contact, "not this time." Heat radiated through her body as she slipped on her jacket. "I'll see you when you get back, okay?"

"Okay," both sighed dejectedly.

CHAPTER 7

With a feather-lite toe, Carsyn slowed to a crawl. Having traveled this road on many occasions, she knew that her turn from the two-lane blacktop to the single-lane gravel was close. Her hitch groaned, navigating the pitch-black corner. As she brought the rig around, her horses moved, shifting the distribution of her load. Her toe lifted, her eyes darting to her smartphone. Gone were the days when she'd have had to find a safe place to pull over to check on their wellbeing, the ceiling-mounted camera having solved that problem. With a glance at her device, she had a three-hundred-sixty-degree view of the equine environment, a Godsend on multiple levels. Satisfied that Lily and Relic were fine, she increased her speed to slightly above her previous crawl. She continued that way for a couple of miles before slowing to her slowest speed of all. Affectionately referred to as 'Deadman's Needle,' the one-mile stretch ran between two dangerously steep drop-offs. It had caused more than its share of fatalities and marked the entrance to the rugged recreational area and campground. *Focus,* she told herself, switching on her floodlights, and willing thoughts of Aki out of mind. *Focus...*

* * *

"Evening," Carsyn greeted, tipping her beaver-felt Stetson as she dropped down from her cab. "Not too nippy, I like it."

"Indian summer," the tall man responded. She'd seen him walking her way as she was backing over the culvert. He too wore a cowboy hat, tipped down. His skin was weathered, and his eyes were wrinkled at the corners. "Lows aren't gonna dip much below fifty all week," he continued, "and the highs are gonna top out around seventy-one."

"Can't get much better than that," Carsyn responded, inhaling woodsy air to the bottom of her lungs. "I love the smell of fall," she added, collecting her picket line.

"Sure can't," the guy answered, following as she stepped to the backside of her campsite. She was looking for what she always looked for—two firmly rooted trees a good distance apart with at least one sturdy limb, seven to eight feet above the ground. She'd selected the site because it had several from which to choose from. "That looks like a good one," he commented.

"Sure does," Carsyn responded, tossing the heavyweight rope over and around. She stretched it to the second tree and ratcheted the cable winch tightly.

"Make it look easy," the guy commented. "Bet you don't get any slack in that one." He smiled, extending his hand. "They call me Ringo," he added, nodding to one side. "The wife and I are camped just over yonder. It's the one with the palominos on the line."

"Fine looking horses," Carsyn responded with a firm handshake. "Got an Appy and a Quarter horse," she added, noting the sound of hooves stomping on the floorboards, "both pretty eager to get out." She shook her head, smiling, and adding, "And probably hoping for a little more supper."

"Well, I'll let you get to it," Ringo answered, stepping off toward his campfire.

"Hey," Carsyn called out, "thanks for coming over. And my apologies in advance for the twenty-plus college students that'll be joining me in the morning."

"Won't bother us at all," Ringo called back with a nod. "You holler if you need anything. Got extra staples, tools, and whatnots."

"Will do. And you too," Carsyn responded, lowering her tailgate to the ground.

* * *

CARSYN BACKED her horses down the ramp, clipping them onto the picket line at a safe distance from one another. "Here you go, Lily," she said, palming a juicy, red apple. "And here you go," she added, palming a yellow one to Relic. No rhyme or reason. It was just the way it turned out. She wiped her hands down her jeans and positioned a wireless camera that would allow her to check the horses from inside. Then, she unloaded the firewood and tugged a picnic table near her door. As she stepped up, her cell rang out from her back pocket. "I figured you'd call," she answered, clicking the door shut behind her. "Nope," she said, "nothing's wrong, I'm absolutely fine. Okay then, I'll see you in the morning." She switched on her generator and set her automatic coffeemaker to brew before sunrise. As she dropped her jeans, she took a soft breath and allowed the memory of Aki's scent to fill her mind. *You can't,* she told herself, crawling under the covers. *You don't even know she's gay.* Her brow furrowed, trying to remember the details of a study examining the relationship between sexual orientation and biology. With Jack as her sibling, would it be more or less likely that she was? She licked her lips, biting her lower one. *Maybe slightly more likely,* she thought, *but she's probably not.* Although, Aki had given off an array of mixed signals—downright flirty and then not at all. *Even if she is,* she thought, *she's Jack's sister, and she's too young for you.* With a soft sigh, she reminded herself that young, beautiful women didn't go for the older ones. *Oh, it happens,* she countered silently. *Let it go,* she told herself, swallowing as she rolled to her side. Dating, she'd tried it a year or so ago, and it didn't work out. She closed her eyes, willing sleep to come, and fantasizing about what it might be like to touch her.

* * *

AKI TURNED BACK the brightly colored hotel spread, tossing two of the three over-stuffed pillows to the floor. She picked up the small clock from her nightstand, setting her alarm, and turning it off. *Take advantage of your time off,* she told herself. She'd been in the habit of maximizing her every waking moment since high school. As she sat down on the end of the bed to untie her Nikes, she considered what had transpired in the hours prior. Meeting Jack, Courtney, and the kids had been wonderful. It felt good to have family even if she was just getting to know them. And then there was Carsyn—*Dear God, Carsyn* —with her cool, fresh scent, and her baby blue eyes. *What was that all about?* She took a breath, holding it. *You know what it's about,* she answered, unclasping her bra. She walked across the room to stand in front of the full-length mirror. *It's about desire. It's about you feeling desire for a woman.* Her insides quivered, palming her left breast, and allowing her fingertips to brush across her erect nipple. Desire, she hadn't experienced it that many times in her life—and never as she had tonight. *Maybe it's that you just learned Jack's a lesbian,* she supposed. *Maybe your mind's playing tricks on you. It's not like anything like this has ever happened before.* Her breathing accelerated. *But it has,* she told herself, feeling the urge to run and hide as she flashed back to her sixth-grade picnic. "Sister Mary Kathleen doesn't count," she said out loud, walking toward the bathroom. "It was a school girl crush spurred on by an imbalance of hormones," she added, turning the knob for a cold shower, "nothing more, nothing less."

CHAPTER 8

"The Wrangler's loaded," Jack announced, stepping into the kitchen from the garage. It was the new model, a red four-door with a black hard top.

"I can't believe I let you talk me into this," Courtney said, shaking her head.

"You didn't let me," Jack answered, gathering her in for a kiss, "I won, fair and square."

"Uh-huh," Courtney responded, pressing into her, "sure you did."

Jack kissed her again, whispering, "Where are the kids?"

"In the backyard," Courtney answered, "giving the dogs one last chance to do their business." She tilted her head, meeting Jack's gaze. "Are you sure it's a good idea to take them?"

"The dogs or the kids?" Jack asked, suppressing a smile.

"Biboon and Niibin," Courtney responded, shaking her head with an eye-roll, "our Siberian Huskies."

"Yes," Jack said, laughing, "we should take them. It'll be fine. I tossed in an extra tent in case we need it."

"Great," Courtney muttered, "camping in frigid temperatures, ticks, snakes, and the prospect of sleeping separately." She shook her head, curling her upper lip. "Just great."

42

Jack pulled her close, meeting her gaze tenderly. "Six years of marriage, two rambunctious kids, and still you want to squeeze into a sleeping bag with me." She smiled, kissing her nose, and then her lips. "How sweet is that?"

"Can I take these?" Charlie blurted out, coming up beside his parents as their bodies separated.

"That's a crowbar, and that's a level," Jack responded with a tilt of her head. "I don't think you'll find them to be of much use on your dig." She lifted the tools from his hands, setting them on the counter. "Carsyn has a toolkit that'll be yours to keep." She mussed his hair with her fingers. "Don't worry, buddy, she'll make sure you have everything you need."

"Cool," Charlie responded, his eyes becoming big, round discs, "hey, Lizzy," he yelled, running down the basement stairs, "I get my own archaeologist toolkit."

"Okay," Courtney said softly, coming in for another kiss, "I concede, this camping trip is a good idea."

"You're such a good sport, Courtie Holloman-Camdon," Jack responded, smiling as she kissed her forehead, "one of the many reasons that I fell in love with you in high school."

"I'm not that good of a sport," Courtney answered. "You know that I'm not. It's just fun to see you and our kids so excited about going." She held her gaze, her lips parting. "We should go more often," she added softly.

Jack closed the distance between their bodies, kissing her slowly.

"Are we ever gonna go?" Lizzy asked, joining them with a loud sigh.

Jack took a breath, releasing it slowly. "Yes, Elizabeth," she answered, "we're going right now."

* * *

"Look, it's that old lady, the one who comes to see you all the time," Charlie announced, pasting his nose to the rear window.

"So, I see," Jack responded, shifting from reverse to drive, and pulling back into the driveway.

"Wasn't she just here last night?" Courtney asked, knowing that she was. Her eyes narrowed as she looked over.

Jack nodded, trying not to engage her wife.

"Okay, so tell me," Courtney continued, her tone lowering, "what could she possibly need that she didn't need last night? It's only been what?" She checked her watch. "Twelve hours?"

"Something like that," Jack responded, still not wanting to engage, but feeling the need to respond. "She's not well, Courtie," she said softly, "and I'm not sure that she has anyone else to help her."

Courtney took a long breath. "Of course not," she responded, "but they're all unwell in one way or another, aren't they?"

"Yes," Jack answered with a slow nod, "but some, more than others." She laid a palm on Courtney's thigh, making gentle eye contact. "I won't be long," she added.

"Go on," Courtney said, her tone and gaze softening, "Do what you need to do; it's fine." She glanced to the back seat. "We'll just play a game of *I Spy With My Little Eye* until you get back." She tilted her head toward Lizzy. "I believe the reigning champion goes first."

As Lizzy scanned for an object to stump her opponents, Jack exited the vehicle. "I'll be right back," she said, catching Courtney's eye.

* * *

JACK INHALED, exhaling as she made her way down the driveway to the sidewalk. "Well, hello," she greeted, smiling. "That's an awfully long trek to make both morning and night." Since the death of the woman's father, two years come May; she'd ridden the city bus to the bridge and walked the remaining two miles to their house.

"Some days, longer than others," the seventy-year-old woman with long, silver locks responded, forcing a smile.

"So, did you drink the tea I prepared for you?" Jack asked. She'd gathered the ingredients early the previous morning, expecting her to stop by.

"I did, Mitä'kwe," the woman answered, dropping her eyes. "It helped me. I saved enough for tonight."

"No saving," Jack responded, opening her medicine bag to replenish her supply. "And I'm not a Mitä'kwe," she added, in no way believing that she had more powerful medicine than other shamans. "The medicine, the Mashkikiwan, it's not my medicine, but the medicine of Kitche Manitou, the Great Spirit, the Creator."

"You're a Mitä'kwe," the woman countered, meeting her eye.

"And did you toss out those sugary donuts?" Jack continued, lifting an eyebrow.

"It was difficult," the woman answered with a soft chuckle, "but they're in the garbage."

"That's good then," Jack responded, smiling. "So, what brings you back to see me before Father Sun has had the chance to journey to see Grandmother Moon even one more time?"

"What happened this morning," the woman answered, swallowing. "I'm sorry to be so much trouble."

"You're no trouble," Jack responded, slipping her arm around her shoulders, and walking. She was becoming increasingly frail, and she was worried about her. "Sit," she said, pulling a chair nearer the porch rail, "and tell me what happened this morning."

"My vision," the woman responded, releasing her grip, and sitting down, "it blurred so much that I could barely see the sunrise."

"You know what I think you need to do," Jack answered, making direct contact. "We talked about it; it's time."

"No," the old woman responded, raising her voice. "No blood test and no white man's medicine. I don't trust any of it. It ruins lives."

Jack knew so little about her, not her given name, not if she had family who looked after her, and not what caused her paranoia. She took a breath, thinking back to the first time the woman had come to her, seeking healing for her father. "I was just remembering White Eagle," she said softly. "You must miss him a lot."

"I do, every day," the old woman responded. "You stayed with us that night," she continued, her tone softening, "the night my father journeyed to the world of spirits to be with my mother. You stayed, even though you didn't have to." She smiled, her eyes taking on a rare sparkle. "He too knew that you were a Mitä'kwe," she added with a nod. "Your medicine is powerful, Mitä'kwe, good enough for him, and good enough for me as well."

CHAPTER 9

*J*ack's gaze drifted, taking in the panoramic view of fall color, lush greens morphing into fiery-reds, burnt-oranges, and yellows. In the distance, an old fire tower thrust through the tree tops.

"Eyes on the road," Courtney reminded, taking a breath, and holding it.

"They are," Jack responded softly, gripping the steering wheel with both hands, and looking forward. "I forget from one year to the next, just how beautiful it is out here."

"You can look once we get past this drop-off," Courtney answered. "Eyes on the road."

"Look," Charlie chirped, pressing his finger to the window, "a deer just hopped over the stream. Look, Mommy, down there."

"I see her," Courtney answered, her eyes darting downward for a fraction of a moment. "Now, let's be quiet so that we don't distract your mama while she's driving."

"Okay, you can breathe," Jack said, winking to Courtney, "it's behind us."

"Thank goodness," Courtney answered, her facial muscles relaxing as they made their way into the campground. "What number are we looking for?"

"Not sure," Jack responded, "but she reserved like almost a whole row." She pointed across and forward. "It's supposed to be over there somewhere, by the burial mounds."

"Okay," Courtney said, a quiet sigh escaping with her response, "I guess I'll start watching for her trailer."

"Won't be too hard to find her," Jack promised, spotting Relic on the line as she turned the corner. "See? Not hard at all."

"I see," Courtney responded.

"Oooh, cooool," Charlie exclaimed, noticing the proximity of the horses to what he assumed would be their campsite. "Look, Mommy," he giggled, "Relic's eating leaves off of a branch by our picnic table."

"I see," Courtney responded, turning in her seat for direct eye contact. "You're not to go around those horses by yourselves. Not Carsyn's; not anyone's. Do you understand me?" She released a breath when both children nodded in unison.

"It'll be fine," Jack soothed, gently touching her leg. "You'll see."

"I hope you're right," Courtney responded, shaking her head, and muttering, "I don't know how I let you talk me into this."

* * *

"Hey, Dr. Camdon," the lanky young man called out, "over here." His hair was uncombed, his pants sagging, exposing his butt, and his orange t-shirt looked as if it had started the day in a wad. He pointed to a large, flat area, recently cleared of sticks, rocks, and pinecones. "Dr. Lyndon says you're supposed to pitch your tent right here," he yelled. His arm motions were exaggerated, so much so that it looked like he was waving in a plane. "Right here," he yelled again.

"Thanks," Jack called back, nodding as she intentionally averted her wife's gaze.

"No problem," the young man responded, turning to make his way up the hill. After a step or two, he turned around, and added, "I'm going over to tell Dr. Lyndon that you're here."

"That's good," Jack answered. "Tell her we'll get set up and either walk over to the site or see her when you guys break for lunch."

"Yeah, okay," he answered, toeing the dirt to kick a stone before stepping off. "I'll tell her."

As Jack shifted to reverse, he came around the front to peck on Courtney's window. With a soft sigh, she rolled it down.

"That is unless you guys need me to help you unload or something," the young man added. "Because if you do, they're just starting to dig."

"No," Jack responded, noting Courtney's frown, "I think we're fine." She cocked her head, meeting his eye. "Wouldn't want you to miss your first big find."

"Yeah, right," he said, his head shaking as he stepped off at a slow walk.

"Good grief," Courtney muttered, rolling her eyes.

"I know," Jack responded, pursing her lips and nodding slowly.

"Watch it," Courtney said, taking a breath as Jack backed toward the rear of the campsite. "For all you know," she added, "you could be rolling toward a drop-off."

"I'm watching," Jack responded quietly, almost certain that the trees she was headed for were barriers between theirs and the next campsite. "We're fine," she added, "everything's fine."

* * *

"BURIAL MOUNDS," Carsyn said, pointing through the lower branches of the towering oaks, dwarfing her natural classroom. "Beautiful cultural treasures," she added, "too often endangered in the name of progress." She shook her head slowly, her voice fading to black, "Roads, parking lots, and shopping centers."

One head popped up, a young woman, her blonde ponytail tucked inside her shirt, and a trowel in her hand.

Then another head.

And another.

And another.

Carsyn continued when she had the full attention of her class. "For thousands of years," she went on, "indigenous people gathered herbs, nuts, and berries right here. They committed to one another, raised children, cared for parents, and grandparents." She squatted, laying her palm on freshly turned soil, warmed by the midday sun. "Right here," she added, allowing a handful to sift through her fingers, "right where your knees are planted." She looked at the river, pausing until her students looked there as well. "They speared fish to feed not just themselves, but their families. They lived their lives in the very spot that you are." Her voice cracked with respect and reverence. "And for thousands of years," she continued, pointing to the winding row of circular mounds, each having a large burial chamber, "they buried their dead right over there." She met the eyes of each student directly. "You kneel at the fringe of sacred ground," she said. "Never forget that."

Jack squeezed Courtney's hand, saying, "She's good, isn't she?" They'd opted to hike on over instead of pitching their tent, figuring that the process of pitching might go more smoothly once their children had joined Carsyn on the dig.

"She is," Courtney answered, squeezing back. "You can see that she really cares."

"About her students as well as their long-gone ancestors," Jack added.

"Can I go over now?" Charlie asked, his eyes widening. "I won't get in the way."

"Let's let Carsyn finish her lesson," Courtney answered, stroking through the back of his hair. "After lunch," she said.

"Did you understand what Carsyn was just saying about those hills," Jack asked, pointing to an area between the burbling river and where they were standing, "the ones right over there?"

"Uh-huh," Charlie answered, "It's like in a cemetery. You know, like when me and Carsyn go visit her mommy and daddy. We can leave flowers, but we can't dig 'cause by accident we might dig somebody up."

"That's right," Jack said, catching Courtney's eye with a smile as she zipped his windbreaker. "You're going to make a fine archaeologist, young man," she added, straightening his collar.

"I know," Charlie giggled. "And that's what I want to be when I grow up."

"I know you do," Jack responded, mussing his hair.

* * *

AWAKE MULTIPLE TIMES during the night, Aki had gotten up much earlier than she'd have set her weekend alarm. She'd gone down for the complimentary breakfast, a scoop of instant scrambled eggs, a day-old blueberry bagel, and a glass of watered-down orange juice, consuming less than half of a small portion. Tomorrow, she'd go out. With a soft sigh, she dropped into the over-stuffed chair by the window, dangling her leg over its arm, switched on her iPad, and selected the journal article on pediatric neuro-ophthalmology—an article that she'd had no intention of reading until she told Jack she was going to. *Pediatric neuro-ophthalmology*, she read, *is recognizably different from adult neuro-ophthalmology because...*She shifted her position, bringing her left leg down, and dangling the other. *Pediatric neuro-ophthalmology is recognizably different from adult neuro-ophthalmology because...* She rubbed the back of her neck, exhaled loudly, and read on...*Because the congenital and acquired disorders, the examination, and the treatment are different.* She leaned back, thinking, *no-brainer,* and stared out the window. She switched off her device, watching a flock of small birds fly by, landing in the parking lot. Then she stood, walked to the dresser, and rummaged through her purse for a package of crackers. Jack and the kids had looked so disappointed when she'd declined that last invitation to go camping. Maybe she should drive out to see them, just for a little while. And...if she landed around mealtime, maybe she'd run into Carsyn. With that thought, she dropped the crackers to the bottom of her purse and headed into the bathroom to take a shower.

CHAPTER 10

"You don't have Sushi?" Aki asked, her mouth slack in disbelief. It was one of her favorite foods and a norm in even the smallest of California delis. Considered somewhat of a delicacy, she'd decided that it would make a nice contribution to dinner, especially since she'd be arriving unannounced.

"No, ma'am," the older woman responded politely. "I'm sorry we don't."

"Are you sure?" Aki asked, stepping closer to the glass, "not even California or Spicy Crab Rolls?"

"No, ma'am," the deli clerk said, "we don't. We used to have it, but it didn't sell well."

Aki pursed her lips, stepping over to examine the choice of fresh fish. "Alright then," she continued, her voice lowering, "I guess I'll have six of your marinated tuna steaks." She looked up. "Could you brush them with a dab of olive oil?" she asked. "We'll be grilling them later tonight."

"Yes, ma'am," the woman responded, carefully removing the pink filets from her refrigerated display case.

Aki slipped her phone from her purse, dialing Jack while she waited. Once again, her call didn't complete. Jack had said they'd be camping in the middle of nowhere and judging from the lack of cell reception, that was certainly the case.

"Here you go, ma'am," the clerk said, handing over a triangular package wrapped in white paper.

"Thank you," Aki responded, smiling, and taking it. "Oh, and I'll need two pounds of Asian slaw, and six pair of chopsticks."

"Yes, ma'am," the woman said.

Aki placed her purchase atop a layer of ice in a small cooler and set her GPS. The device processed for what seemed like hours, but eventually directed that she turn left. She received the same direction, ten miles down the road, slowing, and searching for the corner.

"Recalculating route," the artificial voice barked from her dashboard.

"I didn't see it," Aki barked back, searching for a place to turn around. Unfortunately, the one she found was a dirt road leading back to an old barn, two miles down the road. She pulled in, catching a strong whiff of manure as she backed out. She slowed to a crawl, this time spotting the narrow road that would take her to the campground without any trouble. *Beautiful, but way the hell out here,* she thought, navigating the corner. Then, she pulled over, returning her sunglasses to the glove compartment. The trip had taken longer than she'd expected and she regretted her decision to delay her departure. If she didn't hurry, she wouldn't make it in time for dinner, let alone get there early enough to provide it. She sped up, switching her lights on, and restarting her audiobook. As she did, the road unexpectedly became much narrower. "Oh, shit!" she yelped, applying her brake, and skating across the gravel. Her pulse raced and her lungs threatened to implode as her car rammed into the guardrail. With a whoosh, her airbag deployed. There and gone in the next moment, it served its purpose, protecting her head from the impact of the steering wheel. *You're alive with no serious injuries,* she told herself. *Just breathe and get the hell out of the car.* As she pulled her door handle, the vehicle tipped, taking a downward tumble. She closed her eyes, screaming as branches raked across her windshield, and metal torqued metal.

* * *

"Good God," Ringo mumbled, talking to no one other than his mount. "How are we ever gonna get that poor sucker outta there?" He shook his head, adding, "Lucky as hell he didn't snap that cable or he'd be a goner."

"Help," Aki shouted, hearing movement on nearby ground. "Somebody, please help me."

"Coming your way," Ringo answered. He was surprised, even though he shouldn't be, that it was a woman by herself. He moved in as close as he dared, dropping down from his saddle, and tossing his reins over a nearby limb. "You stay put," he directed, pausing for a split-second to watch his horse latch onto a tuft of grass. "I'm coming your way," he yelled again, grabbing onto whatever he could as he made his way to straddle what he could of the guardrail. "You okay in there?" he asked, peering through the glass.

Aki nodded, saying that she was.

"Okay, well, that's good then," Ringo responded, straining to see the floor of the vehicle. "That's right," he added, "you keep your foot solid on that brake pedal."

Aki nodded, noticing that she hadn't released it since trying to stop.

"Okay, well, I need to go rustle up some help," Ringo said, leaning in without touching the vehicle. "Don't you worry," he added, his eyes narrowing with his nod, "we'll get you outta there." He looked back as both feet touched solid ground. "Now, don't you be moving around while I'm gone."

"Not a chance," Aki responded.

* * *

Carsyn looked up at the sound of thundering hooves. "What's up?" she called out, recognizing panic in the gallop of her neighbor's horse.

"Over yonder," Ringo called back, "there's a lady driver hanging over the guardrail." He yanked up on his reins, skidding to a stop inches from the back door of his trailer. "Come quick! I need you to put Buffy on the picket line," he bellowed, tossing his reins at his wet-haired wife as she pushed open the screen door. With that, he spun, running for his truck. He jumped in, started his engine, and raced to the front of Carsyn's campsite, screeching to a halt. "Come on," he shouted.

As Carsyn got in, she caught a glimpse of Jack and the kids coming off of a nearby hiking trail. "Think maybe we need more help?" she asked, figuring that it wouldn't take long for her pal to leave Lizzy and Charlie with Courtney and climb on board.

"Maybe," Ringo answered, "but I don't think we have time for it. That, and you get too many hands on that car, it might just push her over." Carsyn knew it was true, rescuers unintentionally causing a vehicle to fall. She'd read an article about one such case in the newspaper not too long ago.

"Shit," Carsyn said, a boulder dropping to the bottom of her stomach. "So, what's the plan?" she asked, retrieving her cell from her pocket.

"Don't have one," Ringo responded. "Got tools and chains in the back," he added, meeting her gaze directly, "so hopefully the two of us can come up with something."

Carsyn shook her head, giving up on connecting to 9-1-1.

"Didn't figure you'd get a line out," Ringo commented.

"Not without a tower," Carsyn said. "You'd think they could at least put one out here somewhere."

"Yep, but they ain't gonna," Ringo responded, coming up on the blue Versa Note.

"Precarious position," Carsyn commented, shaking her head. "Be tricky as hell to get her out of there."

"Sure will," Ringo responded.

"Dear God," Carsyn said, pain shooting through her chest for lack of breath, "it's Aki."

"You know her?" Ringo asked, his voice lifting substantially.

"Yeah," Carsyn said, opening her door, and exiting the slow-moving vehicle.

"Hey, wait a minute," Ringo called out. "You gotta be careful," he said, "one wrong move and you're gonna push her over that cliff."

CHAPTER 11

Carsyn stood frozen, praying. The old guardrail dangled, knocked from its base, the wire rope safety barrier groaned, and a dangerously rugged landscape awaited another casualty. That single cable, a cable not designed for the stress of the situation, was stretched beyond its capacity and the only thing holding Aki's vehicle in place. *Please don't let this be a repeat of history,* Carsyn begged. It was a totally different situation—and yet the same. She moved closer, being careful not to touch the precariously positioned vehicle. "Hey," she greeted softly, "you doing okay?"

Aki nodded, taking a breath. When she reached to roll down her window, the car rolled—an inch, another, and then another with an eerie, cat-like screech.

"No," Carsyn exclaimed, her eyes widening.

Aki released the handle, responding, "Okay."

Carsyn blew air between her lips and again asked if she was okay.

"Yeah," Aki said, her voice shaky, "but I'll be a whole lot better when I get out of here."

"I'll bet you will," Carsyn responded, forcing a thin smile, and wanting to hold her more than anything. "And that's exactly what we're gonna do in a few minutes." She held her gaze gently, saying,

"It's gonna be okay." Thank God, she wasn't in a position to see the full gravity of her situation. "I need to grab a couple of tools," she added, "and a flashlight. You sit tight." She smiled, repeating, "It'll be okay."

Aki nodded, swallowing.

Carsyn fought the urge to vomit, making her way up the hill.

"So, what do you think?" Ringo called down from the road.

"I think it'll be tricky," Carsyn answered, reaching the top. She took a breath, and another, willing her stomach to still. "Tricky, but doable," she added, swallowing the pool of moisture in her mouth. She lifted a leg, bouncing into the bed of the truck. "I assume it's okay if I take a look."

"Sure is," Ringo responded, watching as she rummaged through the items in his toolbox.

"How long are these?" Carsyn asked, lifting chains from a box at the front.

"Long enough," he answered, looking over to scan the distance between his truck and the car.

"Good," Carsyn said, laying them out, "I think we'll need both." She straightened, making eye contact. "Maybe wrap 'em around the telephone pole a couple of times," she added, "then hook 'em to her car."

"Oughta work," Ringo responded with a firm nod. "I assume you're gonna try to pull her out through the window."

"Afraid not to," Carsyn said, shaking her head, "afraid if she opens that door to step out, the thing'll roll before she gets out of the way. She'll be safer if I have a good grip on her."

"Yep, I agree," Ringo said. "I'm afraid it could go when she lifts off that seat." He shook his head, pursing his lips. "Could take her leg off if you don't get her outta the way quick."

"I know," Carsyn responded, unable to breathe. She looked off and then at Aki for a long moment. "Okay," she exhaled, looking back. "Give me a couple of minutes to talk with her and then I'll be ready."

"I'll get the chains in place," Ringo said, "and then be in the truck, waiting."

* * *

"Okay," Carsyn said softly, "so it's all gonna work just like clockwork." Her muscles twitched, and her stomach rolled. "In one smooth move, you're gonna turn, put your arms around my neck, and let me bear-hug ya right outta there." She squinted, feeling a tightening in her chest. "But first," she continued with a breath, "we need to roll down your window."

Aki's eyes narrowed, studying her. "I can't ask you to put yourself at risk," she said, "not when you hardly know me."

Carsyn peered into her eyes, deeply enough that it felt as if she could see her soul. "I know you," she responded, low and soft.

Aki's lips parted as their gazes locked.

"Don't ask me how," Carsyn continued, swallowing, "but I know you."

"Okay, how about this?" Aki suggested, her voice jumping an octave higher, "how about you drive back to the point that you have cell service and call 9-1-1? I'll just sit right here, totally still, until help arrives."

"That'd be great if I could be sure that we had time," Carsyn responded, "but I can't. And that being said, I'm not willing to gamble with your life." She took a breath, tugging at the front of her harness. "Besides," she added, forcing a smile, "I've got this on. What could go wrong?"

"A hand-strung harness," Aki said, forcing a thin smile, "oh, I feel so much better."

"It's made of heavy rope," Carsyn added, pressing a piece as close as she dared to the window. "Look."

"I see," Aki answered, her lips pursed tightly.

"It'll be fine," Carsyn said softly. "You'll see, it will."

"I hope so," Aki responded, again forcing a thin smile.

"Okay," Carsyn said, her eyes narrowing, "back to the business at hand."

Aki nodded, meeting her gaze solidly.

"You're gonna turn like this," Carsyn said, demonstrating with her own body, "careful to keep your weight as even as possible." She tipped her head down, maintaining eye contact. "And you're gonna do it, ever so slowly."

Aki nodded.

"Then, you're gonna reach out through the window and put your arms around my neck," Carsyn said, their gazes locked, "fingers clasped, just like so." Again, she demonstrated with her own body.

Aki nodded.

"And after that," Carsyn continued, biting her lip, "I'm gonna bear hug ya right outta there." She lifted an eyebrow, waiting for the nod.

Aki nodded slowly, swallowing.

"So, we're gonna do it," Carsyn continued, "on the count of three." She took a breath, releasing it. "Right after we roll down your window."

Aki nodded, taking hold of the knob.

"Easy and slow," Carsyn said.

"Easy and slow," Aki responded.

* * *

CARSYN GLANCED OVER HER SHOULDER, watching for Ringo's nod. When she got it, she looked back to Aki. "You ready?" she asked.

"I'm ready," Aki responded, her voice quivering ever so slightly. She was a strong, beautiful woman.

"Okay then," Carsyn said with one last check of her harness and an adjustment of her footing. "Here we go."

Aki nodded, alert and focused.

As Carsyn tipped her shoulders back, she met her gaze. "One," she said softly.

Aki sucked in air, mouth wide open. She shifted, preparing to reposition quickly.

"Two," Carsyn continued, her chest puffed with increased stamina and strength.

Aki nodded, still holding her gaze.

"Three," Carsyn said, her attention momentarily shifting at the sound of a high-pitched whistle as the cable whipped free. "Gotcha," she exclaimed, lifting Aki. As she pulled her foot through the window, the tow chain snapped, the car lurched forward, and she couldn't breathe. "Oh God," she gasped, stepping them from the path of the telephone pole, about to give way.

"Thank you, thank you, thank you," Aki squeaked, kissing her neck, and clinging.

As Carsyn lowered her to the ground, she slid her palms down her backside, over the rounded pockets of her jeans, gently squeezing. "Oh, God," she said, "I'm so sorry." She shook her head, looking down, and stepping away.

Aki took a breath, saying, "Don't be."

CHAPTER 12

Triggers, Carsyn did everything she could to avoid them. She took a different route when she saw flashing lights and avoided that intersection, the one that changed her life, at all cost. But despite her best efforts, there were still times when encountering those things, the ones that pushed play on her tape of flashbacks was inescapable. A locomotive would appear out of nowhere, blasting his horn. A driver would slam on her brakes—too late. She cringed, seeing rubber on the pavement and caught a sickening whiff of burning flesh. *It's not real,* she told herself. *It's not real. Make it go away.* Sweat droplets popped onto her forehead, trickling down her temples, and she reached for her handkerchief. *You're almost back. Hold on. You're okay.* She closed her eyes tightly, feeling her pulse race.

"What's going on with you?" Aki asked softly. Her eyes narrowed, leaning her way.

"Good thing you went off so close to the campground," Ringo blurted out. "Otherwise, I might not have run across ya."

"Yes, it was," Aki responded distractedly, "thank you." She wrinkled her brow, leaning closer to Carsyn. "Are you experiencing pain?" she asked quietly, turning in her seat.

"No problem at all," Ringo answered. "Better world when we help each other out, I think."

"Yes, it is," Aki responded flatly, positioning her fingertips on the inside of Carsyn's wrist. "Where do you hurt?" she asked quietly. "Can you tell me?"

"I'm fine," Carsyn said curtly, moving her arm from Aki's grasp.

Aki's mouth opened, but she didn't say anything.

"It'll pass," Carsyn added, her tone softening as she met her gaze. "Really, it's nothing you need to worry about." She caught her breath, swallowing self-loathing and nausea. Dear God, did she have to grab her ass? It was totally unlike her. If only she could undo what she'd done, but she couldn't, could she. What she could do though, was to assure that it didn't happen again.

"Looks like your mare needs some untangling," Ringo announced, bouncing through a pothole at the corner. "Let me know if you need some help gettin' her outta that fix."

"I'll handle it, but thanks," Carsyn responded, pulling the handle on her door when the truck halted in front of her trailer. "Glad everything turned out okay," she said, pausing to meet Aki's gaze. "Jack's next-door," she added, "Ringo will drop you off on his way."

"Are you sure you're okay?" Aki asked with a soft breath.

Carsyn nodded. "Yeah," she said quietly, "I'm okay." She smiled thinly, turned, and walked toward the red trailer.

* * *

"You okay getting back there by yourself?" Ringo asked, placing his foot on the brake pedal.

"I'll be fine," Aki answered, getting out of his vehicle. "Thanks again."

"No problem," Ringo said. "Glad everything worked out okay."

"It wouldn't have without your help," Aki responded, holding his gaze. "Again, thank you." She shut the door, staring into his taillights as he drove away. Then she turned to study movement around the red trailer. She watched Carsyn untangle the bay with what appeared to be minimal effort, relieved that she didn't seem to be experiencing pain.

"Aunt Aki," Charlie squealed, running her way.

"Well, aren't you cute, all decked out in your camo," Aki greeted, smiling. It was so much fun to have a niece and nephew, and would be even more so during the holidays. "So, how's the birthday outing?" she asked. "Are you having a good time?"

"Uh-huh," Charlie answered excitedly. "I already found two arrowheads—and maybe a dinosaur bone!"

"A dinosaur bone," Aki responded, lifting an eyebrow. "Wow, I'm impressed."

"Yeah, maybe," Charlie chirped, reaching for her hand. "Carsyn says the jury's still out though."

"Guess we'll have to wait and see then, won't we?" Aki responded, winking.

"Uh-huh," Charlie said, approaching the campfire.

"Hi," Aki greeted, trying not to look as exhausted as she felt.

"Hi," Jack said, smiling broadly, "I'm glad you decided to come out." She cocked her head, meeting her eye, "Kind of dangerous after dark though." She furrowed her brow, looking at the road. "Where's your car?"

"It's a long story," Aki responded, shaking her head slowly. "The short version," she continued, "is that it's precariously positioned about a half-mile from the entrance." She took a breath, allowing it to escape slowly.

"Oh my gosh," Jack exclaimed, her eyes widening. "Are you okay?"

Aki nodded. "Yes," she said, "a little sore, but otherwise fine. I'm in a whole lot better shape than my rental." She smiled thinly, her eyes darting to the red trailer, watching Carsyn wrench her picket line a bit tighter. "Thanks to Carsyn," she added, biting her lower lip. "I just hope I didn't wear her out." She took a soft breath. "She doesn't have a heart condition or something like that does she?"

Jack made a face, shaking her head slowly. "Carsyn? No," she said, "she's healthy as a horse."

"That's good," Aki said, still aware of the knot at the pit of her stomach. She considered asking if Jack had observed Carsyn to have symptoms, but opted not to, feeling that it wasn't appropriate. *She's probably fine,* she thought, concluding that what she'd observed had probably been a spike of adrenaline.

"Aki," Courtney greeted with a warm hug, "how wonderful." She smiled at Jack. "Look, honey, a kindred spirit has joined the party."

"I know," Jack responded, slipping her arm around her waist with a hug, "wonderful is right." She looked at the crackling wood fire and then to Aki. "Hot dog or brat?" she offered.

Aki swallowed, trying not to curl her upper lip. "Hotdog," she responded.

"So, where's your car?" Courtney asked, furrowing her brow.

"It's a long story," Jack answered for her. "The short version is that she left it on the main road."

"Left it near the main road," Aki corrected, meeting Courtney's eye. "And don't get your hopes up," she added, "because I'm not necessarily staying the night."

"Oh, but you are," Jack responded, her voice lowering with serious eye contact. "It's too risky to take you back." She shook her head, adding, "Not tonight." She caught her wife's eye. "You two are about the same size," she continued. "You think you could come up with something for her to sleep in?" She wiggled her eyebrows. "I'm sure you've got extras in at least one of those three suitcases I carried out."

"Perhaps," Courtney responded with a slow wink and a smile. "Let me see what I've got."

"And while she does that," Jack continued, "I'll pitch the second tent for you. It's a dome with a nylon floor so it'll be airtight."

With the accident in recent memory, Aki's worries of ticks, spiders, and snakes seemed almost nonsensical. "Thanks," she responded.

"You're quite welcome," Jack said with a warm smile.

"Can I sleep in Aunt Aki's tent?" Lizzy asked, skipping behind her mama.

"Me too," Charlie whined, coming up on the other side.

"If it's okay with your parents," Aki said, nodding, "it's okay with me."

"I suppose so," Jack answered, pausing for direct eye contact, "but you have to go to sleep when she tells you it's time; no keeping her up half the night."

"Okay," Lizzy promised.

Jack tipped her chin down, lifting an eyebrow at her son.

"Okay," Charlie responded.

"Sorry to cause you extra work," Aki said, stepping in to watch Jack empty and sort through the contents of the long, slender carton.

"You didn't," Jack responded, looking up, "I invited you so I would've been pitching this tent no matter what." She rubbed her temple, studying the diagram included in the instructions. Then, she walked over to pick up the box. She scratched her head, examining the webbing and grommets.

"Have you done this before," Aki asked, bending down to analyze the available parts.

"Yeah," Jack answered, nodding, "but it's been a long time." She frowned, staring at the picture printed on the front of the box. "I just need to figure out what's what."

Aki nodded, her eyes narrowing as she considered the collection of items on the tarp. "So, some of these are silver," she said thoughtfully, "some are blue, and some are gold. So, what if we match them up?" she asked, pairing poles, grommets, and webbing, "like so."

"You're a genius," Jack exclaimed, "but I should've expected that," she added, grinning, "because we're sisters."

"Right," Aki responded with a chuckle.

"Trouble with the tent?" Courtney asked, stepping out.

"Not anymore," Jack responded.

CHAPTER 13

Courtney stepped across the zippered threshold, securing the removable fly. "You think we should close the roofing vent too?" she asked, looking over. Their tent was a large ten-man with separate sleeping areas.

"It's gonna be in the fifties," Jack responded. "If we close it, we won't get much circulation."

"Perhaps," Courtney said, "but we won't freeze to death either."

"Good point," Jack answered, smiling. "Do as you like."

With a zip, Courtney made sure their sleeping accommodations were airtight. She slipped off her sweatshirt and jeans, shimmying into a lace-trimmed flannel nightgown.

"I haven't seen that one since the dead of last winter," Jack commented, a slow smile eclipsing her mouth, "I like it."

Courtney tilted her head. "I considered long underwear," she responded, meeting her eye.

"Now that wouldn't have been any fun," Jack said, patting the soft quilted area beside her. Their sleeping bag was a two-person, rated for zero degrees Fahrenheit.

Courtney peeled back her corner, sliding in beside her.

"See, not so bad," Jack said, pressing tightly against her body. "Cuddling makes it all good, doesn't it?"

"I have to admit it's the best part," Courtney responded, kissing her mouth.

Jack kissed her back and nibbled her earlobe. When she moaned, tipping her neck upward, she wiggled her eyebrows. "There's more where that came from if you're interested," she offered. In the early days, before they'd had kids, they'd made love every night.

"I don't think we should," Courtney answered, shaking her head slowly. "You pitched your sister's tent so close to ours that it'd be like having them in here with us."

"They'll be asleep by now," Jack responded, unbuttoning the top two buttons of her wife's nightgown with intense eye contact. "Mmm," she purred, brushing across her nipples, "you're so responsive."

Courtney sucked in a breath, arching, and murmuring, "That feels nice." She held her gaze, feeling warm inside. "We'd have to be really quiet," she said, unbuttoning her remaining two buttons. She exposed her right breast, beckoning Jack's mouth.

"There's no we about it," Jack responded softly.

"I'm not the only one who gets loud," Courtney answered, biting her lower lip as Jack licked and nibbled.

"Yes, you are," Jack whispered, her warm breath teasing her wife's nipple. She held her gaze, capturing it between her teeth.

Courtney gasped. "Oh, Jack," she moaned as she raked her fingernails through her hair and down her back. "Ohhhh…"

"Shhhh," Jack reminded, suckling each nipple with focused intensity.

When Jack's hand slid downward, Courtney writhed beneath her. "I need you inside me," she begged, lifting her nightgown.

"In due time," Jack murmured, kissing her abdomen, and massaging her hips and buttocks. "God, you're wet," she moaned, pushing inside her. She pulled out, pushing in deeply.

"Ohhhhhhhh…"

"Shhhh…"

"Ohhhhhhhhhh..."

"Shhhhhhh..."

"Ohhhhhhhhhhhh..."

"Shhhhhhhhhhhh," Jack said, making eye contact, and whispering, "Courtie, they're right next door."

"Ohhhhhhhhhhh," Courtney moaned, spasms taking hold. "Oh—Dear—God—Jack—Yes—Harder—Oh, God—I'm coming..."

"I know, baby," Jack said, kissing, and holding her. She brushed a lock of hair from her eyes, murmuring, "I know...Shhhh."

"Damn, that was good," Courtney panted, her breathing starting to slow.

"Not bad for sleeping bag sex, huh?" Jack responded.

"Not at all," Courtney chuckled, reaching over to untie her wife's pajama bottoms. "Time for act two," she said softly. As she kissed Jack's nipple through her t-shirt, she slid her hand down the front of her pants.

"I was hoping you'd be in the mood for a two-act show," Jack said, moaning. She sucked in air as Courtney's fingertips found her prominence. "God, you've got that down to a science," she murmured.

"Uh-huh," Courtney answered, stroking in a steady circular motion, and peering into her eyes. "I know what you like."

"You always have," Jack answered, her breathing coarse.

Courtney bit her lower lip, whipping harder. "I love you, baby," she murmured, pushing inside her, "I love you so much."

"I love you too," Jack responded, stiffening under her touch.

Courtney closed her eyes, relishing the moment.

"Oh God," Jack groaned. "Courtie, I'm coming..."

"I know, baby," Courtney answered, easing and slowing. She nestled against her breast, kissing inked skin, two hearts adorned with wedding bands and their initials, marks of their love. Euphoria, this was euphoria.

* * *

AKI CRAWLED from the blue vinyl to the cold ground, pausing for one last look at her niece and nephew, before zipping the rounded door closed. She smiled, thinking that they represented living proof that kids could sleep through any amount of commotion. Unfortunately, she could not. Anything and everything roused her—a dripping faucet, a cricket chirping in the distance, a socked foot on the stairway—a woman screaming during orgasm. Until tonight, in spite of the literature, she'd never believed that the earth-shattering variety existed. Two well-adjusted kids, smart and good-looking, a beautiful home, a good job, and a spouse who screamed her name during sex. It couldn't get much better than that. Her sister was one lucky woman, luckier than she dared hope for. At thirty-five, getting a good job, and eventually, a nice house, was her best-case scenario. She glanced at Carsyn's trailer, noticing that a light was still on, and pulled her blanket around her shoulders. With a shiver, she stepped several paces to the wood pile. Larger than she'd have expected for a week-long outing, it offered split logs in all shapes and sizes. She selected a small one, clean, and free of spider webs, setting it gently atop the glowing orange embers. As flames crackled around it, she settled into a seat.

"You heard us," Jack whispered, coming up from behind, and straddling the adjacent camp stool.

"Possibly," Aki responded, suppressing a smile.

"Probably," Jack countered, shaking her head slowly. "I'm sorry," she added, her cheeks flushing, and a dimple appearing as she dropped her eyes.

"It's okay," Aki answered. "It was probably just me, sleeping lightly." She lifted an eyebrow, adding, "The kids didn't stir at all."

"They're used to it," Jack responded, biting her lower lip, and staring at the fire.

"I'm glad you came out to join me," Aki said, smiling.

"Me too," Jack responded, lifting her eyes. "So, how's the ankle?" she asked, changing the subject.

"Swollen, but fine," Aki responded. "I wish I'd have had the forethought to toss my bag to Carsyn before she pulled me out."

"That, and your tuna steaks, huh?" Jack answered, winking.

"It was that obvious, huh?" Aki responded, smiling thinly. "I'm not much for greasy processed food," she added.

"Probably because you know how bad it is for you," Jack responded. "I'm not much for it either," she added. "And really, we don't indulge that often."

"That's good," Aki said, nodding.

"We'll fix something healthy tonight," Jack continued, meeting her eye. "You are gonna stick around, right?"

Aki's gaze drifted to the red trailer as she poked the fire. "We'll see," she answered quietly.

Jack got up, collecting a thick log, and tossing it on.

"You think Carsyn will eat here tonight?" Aki asked, "or will she eat by herself?" She'd been disappointed when the evening passed without her coming over.

"Probably eat with us," Jack answered, her brow furrowing, "why?"

"Just wondered," Aki said. "I want a chance to thank her properly." She looked off and into the fire. "You know," she added, "now that I've got my wits about me."

"Sure," Jack said, nodding.

"That's if I decide to stay," Aki added.

"Sure, I get it," Jack responded.

"But I might not," Aki said, her lips parting.

"Sure," Jack said, her eyes narrowing. "Whatever you decide to do is fine."

"That's good," Aki answered, licking her lips when Carsyn stepped outside. "That's good," she repeated absentmindedly.

Jack cocked her head, lifting an eyebrow. "She's probably just checking on the horses," she said quietly.

CHAPTER 14

Carsyn missed the first step, catching her balance before her knee hit the ground. As she straightened, she looked toward the blazing fire. *She didn't notice,* she told herself, not that it mattered because Aki wasn't gay and she was too old. When Aki tipped her head back, laughing, she smiled. It pleased her that she and Jack had hit it off so well. She switched on a second light, stepped inside and collected her bottle from the counter. As she slid into the custom-made dining nook, maple with red padded seats, she poured another glass of Jack Daniel's. She swirled the golden liquid, swished it around in her mouth, and swallowed. She'd had an alcoholic beverage or two when she was in college, none before, and more than she could count since the funerals. Nights were the hardest. Sleeping led to nightmares. Nightmares led to whiskey. Rinse and repeat—over and over. It was worse after being triggered—and seeing Aki nearly go over the edge had been like reliving the horror. She poured, swished, and swallowed, pushing aside the curtain to peek out.

Aki rested her poker against a log, looking over.

Carsyn sucked in a breath, leaning back so as not to be visible. *Just stop,* she told herself. *Stop torturing yourself. She's too young, you're too* old, and she's Jack's sister. She exhaled, staring into her glass. *Plus, she's not gay...and even if she was, you don't date anymore.* She poured, swished, and swallowed. "I date," she mumbled. "I date when it feels right." *Which is never,* her mind responded, *not since that one time.* She tipped the bottle, allowing the last drops to fall into her glass. "I date when it feels right," she mumbled.

* * *

"So, is she married?" Aki asked, watching a second light come on in the window, probably a lamp on the table.

"Who?" Jack responded, cocking her head.

"Carsyn," Aki answered, feeling a quiver in her stomach.

"No," Jack said quietly, her head shaking slowly as she stared into the flames. "But she used to be," she added, her brow furrowing. "Why do you ask?"

"No reason," Aki responded, "I was just curious. She didn't have anyone with her at your house, and no one seems to be with her in her trailer." She swallowed, holding her hands over the fire for a minute. "Well, that's about all for me," she said, standing. "I'm headed in for what I hope will soon be a warm sleeping bag."

"I enjoyed our talk," Jack said, holding her gaze, "and I hope you decide to stay."

"I may," Aki answered, folding her blanket across her arm. As she unzipped her tent door, she took one last look at the flashy red trailer with the golden trim. "What's wrong with you?" she asked under her breath. She checked on the children, slipped inside her insulated cocoon, and pushed her mind to distraction. *Think,* she told the organ. *Think of anything, absolutely anything, anything but the woman whose neck you kissed so naturally—Sclera, cornea, anterior and posterior chambers, iris, pupil, lens, vitreous humor, retina, fovea, and macula.* Parts of the eye, she shook her head remembering how she'd forgotten to list retina on her first exam. She tugged her blanket, covering her ears, and rolling to her side. It was chilly, especially in a nightgown, but not nearly enough to be an adequate distraction. As she drifted off, *the white eagle swooped low in the valley from a high branch.*

* * *

"Come, Biboon," Jack whispered, meeting the eye of their oldest dog. "Come, Niibin." The huskies yawned, standing and stretching, the jingle of their tags being the only sound as they made their way around the air mattress. As she clipped on their leads, she reminded them to be quiet. Courtney had slept fairly well and she wanted her to sleep a while longer. She unzipped and zipped the door, one tooth at a time. "Come on," she whispered, tugging. As she took off, she held two leashes in one hand and a bucket in the other. "You're up early," she called out, passing the shower house.

Carsyn nodded, saying, "It was one of those nights." She smiled thinly, tipping her head in the direction of the mounds. "Already took some tools over to the site," she added. "Can you believe a couple of my students were already there waiting for them?"

"Unbelievable," Jack responded, shaking her head. "So, you're digging today?" she observed, crinkling her brow. It was Sunday—and three years to the day since she'd lost her parents and wife.

"Yeah," Carsyn responded, pressing her lips together. "It's better if I stay busy, you know?"

"Yeah, maybe so," Jack responded, patting her shoulder. She met her eye, adding, "Missed you at dinner last night."

"I wouldn't have been good company," Carsyn responded, looking over.

"Wouldn't have mattered," Jack countered. "Maybe tonight?"

"Yeah, maybe," Carsyn responded with a thin smile, "Or at least we'll shoot for it."

"Aki told me what you did," Jack continued softly. "Thank you," she added, meeting her eye.

"Yeah, well, you'd have done the same for me," Carsyn responded, swallowing. "How's she doing this morning?"

"Haven't seen her yet," Jack answered. "She got to bed pretty late, so I might not for a while. My best guess? Her ankle will be even more swollen."

"She hurt her ankle?" Carsyn asked, her forehead wrinkling and her mouth falling open.

"Yeah," Jack said, nodding, "I guess her foot got caught on the mirror or something when you were pulling her out. She said it wasn't fractured," she added, "and didn't want to go to the hospital. I offered to make her an arnica poultice, but even after I went on and on about how the herb had been used by Native Americans for centuries as an anti-inflammatory, she didn't want any part of it. I guess she's one of those Docs who sees no value in traditional healing."

"Or," Carsyn responded, lifting an eyebrow, "she just didn't feel like she needed an arnica poultice at the moment." She sighed, shaking her head, and looking off. "God, I feel bad I injured her ankle," she added softly, "I should've been more careful."

"You did the best you could," Jack responded, locking gazes, "and you don't need to feel bad, because what you did, saved her life."

"I suppose you're taking her back to her hotel this morning," Carsyn said, her voice fading off.

"I don't know, maybe," Jack responded. "I think it'll depend on how sore she is and how well she slept on the hard ground. At the very least, we'll have to drive in to arrange for a tow truck, and maybe another rental."

Carsyn took a breath, turning toward her trailer. "Well, I've got lots to do," she said, "better catch you later."

"Yeah, later," Jack responded, heading toward the water spigot between the two campsites. She filled her bucket, built a fire, and made coffee. As she sipped from her copper mug, arms came around her from behind. "Hi," she said softly, smiling.

"Hi," Courtney responded, kissing her lips, and pouring coffee. "You're up early," she said, pulling a campstool over, and sitting beside her.

"Yeah, the crack of dawn," Jack responded. "Did you sleep well?" she asked quietly.

"Like a baby," Courtney responded, resting her head on her shoulder, and kissing her another time. "Better than I thought possible."

"Morning," Aki greeted, joining them. She grimaced, saying, "I think I'll take you up on your arnica poultice."

"Coming right up," Jack responded with a smile.

CHAPTER 15

"Okay," Jack said softly, lowering onto her knees, "let's see that ankle."

"It's a sprain," Aki responded, removing her unlaced tennis shoe and sock.

"Wow, I'm surprised that you could even bear weight on that last night," Jack said, examining her ankle. "I mean, judging from the amount of swelling and depth of the bruising," she added, looking up, "you should've been experiencing quite a bit of pain."

"It worsened overnight," Aki admitted.

"You noticed it overnight," Jack corrected.

"You're probably right," Aki said, nodding, "probably once the shock wore off." She pursed her lips, taking a breath. "I should've listened when you told me not to take off the ice pack."

"Yes, you should've," Jack said, lifting an eyebrow. She slid her fingers up Aki's lower leg and back down. "And you're sure you don't need an X-ray?" she asked, frowning.

"No," Aki answered, "I think it'll be fine. I didn't see any sign of a fracture."

"You're the Doc," Jack responded, maneuvering her leg to stretch a ligament.

"Ouch," Aki responded. "You know what you're doing," she commented.

"Thanks," Jack answered, smiling. "Coming from someone with your level of training, that's a real compliment." She met her gaze, adding, "And since you are so well-trained, I probably don't need to tell you what you need to do here."

"Nope," Aki responded, shaking her head, "RICE—rest, ice, compression, and elevation." She smiled back, wiggling her eyebrows. "And of course," she added, "your magic poultice."

"Exactly," Jack answered, winking. She prepared the warm herbal paste, wrapped it in cloth, and placed it on the top of Aki's ankle. "We'll need to leave it on for a few hours," she added, standing.

"After which time," Aki said, looking up, "I'm hoping to talk you into giving me a lift into town."

"My pleasure," Jack responded, lifting the black pot from its rack over the fire. "More coffee anyone?"

"Absolutely," Aki said, "I may as well enjoy a second cup since it seems I'm going to be sitting here with my foot elevated for a while."

"None for me, thanks," Courtney responded, dropping her mug into a tub of soapy dishwater that she'd just placed on the end of the picnic table. She kissed Jack's lips, adding, "I need to get our son up and dressed for his second day as an archaeologist."

"Be in shortly," Jack answered, turning her attention to Aki. "So, did you get any sleep last night?" she asked. She filled their cups and set the percolator back down. "I hate that we woke you up."

"As I told you," Aki responded kindly, "it wasn't a problem." She shook her head, glancing at the fire, and then the trailer. With no sign of activity, she looked back. "I just kept waking up," she added. "Nothing new, and nothing I seem to be able to do about it."

"Pain?" Jack asked, furrowing her brow.

"No, not really," Aki responded. "I mean I had some last night, but not so bad that I couldn't have slept through it." She took a breath, releasing it with a heavy sigh. "It's these crazy dreams I keep having," she added. "They've been waking me up for months and months and months."

Jack squished her eyebrows together. "I thought you said it'd been a month since your last one," she clarified.

"Since my last one about you," Aki responded, her chin dropping as she met her eye. "Unfortunately," she added, "I have other recurring nighttime dramas." She sipped the steaming black liquid, palming the sides of her cup. "I had high hopes that our meeting, and of course finishing my fellowship, would put an end to all of them." She exhaled, adding, "But I guess not."

"Tell me about them," Jack said, leaning toward her.

Aki shook her head, saying, "No, I don't think so."

"Dreams are important," Jack continued softly, "you don't need to be embarrassed that you have them or about sharing their content. They're conduits to a nonphysical realm that allow us to communicate with our guardian spirits. They're important."

Aki turned, staring incredulously.

"You think I'm nuts," Jack responded, swallowing. "Don't worry; you're not the first."

"No, I don't think that," Aki said, shaking her head, "I was just processing." She lifted both eyebrows, tilting her head slightly. "It's actually an interesting concept."

"More than interesting," Jack responded, her tone lowering. "It's central to an Ojibwe's spiritual life."

"I didn't mean anything by it," Aki said, "it's just not a topic that I'm familiar with, that's all."

"It's okay, I get it," Jack said, her lips pursed, and nodding. She took a breath, adding, "It was that way for me at one time, a long, long time ago." She exhaled, looking off and flashing back to the Black Bear's first appearance during her slumber. It was in the month following her graduation from high school. Courtie had disappeared, and that night she'd been missing her more than anything in the world. As she'd unscrewed the cap on a bottle of her dad's heart medication, prepared to take her life, the bear came to her. He came and saw her through. In the years that followed, he led her to her people, sharing his gifts, and teaching her to be a healer. And decades later, after hope of seeing Courtie again had all but vanished, he stood with them at the time of their reunion, continuing to walk with them as they raised their children.

"I'm sorry," Aki said, touching Jack's knee. "I didn't mean anything by it. Really."

"I know you didn't," Jack said, her gaze lifting from the fire, and her attention returning to the present. "I was just thinking, thinking about a dream I had long ago, one that changed everything." She bit her lip, looking at her. "You wouldn't happen to be dreaming about an animal or animals, would you?"

Again, the incredulous stare. "How could you possibly have known to ask that question?" Aki inquired, her lips parting. "How in the world could you possibly have known that?"

Jack smiled thinly, nodding. "I wondered if that might be the case," she said softly. "The teachings, they tell us that we have two souls," she continued, "one, a night traveler who makes her home in our dreams, and the other a day traveler who makes her home in this world. At the time of creation, our spirit animals were given special gifts, including knowledge of the future. They exist in that non-physical realm."

"So, you think my dreams are like messages from this other world?" Aki asked, her mouth open, and her brow furrowed.

"It's a possibility," Jack answered, nodding. "The guardian spirits could be trying to tell you something."

"Well, if they are," Aki muttered, "they need to do it so that I can figure it out." She caught her breath, flushing when she met Carsyn's eye. "Hi," she said softly, moistening her lips, and swallowing.

"Hi," Carsyn responded, her voice lowering as she moved closer.

"Hey there, pal," Jack greeted, "I figured you'd be at the site by now."

"No, not yet," Carsyn responded distractedly. "I thought I'd better come over and check on somebody's ankle." She held Aki's gaze, saying, "I'm so sorry."

"It's fine," Aki responded, touching her neck, and swallowing. "Just a little sprain, that's all." She licked her lips, adjusting the neckline of her robe. "Sit with me," she invited softly, tugging the adjacent camp stool closer.

Jack cocked her head, inwardly lifting an eyebrow.

"I can only stay for a few minutes," Carsyn responded, brushing against Aki's thigh as she sat down. "Then," she added, smiling, "I really do need to go."

"You know what?" Jack blurted out, clearing her throat, "I think I need to check on something." She stood, looking to Carsyn. "You keep Aki company, okay, pal?"

"She will," Aki responded, removing her perfectly placed poultice to show Carsyn her ankle.

"Sure," Carsyn said, gently touching it. "Aww," she cooed, "it's so swollen."

"It'll be reduced by tonight," Aki responded, touching her mouth.

Not if you don't keep that poultice on, it won't, Jack thought, stepping off.

* * *

"Well, I'll be darned," Jack said, unzipping, and coming through the door.

"What?" Courtney asked, coming to her.

"I'm not one-hundred-percent sure," Jack answered, smiling, "but I think my sister and Carsyn might be interested in one another."

"Wishful thinking," Courtney responded with a roll of her eyes. "Aki's not a lesbian, honey," she proclaimed decisively. "You should've seen her reaction when she learned that you had a wife."

"I wouldn't be so sure about that," Jack said, a playful lift dancing in her voice. She wiggled her eyebrows, adding, "I wouldn't be so sure at all."

"Uh-huh," Courtney responded, kissing her lips, "well, wishful thinking gets my vote."

CHAPTER 16

"I appreciate the ride," Aki said, looking away as they drove past her crash site. It made sense that Courtney was driving her to town. With the temperature predicted to dip into the low forties, Jack's time was better spent splitting logs. She probably would've gone ahead and taken her had she not decided to stay a couple more nights. It was freezing cold, the ground was hard, and the food to this point had been unhealthy—but Carsyn was next door.

"Not a problem," Courtney responded, her hands gripping the steering wheel, and her eyes fixed on the road.

"I'll sit quietly," Aki said, recognizing her symptoms of anxiety for what they were. "We can talk once you get on the blacktop."

"I hate this stretch," Courtney muttered, "and I'm not fond of driving this vehicle either."

"I understand," Aki said quietly, eyes forward.

"There," Courtney sighed, her shoulders relaxing.

"We made it," Aki responded. "It's a nerve-racking road," she added, touching her ankle. "They should widen it or something."

"Yes, they should," Courtney agreed, looking over. "So, how is it?" she asked softly.

"Better by the hour," Aki responded, smiling. "Still sore, but definitely not fractured." She tilted her head, adding, "Jack's poultice helped."

"I'm sure it did," Courtney responded, passing a slow truck. "She studies all the time," she added, "and she's gotten really good at what she does."

"She is good," Aki agreed, having not thought much of traditional medicine until the last twenty-four hours.

They traveled the next leg in companionable silence. "So, how'd you meet Jack?" Aki asked warmly.

Courtney took a soft breath. "We went to high school together," she answered quietly, "high school sweethearts."

"Awww, high school sweethearts," Aki responded, smiling. "That's nice, but a long time to love the same person."

"Not so long," Courtney responded, slowing behind a large piece of farm equipment, "not if that person's the one." Her eyes moistened. "Not only is it not a long time," she added, "but for us, it'll never be long enough." She took a soft breath, releasing it as they came to a stop. "She swept me off my feet," she continued, touching and turning her wedding band, "and from that moment, I couldn't imagine loving anyone else."

"That's sweet," Aki said, feeling a pang in her heart. "So, did you always know?" she asked, her eyebrows furrowing, and releasing. "I mean before you met Jack?"

Courtney tilted her head. "Are you asking me if I always knew that I was a lesbian?"

"Yes," Aki said, meeting her gaze with surprising directness.

"No, I didn't," Courtney answered, chuckling softly. "I guess I figured it out as Jack was sweeping me off my feet. I must say though, I've never looked back."

"That's funny," Aki said, chuckling with her.

"I'm dead serious," Courtney added. "The day before we became an item, I was a cheerleader, just like all the others, drooling over the football team." She bit her lower lip, remembering. "And then..."

"I'd say my sister made quite the impression," Aki said as her mind flashed back to Friday evening.

"Yes, she did," Courtney said, reducing speed as she approached a stoplight. "Where would you like to go first," she asked, "your hotel or the car rental agency?"

"Car rental agency," Aki answered. "That way, you can go on back while I finish up my business." They discussed what each family member liked to eat as she was preparing to step into the parking lot. "And what about Carsyn?" she asked, "What would she like?"

"Probably a tuna steak," Courtney responded. "I don't think I've ever seen her eat a hamburger."

"Okay," Aki said, smiling as she summarized their order. "So, we've got three hamburgers, one chicken breast, and two tuna steaks," she reported. "Now, how about dessert?" she asked. "Judging from the layer of icing on my nephew's birthday cake, I'm fairly certain that I've joined a dessert eating family."

"That you have," Courtney responded, adding, "some kind of pie. Jack's favorite's pecan."

"And Carsyn's?" Aki inquired, lifting an eyebrow.

"Chocolate cake or s'mores," Courtney responded.

"Okay then, I'll see you back at the campsite," Aki said, opening her door.

"Drive carefully," Courtney said with eye contact.

"You know I will," Aki responded. "No multi-tasking," she added, "especially on that road, not anymore." She walked off and turned around. "Hey, stick around for a minute, would you?" she called out. "I want to make sure they'll rent me another car after I tell them their other one is dangling over Deadman's Bluff."

"I'll be right here until you wave me on," Courtney responded, swiping the screen of her smartphone.

* * *

"That's right," Aki said, nodding, "I'm checking out early."

As the clerk tallied her bill, he asked about the quality of her accommodations.

"They were great," Aki responded. "I'm cutting my stay short to stay with family." Just stringing the words together in the same sentence brought pleasure.

"Excellent," he responded, handing her a receipt. "We hope you'll stay with us should the need arise in the future, Dr. Williams."

"I'm sure I will," Aki responded, smiling politely. She followed her luggage cart through the revolving door, watching as the young bellhop unloaded it.

"There you go, ma'am," the woman announced, gently closing her trunk.

"Thank you," Aki responded, noticing that the woman's hair was short like Jack's—and Carsyn's. She handed her a twenty-dollar bill, entered the address of the supermarket into her GPS, and parked her midsize rental near the door. Leaning on her cart, she made her way around the store.

"One pound of ground sirloin, one chicken breast, and two choice tuna steaks," the older woman said, handing over three white packages. "They didn't care for the marinated, huh?"

"I beg your pardon?" Aki responded, cocking her head.

"Tuna," the clerk added, "the marinated tuna steaks. I waited on you before."

"Oh yes, I remember," Aki responded. "And, I have no idea as the steaks didn't actually make it to the table."

"Dropped 'em, huh," the woman said, nodding. "Happens to the best of us."

"Something like that," Aki responded, wishing her a good day. She collected graham crackers, chocolate bars, and marshmallows along the same aisle and rolled to the bakery. "I'll have a pecan pie; the one right there," she said, pointing through the glass, "and a good-sized slice of your triple-layer, chunky-chocolate cake."

* * *

"Need help?" Jack asked, rolling down her window.

"Nah," the tow truck driver answered, unbothered by the situation. "Hardest part'll be getting this baby backed in at the right angle." He patted the pink, six-wheel vehicle with an idling diesel engine. "You know, around the chain." He met her eye, nodding. "Good idea by the way," he added, "the telephone pole, I mean." He cocked his head toward the road. "You back on outta the way," he said, "and I'll have your car up in a jiffy."

"Good deal," Jack answered, moving to the safer location. "So, I've got a professional question," she said, meeting Aki's gaze, "if that's okay, I mean."

"Of course, it's okay," Aki responded, making a face. "Ask away."

"So, I've got this patient, an older woman," Jack began. "Treated her for years."

"Okay..."

Jack sighed, continuing. "And I'm afraid she's going blind," she said, "and I don't know what to do for her."

"She needs to make an appointment to see an ophthalmologist," Aki responded.

"I know," Jack sighed, "but she refuses. She's one of many who don't trust the white man's medicine."

Aki looked upward, shaking her head.

"Many don't, you know," Jack added.

"I know," Aki said, her tone softening. "I've read the studies, those that recommend the integration of traditional healing practices into mainstream medicine. For some reason, when doctors and tribal healers work together, their Native American patients have better outcomes."

"I've read similar studies," Jack said, taking a breath, "and know from personal experience that there are times when a patient needs more than a tribal healer has to give them, times when she needs modern medicine." She swallowed, looking out her window. "And it's so frustrating," she continued, her voice cracking, "so incredibly frustrating when I can't get her to see that."

"Tell me more," Aki responded, resting her hand on Jack's wrist.

"She's seventy," Jack said. "I suspect she's diabetic although I've not been able to talk her into going in for a blood test. She has peripheral neuropathy."

"Hands, feet, or both?" Aki asked.

"So far, just her feet," Jack responded. "With regard to her eyes, her vision is blurred, and she reports seeing floating dark spots. So far, they've cleared on their own."

"The bleeding will recur," Aki said, "and without treatment, you're right, she's going to have a permanent reduction in her vision."

"I know," Jack said, shaking her head. "I just don't know what to do to help her."

"Let me think about it," Aki responded, looking over at the sound of the tow truck's first tug.

Wumpth—the tow truck lurched forward.

"Scares me to death to think what almost happened here," Jack said, swallowing hard.

Wumpth—it lurched again.

"It could've been bad, that's for sure," Aki responded. She met her gaze with a thin smile. "But you should've seen Carsyn," she continued softly. "She was absolutely amazing." She bit her lower lip, her eyes brightening. "Steady and strong through the whole ordeal."

"I'm not surprised," Jack responded, smiling.

Wumpth—the bumper bounced over.

"Here it comes," Jack announced, stretching upward to see the rest of the vehicle.

"I don't think it's totaled, do you?" Aki asked, her brow furrowing.

"No, I don't think so," Jack responded, shaking her head slowly. "It'll have some hefty repairs though."

"Yes," Aki sighed, "I think so." She pulled her door handle. "I need to get my bag before he pulls off," she announced, "oh, and my cooler."

"You sit tight," Jack responded with a pat on her leg. "I'll get 'em for ya."

CHAPTER 17

"Ahem...did you forget someone?" Courtney asked. Her eyes widened, tilting her head.

"What?" Jack asked playfully. "You want one? Why I had no idea that roasting a marshmallow would be worth risking those beautifully manicured nails." She laughed, revealing a sixth whittled green stick from behind her back. "Only my wife," she added, "would have her nails done in the middle of a camping trip."

"See what I put up with?" Courtney asked, shaking her head. "It's worth it, baby," she shot back with serious eye contact. "Come on," she said, "hand it over, handsome."

Jack skewered a marshmallow. "Here you go," she said, laughing.

"It won't work," Lizzy huffed as hers caught on fire, turning the color of charcoal. "Mama would you do mine?" she whined.

"You have to hold it high above the flame and be patient," Jack responded, moving closer. "Here, let me show you."

"It's trickier than one might think," Aki said, watching hers drop and sizzle.

"Here," Carsyn offered softly, "I'll show you." She scooted close and then closer, folding her hands around Aki's to slow-roast a perfectly golden marshmallow. Then, she broke off a piece of chocolate, laid it on a graham cracker, pulled the marshmallow from the stick, and laid it on top.

"You eat it," Aki said, smiling as she squished on the second graham cracker. "I'll eat the next one."

"No way," Carsyn responded, smiling back, "this one's all yours." Her eyes twinkled, watching Aki take her first bite. "Good?" she asked, cocking her head, and grinning.

"Mmmm, really good," Aki answered, giggling as she wiped marshmallowy-chocolate from her mouth.

"I love your cologne," Carsyn murmured, handing her a dampened washcloth, "spicy like warm apple cider."

"Thanks," Aki responded, swishing her hair back and forth. Her gaze lingered with a need to be touched. *What are you doing?* she asked herself. *You're playing with fire, that's what.* She swallowed, trying to think as blood pounded against her eardrums.

Carsyn's lips parted. She took a soft breath, moistening them with her tongue as she moved closer.

Dear God, Aki squeaked in her thoughts, *she's going to kiss you.* Her breath burst in and out. *She's going to kiss you. Then what?* Her heartbeat raced, glancing away, and putting considerable distance between their bodies.

Carsyn's smile stiffened, she clenched her jaw, and her face lost color. "I think it's about time for me to call it a night," she announced, swallowing.

"You didn't even eat one s'more," Jack responded, frowning. "You okay, pal?"

"I'm fine," Carsyn said, forcing a smile. "I have a lesson plan to do before I turn in and with tonight's dinner, I've already had plenty."

"If you want, I'll make you one," Jack persisted, reaching for the bag of marshmallows.

"No," Carsyn responded, "I really have had enough." She walked off without further eye contact, her shoulders slumped.

"Carsyn, wait…" Aki called out, her mouth filling with imaginary cotton balls.

"I'll catch you tomorrow or the next day," Carsyn responded, turning back briefly, and forcing another smile.

Jack's brow furrowed, watching the scene unfold.

"Can we sleep with Aunt Aki tonight?" Lizzy asked.

"Yeah, Mama," Charlie whined, "can we?"

Jack shook her head, saying, "No, not tonight." She looked at Courtney, communicating with her eyes. "I think your mommy has a special camping story that she wants to tell you."

"That's right, I do," Courtney answered, smiling, and nodding to Jack. "Come on, you two," she added, collecting her children with a gentle nudge. "Let's get our pajamas on."

"Night," Lizzy said, hugging her mama and aunt.

"Night," Charlie echoed, following suit.

"Night, angels," Aki responded. As they moved off, she looked over, watching Carsyn.

"Can we sleep with Aunt Aki tomorrow night?" Lizzy asked hopefully.

"Yeah, can we?" Charlie echoed.

"We'll see," Courtney responded, zipping the tent door closed. "You can talk with your mama and Aunt Aki about it tomorrow."

* * *

JACK GOT UP, returning food items and utensils to their containers. "Is everything alright?" she asked, sitting back down. Her tone and demeanor were gentle and kind.

Aki nodded, saying, "I hope so." She turned, meeting her eye. "I'm not gay," she blurted out.

"Okay…" Jack said quietly. She poked the fire and added another log.

"At least I didn't think that I was," Aki added with a swallow. "Now, I don't know."

"Does it matter?" Jack asked tenderly, "I mean, whether you are or whether you aren't?"

"I'm not sure," Aki answered, her gaze dropping to the fire for a long moment. "I don't think so," she added, taking a breath, and holding it.

"Straight, gay, or somewhere in between," Jack said, "to me, it doesn't matter." She held her gaze. "I love you just the way you are. I love you and I feel so blessed that we've been given the chance to know one another."

"I feel the same way about you," Aki responded, smiling thinly.

"It's weird, isn't it," Jack commented, her head shaking slowly, "to have just met someone and feel a connection like you've always known them."

"It is," Aki responded, "weird, but wonderful." She swallowed, again staring at the fire. "I think it might matter," she added, looking up.

"Because of Carsyn?" Jack asked quietly.

"Yes," Aki said, pressing her lips together, "and I need to go. I mean I need to go check on her."

"I knew what you meant," Jack answered, retrieving the chocolate bars, the graham crackers, and the marshmallows. "She really did want one of these, you know."

"I know," Aki responded, spearing the plumpest one, and roasting it just as Carsyn had shown her. "Don't wait up for me," she added, feeling good about the quality of her solo s'more.

"I won't," Jack responded, squeezing her hand. "Be careful walking across that rough ground."

"I will," Aki said, wrapping the treat in aluminum foil.

"See you in the morning," Jack called out.

Aki paused, looking over her shoulder. "I'm sure I'll be back before then," she responded.

"I'm sure you will," Jack answered with a soft chuckle.

* * *

COURTNEY SMILED, gazing at her sleeping children before switching off the lantern. "This was a good idea," she whispered, zipping herself in beside Jack.

"Yeah, they're having a good time, aren't they?" Jack said, pulling her close, and kissing her lips. "You are too," she added, smiling.

"I have to admit that I am," Courtney answered. "It's been fun watching you with your sister."

"She's a sweetie, isn't she?" Jack responded, draping her arm around Courtney's abdomen, and squeezing gently.

"She is," Courtney said. "What a shame that you two didn't get the chance to know one another growing up." She met her gaze. "And in spite of that unfortunate circumstance," she added, "look how much you have in common."

"Yeah, we do have quite a few similarities, don't we?" Jack agreed, her eyes twinkling with her smile.

"I mean, it goes way beyond appearance," Courtney continued, her eyes widening. "It's your food preferences, your taste in music, your mannerisms, and that you both became healers." She pursed her lips, her head shaking gently as she repeated, "Such a shame that you didn't get the chance to know one another as children." She glanced across the tent to the small adjacent sleeping bags. "I think you'd have been the best of friends like our babies."

"Yeah, I think we would've," Jack responded with a soft sigh. "But a kid can't be best friends with a sister until she knows she exists. There should be a requirement that if another child is born, the older sibling's adoptive parents get notified." She swallowed. "Had that been the case," she added, "I'm one-hundred percent certain that we'd not only have known one another as children, but we'd have grown up in the same household."

Courtney became unnaturally still, feeling tightness in her chest.

"Oh well," Jack continued, "there's nothing we can do about that now." She smiled, squeezing and planting a kiss between her wife's shoulder blades. "I'm just glad that Aki has dreams like I do. Otherwise, we might never have met one another."

"Me too," Courtney responded, reaching for her prescription antacids, and debating how much, if anything, she should tell her.

CHAPTER 18

At the sound of nickers, Carsyn looked out the window. "Shit," she muttered, closing the blind, and running to close the others. She caught a glimpse of Aki looking up as she twisted the last handle. "Shit," she muttered again, holding her forehead, and sliding her knees under the table.

Knock, knock, knock.

Carsyn sucked in a breath, holding it.

Knock—knock, knock, knock.

"Carsyn, please open the door," Aki called out. "I know you're in there," she added. "I saw you."

Carsyn swallowed, considering her best course of action.

"Carsyn, would you please come to the door?" Aki asked firmly. "I need to talk to you for a minute." Her tone softened. "And, I have something for you."

Carsyn sat, not moving a muscle. *Coward,* she thought. *Just face her. Tell her you're busy, she'll leave, and that's all there'll be to it.*

"Alright," Aki sighed, "it's on the step."

Carsyn exhaled, relieved that she'd given up so easily.

"If you change your mind," Aki added, "I'll be awake for a while. Come over if you want."

Carsyn listened for her to step off before opening the door. She smiled, bending down to retrieve the warm s'more. As she straightened, Aki reemerged from around the corner. "Shit," she muttered.

"Busted," Aki said, lifting an eyebrow.

"Come in," Carsyn answered, holding the door open.

"I thought we should talk," Aki said with a thin smile.

"Yeah, sure," Carsyn answered. She slid her hands into her pockets and leaned against the stove. "I'm sorry I got out of line tonight," she added.

"What?" Aki answered, squishing her eyebrows together. "What makes you say that?"

Carsyn looked away, feeling heaviness in the bottom of her stomach. "I don't know," she responded, brushing cake crumbs into her palm. "Can I fix you a drink?" she offered.

"No, but you go ahead," Aki responded with a slight pinch of her brow.

"No, I don't need one," Carsyn said with a nod toward the small sofa. "Have a seat," she offered, standing until Aki sat down.

"I could almost enjoy camping in a trailer as nice as this one," Aki complimented.

"I like it," Carsyn said, clearing her throat, and stepping back to the counter for her s'more.

"It's probably cold by now," Aki commented.

"Maybe, but it doesn't matter," Carsyn said. "Warm, cold, or room temperature, I've always loved them." She held Aki's eye. "Thanks for bringing it over."

"You're welcome," Aki said, smiling. "I hope I got the marshmallow right."

"You did," Carsyn said, taking a bite. "There's no way to eat these without getting them all over you," she added, laughing and wiping her mouth.

"So I found out," Aki responded, returning to the prior topic. "What made you say that you got out of line tonight?" she asked, slipping off her jacket.

"Gosh, where are my manners?" Carsyn blurted out. "I'm sorry. I should've offered to take that." She collected the jacket, hanging it on a hook by the door.

"There's no reason for you to be sorry," Aki responded. "It's not your responsibility to see to my jacket."

"Maybe not," Carsyn countered, "but it's the polite thing to do, especially after you were so kind as to roast and deliver a warm s'more."

Aki held her gaze, taking pause. "You haven't answered my question," she continued softly. "What made you think you were out of line tonight?"

Carsyn exhaled, meeting her eye. "Pure and simple?" she responded with a shrug of her shoulders, "a beautiful young woman shouldn't have to fend off unwelcome advances." She shook her head adding, "It's okay, I get it, really I do."

"No, I don't think so," Aki responded directly.

"I get it," Carsyn persisted. "You could have anyone you want," she said, "the last thing you need is some old butch coming onto you."

"Good grief," Aki responded, shaking her head slowly. "Some old butch?" she repeated with an eye roll. "Where in the world did that come from?" She shook her head. "You think that's what happened? That I was put off because you were older?" She exhaled, mumbling, "God, I have no idea where to begin this conversation."

"It's okay," Carsyn said, "you don't have to say anything. I get it, I do."

"I guess from the beginning," Aki continued, exhaling. "Here's the thing," she added, making direct eye contact, "I'm not gay, Carsyn."

Carsyn tried to breathe, but couldn't—having taken the sucker punch in the middle of her gut.

"At least I wasn't," Aki continued, her head shaking and her gaze becoming unfocused. "Now, I'm not sure." She bit her lip, looking at her. "What you saw earlier," she said softly, "was fear. What I was feeling was all new, and I needed a minute to think about it, to consider what I was about to do."

Carsyn scooted closer. "I'm sorry I overreacted," she said softly.

"I was so afraid that you were going to kiss me," Aki went on, "so afraid and I didn't know what would happen afterward."

"I get it," Carsyn responded, slipping her arm around her. "And I was going to kiss you," she added, her gaze lingering for a long moment. "Are you still afraid?" she asked softly.

"No, not at all," Aki responded, her lips parting.

"That's good," Carsyn murmured, moving closer, "because I am going to kiss you." She peered deeply into her eyes. "I'm going to kiss you right now." She was so close that she could feel Aki's quickening breath on her mouth. "That is if you want me to," she added softly.

"I do," Aki responded, closing her eyes as their lips came together. The kiss was tender, like gentle waves licking the shoreline on a windless day.

Carsyn paused for a millisecond, as if an ebbing tide, and then continued kissing her. When she pulled back, allowing their lips to separate, she sneaked another quick kiss, nuzzled their noses, and gathered her into her arms, asking if she was okay.

"My heart's racing," Aki answered, "I'm confused and a little dizzy, but I'm okay." She swallowed, straightening her posture. "I should be going," she added, standing.

"I hate to send you back to sleep in a cold tent," Carsyn said, holding her gaze. "I've got plenty of space."

"It's okay," Aki said, "I've got a warm sleeping bag and Jack will be listening for me."

"Let me at least walk you over," Carsyn said, helping her with her jacket.

"I'd like that," Aki answered, smiling thinly.

* * *

Carsyn twitched her nose, smelling fresh manure as she passed the picket line on her way back. "I just scooped," she grumbled. She considered leaving the pile until tomorrow but decided it'd be better if she took care of it. If she left it, Relic would lay down and have it all over him. "You're such a slob," she said, scratching his forehead on her way by. "Why can't you drop it off to the side like Lily does?" As she collected her pitchfork from the rear of the trailer, she noticed Aki watching her. She'd seen her to the door of her tent, but she'd come back out to sit by what was left of the campfire. "How about you and I go for a moonlight ride?" she asked, patting Relic's shoulder. She palmed both horses an apple, telling Lily she'd be staying back to hold down the fort. Relic snorted when she released him from the picket line, leading, and re-clipping him to the hitching post. "Stay put," she told him, stepping off to get his saddle and bridle from the tack compartment. She gave him a quick brushing, placed a pad on his back, and positioned his saddle behind his shoulder blades. Then, she tightened the cinch, slid a bit into his mouth, and mounted. "Come on, let's go this way," she said, using her reins to put pressure on the left side of his neck. He hesitated, knowing that their route to the trail was in the opposite direction. "Quick detour," she explained, kicking gently. With that, they trotted across the campsite, slowing to a walk as they approached Aki. "Not tired, huh," she greeted, coming to a stop.

"No," Aki responded, meeting her gaze. "It seems you left me with much to think about."

"But you're okay, right?" Carsyn asked gently.

"I'm okay," Aki said, taking a breath. "I guess you weren't tired either, huh?"

"No," Carsyn responded with a slow shake of her head. "I'll sleep better with a bit of saddle time."

"Be careful," Aki said, concern in her eyes.

"I'll be careful," Carsyn promised. "But you don't have to worry," she added, "it's like second nature when you've been riding as long as I have."

"I'll bet since you were a child," Aki responded with a slow smile.

"Yep," Carsyn said. "In fact, some of my earliest memories are in a saddle." She smiled, patting Relic's shoulder. "This guy stays in the same stall as my first pony. Don't ya, buddy?"

"That's nice," Aki responded, her gaze lingering, "to still have that connection to your childhood."

"If you're still up when I get back," Carsyn said, "I might stop by."

"I probably won't be," Aki responded, glancing at the fire ring. "It's too chilly for my liking, and this fire's about out."

"Sure, I get it," Carsyn responded, her belly knotting as she pulled her reins to one side.

"See you tomorrow?" Aki asked, stepping closer, and catching her eye.

"Yeah, sure," Carsyn responded, swallowing. "We could go for a ride if you want," she offered. "I get out of class around one."

"Oh, I don't know about that," Aki answered, crossing her arms. "I've ridden like two, maybe three times." She shook her head, adding, "And that was at the county fair. Let's see; I would've been about five."

"So, you've been riding since you were a child," Carsyn responded, smiling.

Aki laughed, saying, "Yeah, right."

"I'll stop by," Carsyn said, holding her eye. "If you want to go, we'll go; if not, that's fine." As she trotted off, her mind filled with thoughts of self-loathing. *You're doing it again,* she told herself. *You can't change what happened but you don't have to make the same mistake twice.* "Get up," she said firmly, heeling Relic's gut. If Aki said yes, she'd take her for a ride, but that had to be the end of it. Her breath hitched, galloping into the night.

CHAPTER 19

Aki stood by the fire, listening until she no longer heard hooves in the distance. She bit her lip, dropping her cup into the suds, and thinking about Carsyn—specifically, her body. Her breasts were small, barely noticeable under her loose-fitting flannel. Her shoulders, upper arms, and thighs were muscular. And her beautiful baby blue eyes... *Mmm, those eyes*...made her chiseled jawline even more striking. She caught her breath, feeling electrical impulses at the cellular level. Where had this come from, this newfound interest in women? She'd dated only boys in high school, sweet boys, polite and respectful. She squished her eyebrows together, trying to remember at least something about each of them. Andy was a good speller. Jacob was on the swimming team. Greg drove a blue Mustang. They'd described themselves as boyfriend-girlfriend, but what they really were, was friends. In college, she didn't date anyone. Relationships weren't worth the distraction. She kept her eye on the ball, the ball being the practice of medicine. She grimaced, remembering her two sexual experiences. Painful as they were, she'd learned from each of them. Mistake number one occurred at a sorority party. That was the night she lost her virginity to a man she didn't find the least bit attractive. Never again would she drink to intoxication. Mistake number two occurred during her first year of residency. That was the day she was assigned the first surgery under a cloud of guilt and shame. Never again would she sleep with a superior, not for anything. Through all of it, this notion that she might be a lesbian had never crossed her mind. *So, maybe it's just Carsyn?* she supposed. *Maybe you have a hormonal imbalance, and your body's reacting to the masculine way she carries herself.* Her breath quickened, hearing distant hooves on the gravel. She switched off her lantern, stepping inside before Carsyn got close enough to spot her. As she gathered her night clothes, adding an extra layer for warmth, she heard a series of whinnies, loud and long.

"Are you still there?" Relic asked in her imagination.

"I'm still here," Lily answered. "Don't worry, my love, you're not alone."

Aki swallowed, thinking how nice it would be to have someone who loved you enough that she eagerly awaited your return home. She burrowed into her pillow, closing her eyes and tugging her sleeping bag up to her nose. *What would people think?* she asked herself. Her eyes snapped open, staring at a double-stitched seam, and deciding that if anything happened, no one would have to know. Her stomach fluttered as she drifted off—*And the white eagle swooped down from his high branch, clawed a piece of sod, and dropped it before her.*

"What's this?" Aki asked, her head tilting. As she picked it up, a deer came toward her.

"You don't know?" the eagle responded. He flew into her hair with a screech and then sailed upward. It was odd, but his action didn't frighten her. At some level, she knew that he meant her no harm. He was just trying to wake her up.

"No," Aki answered, her gaze lifting to the clouds. "But I wish I knew," she called out. Her voice was almost childlike. As she listened to her words, she wondered why she didn't sound like herself.

"And so it shall be," the eagle screeched.

Aki watched in horror as his body exploded, becoming white dust.

"No," she screamed. "You can't go! I need you to tell me what this is all about." When she reached upward, dust particles banded together to form a cloud. Inside the cloud was a handsome mounted brave, a spirit statue on a hill.

"You okay in there," Jack called out.

"I'm okay," Aki responded, catching her breath. "Sorry to wake you guys up."

"Not a problem," Jack said, "I just wanted to be sure that you were okay. Go back to sleep. I'll see you in the morning."

"Come in if you want," Aki invited, rubbing her eyes, and sitting up.

Jack unzipped the door, stepping inside, and zipping it shut. "Have another bad dream?" she asked softly.

"Yes," Aki sighed, "the one that I have over and over and over."

"I'm sorry," Jack whispered, sitting cross-legged on a pillow beside her. "You want to tell me about it?" she asked gently. "Who knows, I might be able to help you figure out what it's about."

"No," Aki said, shaking her head strongly. "I want to forget the crazy details, not talk about them."

"And therein lies the problem," Jack responded.

* * *

AKI'S EXPRESSION must've told the story.

"No oatmeal in the wilderness," Jack said, smiling. "It's Courtney's rule; you can't eat healthy on a camping trip."

"It is, huh," Aki responded, her eyes squinting with a twinkle of mischief. "That means when we get back, we should have a couple of days of fish and salad."

"Mmm, something to look forward to," Courtney responded, rolling her eyes.

"Yes, it is," Aki said, grinning. "Oh, and sushi," she added, "I've been craving it since Friday." She glanced at the red trailer, watching Carsyn step out, and toward them.

"She's probably already eaten," Jack commented, "cereal or toast, most likely." She paused. "But we could invite her to join us if you want. Never know," she added, "she just might be in the mood for the breakfast of champions—bacon, eggs, and potatoes over the campfire."

"I need to run into town this morning," Aki said, her eyes still on Carsyn. "Do you need me to pick anything up?"

"I could take you in if you wanted," Jack offered.

"No," Aki responded, "but thank you. I have a couple of errands to run. I think I'll just run them and come on back." She glanced at the door of the larger tent. "Kids sleeping in, huh?"

"Oh yeah," Courtney responded. "Already, they know to take full advantage of a school break."

"It's an odd time for school to not be in session," Aki commented.

"It's a private school," Jack interjected. "And schools like ours," she added, "well, let's just say they march to the beat of their own drummer."

"Church-affiliated?" Aki asked, crinkling her brow.

"No," Courtney responded. "It's an independent elementary that focuses on academic achievement, creativity, and critical thinking."

"Ahh, excellent," Aki said, smiling, "only the best for my niece and nephew." She caught her breath when Carsyn straddled the stool beside her. "Hi," she said softly.

"Hi," Carsyn responded, peering into her eyes. "Did you sleep well?"

"About average," Aki responded, swishing her hair to one side. "Are you hungry?" she asked. "I think Jack made plenty if you want to join us."

Carsyn glanced at the cast iron skillet, its greasy contents sizzling over the robust fire. "I'm hungry," she responded, leaning into Aki with a slow smile.

Jack's eyes narrowed, meeting Courtney's.

Courtney tilted her head, lifting a shoulder.

"You gonna ride with me this afternoon?" Carsyn asked quietly.

"I'm not sure that I'd be able to get on, you know, with my ankle," Aki responded. "Could I have a raincheck for tomorrow?"

"Yeah, sure," Carsyn said, leaning back, her facial muscles tightening.

Aki bit her lip, noticing when her gaze dropped to the ground. "Maybe we could do something else," she suggested softly. "I have to run a couple of errands this morning, but maybe when I get back, I could come over and sit in on your class for a little while."

"I'd like that," Carsyn responded, her eyes brightening.

"Do you like sushi?" Aki asked hopefully. "If you do, I could pick some up while I'm in town."

"I love sushi," Carsyn responded, chuckling softly. "It's funny you should mention it because I've been craving it something terrible."

"Name your roll," Aki said, grinning, "and you'll have it for lunch."

"Spider Roll," Carsyn answered, her smile widening.

"Mmm, one of my favorites," Aki responded.

"There's a nice little sushi bar on your way in," Carsyn said. "I'll jot down the directions." Her upper lip curled as she filled her plate.

"My sentiments exactly," Aki whispered.

"Tabasco or ketchup," Jack offered, meeting one and then the other's gaze.

"None for us," Carsyn responded, not thinking.

"None for us," Aki echoed with a wink.

CHAPTER 20

Aki dropped two quarters into the meter, looking both directions before crossing the terra cotta street. Bricks, like relationships, stood the test of time. A bell jingled above her head as she entered the establishment. It was a charming business, one that she'd never have patronized had she not been looking for a specific item.

"May I help you find something?" the woman asked. She wore two strands of beads, and her hair was tied back into a ponytail.

"No, but thank you," Aki responded, smiling politely. "I believe I'll just browse." She made her way past a small sitting area with a worn paisley print sofa, a matching chair, and a hunter green ceramic tile fireplace.

"Come back on a cold day," the clerk said. "It's beautiful with a crackling fire."

"I'll have to do that," Aki responded, wishing that the woman would stop following her. "I'll just browse," she repeated, making, and then breaking eye contact. On another day, she might have had a scone and a cup of coffee, pausing to enjoy the magical ambiance of the quaint little bookstore.

"As you wish," the woman responded with a warm smile.

Was she a lesbian? Aki wondered, turning down the first of several narrow aisles. The shelves were floor-to-ceiling, old, but with a fresh coat of varnish. The collection of books was a balanced mixture of new and used, categorized by subject. She scanned peripherally, so as not to be noticed.

Cultural Studies—She didn't think so, glancing downward.

Relationships—She pursed her lips, moving on.

Self Help—She pushed up her glasses, realizing quickly that the topics were of a psychological nature.

Sexuality—*Hmmm, now that's a possibility,* she told herself, stealing a quick glance over her shoulder. With no one nearby, she resumed her perusal of titles. She startled, looking up when the floor creaked under what sounded like footsteps. The clerk was behind the counter, she saw no sign of other patrons within proximity and returned to her consideration of the available books. When the bell jingled, she again looked up, watched until the new customer settled in the front of the store, and returned her attention to the categories.

Gay, Lesbian, Bisexual, Transgender—*Bingo,* she thought, smiling even though she wished the shelf label hadn't been so bold and visible. *Gay marriage is the law of the land,* she told herself. *You're being ridiculous.* Her eyes narrowed, giving serious consideration to the small collection of titles.

Lesbian Sex: The Complete Reference

Lesbian Sex Positions: Let's Get Naked

Your First Lesbian Experience—She glanced over her shoulder, removing the title from the shelf, biting her lower lip as she cracked the cover.

"Find what you were looking for?" the chirpy clerk asked.

Aki gasped audibly, nearly losing control of her bladder.

"I'm sorry," the woman said, "I didn't mean to scare you."

"It's okay," Aki responded, catching her breath. "I didn't hear you come up. Her pulse raced, shoving the book that she'd been reading into a vacant slot. "I'm just browsing," she added, stepping down to Cultural Studies.

"That's fine," the clerk responded, smiling kindly. "Just let me know if you need some help."

"I will, thank you," Aki said, waiting until she was out of sight to collect two, and then three of the titles. She tucked them under her arm and made her way down the remaining six aisles. In five minutes, she randomly selected an additional seven books on topics ranging from astronomy to zoology, hoping that her interest in lesbian sex wouldn't stand out.

"Will this be all?" the clerk asked, smiling as she moved Aki's stack closer.

"Yes," Aki responded, averting her gaze. "Quite enough, I think."

"Oooh, good choice," the clerk commented, scanning the first book.

Aki took a breath, holding it.

"Oooh, and this one too," the woman added, smiling as she flipped through the middle section of full-page graphics.

Aki considered bolting but didn't.

"Wait right here," the woman said, touching her arm. "I've got another one for you, just came in yesterday."

Aki pushed down nausea, wishing that she was anywhere else.

"Here you go," the clerk announced, handing over the book. *The Lesbian Tongue: Wild and Free,*" she added, smiling with direct eye contact. "It's on the house."

"Thank you," Aki responded, her mouth as dry as dust, "but I'll pay for it."

"Suit yourself," the clerk said, re-picking up the book. "Don't you just love the cover?" she asked, her eyes wide with enthusiasm. It was an image of a pierced tongue and not much else.

"Love it," Aki responded, forcing a thin smile. *Speed it up,* she thought, *before I vomit.* As her items were checked out, the clerk offered a commentary on each and every one of her books.

"Oh my," the clerk said, giving the total, "you do have a wide variety in your taste in literature, don't you?"

"I guess so," Aki responded, thinking, *please hurry.* She set her package in the trunk and was smiling by the time she left the city limits. It'd been a challenging experience, but she'd come away with lots of reading material.

* * *

"Aunt Aki," Lizzy squealed, running toward her.

"Not digging this morning?" Aki asked, glancing over to see if Carsyn was around.

"I decided not to stay," Lizzy responded.

"Too muddy for your liking?" Aki guessed.

"Uh-huh," Lizzy answered, adding, "Mommy told Charlie that if he decided to stay, he had to take a shower before he got to eat lunch."

"Wow, that is muddy," Aki responded, unsurprised, having experienced a downpour on her way to and from town.

"Uh-huh," Lizzy responded, noticing the large brown paper bag on the passenger side. "What's that?" she asked, pointing across.

"That's our sushi," Aki answered. "You want to try one?"

"Huh-uh," Lizzy said, making a face, "me and my mommy don't like it."

"Well, Carsyn and I do," Aki responded, lifting an eyebrow. She got out and hugged her. "In fact," she added, "that's what we're having for lunch." She set her bag in the cooler and changed her shoes. "No need to walk over for Charlie," she called out to Courtney, "I'll bring him back."

"Okay, thanks," Courtney called back, her expression suggesting that she had more than a clue.

The smell of wet earthy leaves awakened Aki's senses as she moved in the direction of Carsyn's voice. She felt alive, more than she had in years. She settled next to a tall tree, listening and watching.

"To be an archaeologist," Carsyn said, "you have to enjoy getting dirty and working hard." She paused, chuckling when one of her students unintentionally unloaded a small shovel of mud onto another one's hand. "A special thanks to these two for making my point," she added, chuckling. "It's a profession," she continued, "where athletic ability is an asset."

"And if you don't have muscle already, you build it," a young man called out, flexing his bicep.

"Yes, you do," Carsyn responded, playfully flexing hers in response. Aki stroked her throat.

"And along that line," Carsyn continued, smiling broadly, "it's a profession that'll help you stay fit, even when you get to be as old as I am." She caught Aki's gaze, falling speechless for a moment. "So, anyway," she stammered, "your journal assignment is to relate the artifact that we found today to something in your life." It was a piece of jewelry, most likely dropped on the way to one of the nearby mounds. "Let's call it a day," she said, no longer able to focus with Aki nearby. She washed her face and arms in ice cold water and moved toward her.

"You make me want to get dirty, Dr. Lyndon," Aki greeted with a slow smile.

Carsyn lowered her gaze, slowly bringing it back up, scanning Aki's body. "You are dirty, Dr. Williams," she said flirtatiously. "I believe you found a mud puddle on your way over."

"I did," Aki said, giggling as she looked down. "I have sushi," she blurted out, feeling butterflies in her stomach. "And chopsticks."

"That's good," Carsyn responded, her voice lowering with insanely firm eye contact, "because I've been thinking about sushi all morning."

"Aunt Aki," Charlie squealed, running toward her.

"Well, if it isn't Indiana Jones," Aki greeted, taking a breath as she lowered to his level. "Did you have a good time?" she asked, wrapping her arms around him.

"Uh-huh," Charlie answered. "And I helped find a buried treasure too," he added, looking to Carsyn. "Didn't I?"

"Yes, you did," Carsyn responded, mussing his hair with the tips of her fingers. "Rain's starting back up," she said, glancing at Aki as they walked toward the campground. "How about we eat lunch in my trailer?"

"Sure," Aki answered, swallowing. "I'll grab our sushi and be over."

Carsyn locked gazes, saying, "Don't be too long."

"I won't," Aki responded, her gaze lingering as she and Charlie stepped off.

CHAPTER 21

Carsyn sprinted to the door, peeking out, opening it, and leaving it ajar. She dried her hair with a bath towel, returning to the bedroom. She'd had no choice but to work in a shower before Aki got there. She zipped her jeans and slipped into a black shirt, leaving the tail out. As she combed her hair, she took another look out the window, catching sight of Aki moving across the campsite toward her. God, she was beautiful, even under the hat of her slicker raincoat. She watched for a moment before sitting on the edge of the bed, tugged on her boots, and fingered through her hair. At the sound of a knock, she said, "Come in," and stepped out.

"Well, hello there," Aki said. "You showered and dressed in less than ten minutes; I'm impressed."

"I had a lunch date," Carsyn responded, winking, and taking her coat. "Hot tea or coffee?" she offered, moving to the counter.

"Tea, I think," Aki answered, sliding into the booth. Within seconds, a steaming cup of the beverage appeared before her.

"This was a great idea," Carsyn said, pouring one for herself.

"The sushi?" Aki clarified, unwrapping her chopsticks.

"Yeah," Carsyn answered, nodding. "And the lunch."

"Yes, it was," Aki agreed with lingering eye contact. She moved her top chopstick up and down to collect three pieces of sushi and one slice of mango. "I've been so hungry for this," she said, taking her first bite. "You think I should've ordered an extra roll?" she asked, her brow furrowing as she looked up.

"No," Carsyn said, "I think we'll have enough." She reached into the container, fingering one piece and then another into her mouth.

Aki lifted an eyebrow.

"What?" Carsyn asked, cocking her head.

Aki cleared her throat, nodding at the unopened pair of chopsticks.

"According to sushi etiquette," Carsyn responded, "either way is perfectly acceptable. Google it. See for yourself."

"If you say so," Aki answered, frowning. "And I think I will," she added, "just as soon as I have bars on my cell phone."

"You let me know what you find," Carsyn answered playfully.

"You can be assured that I will," Aki responded in kind.

"Although," Carsyn continued, her word dragging out, "your way is a lot sexier." She rested her index finger on her chin. "Maybe I should just start using them."

"Maybe you should," Aki said, taking a breath as she watched her expertly use her chopsticks to place a slice of mango into her mouth.

Carsyn winked, catching her eye. "So, seafood's supposed to be an aphrodisiac, right?" she asked, regretting the words the second that they escaped her mouth. *Oh—dear—God*, she cringed, *she's gonna answer you now.* This flirting, she couldn't seem to stop herself.

A slow smile eclipsed Aki's mouth. "Well, not all seafood," she responded, "but there are definitely some varieties that can have that effect. Unfortunately, crab hasn't been shown to be one of them. And as you know," she continued, "that's what's in a spider roll." She bit her lip, holding Carsyn's eye. "So, with that in mind," she went on, playing with her as if she were a mouse, trapped with nowhere to go, "you'll want to select a roll with scallops, clams, or lobster to increase your sexual arousal."

Carsyn swallowed, feeling flush creep down her neck.

"Or even better," Aki continued, her eyes sparkling with mischief, "maybe you should add an order of raw oysters on the half shell." She winked slowly, having no idea that she was playing with fire. "I'll bet you didn't know that Casanova, you know the eighteenth-century lover, well, he used to eat fifty of them for breakfast each morning." She twisted her hair, peering into her eyes. "They had beautiful lobster rolls at that little sushi bar," she added. "Maybe we should have them and a few raw oysters next time."

"Look, fortune cookies," Carsyn blurted out, emptying the bag onto the table.

"Go ahead," Aki said, chuckling, "choose your fortune."

Carsyn unwrapped the closest one, reading it silently.

"So, what's it say?" Aki asked, her eyes widening.

"Nothing," Carsyn responded quietly, preparing to slip the paper into her pocket.

"Come on, it's a rule," Aki said, "you have to read it out loud and add 'in bed' to the end."

Carsyn met her gaze but didn't comply.

"Hand it over," Aki directed, holding out her upturned palm. "If you're not going to read it, I will."

Carsyn took a breath, following her direction.

Aki pushed up her glasses, reading, "Your ravishingly beautiful girlfriend will agree to be your wife—in bed." She looked up, adding, "I'm almost afraid to open mine."

"I'll bet you are," Carsyn responded, looking off.

"I didn't mean it that way," Aki said softly.

"Of course, you didn't," Carsyn answered, her jaw clenched as she gathered their trash.

"It's just a saying," Aki added, touching her forearm, "I wasn't talking about us."

"Of course, you weren't," Carsyn snapped, walking to the trash can, "because there is no us." She took a breath, locking gazes as she leaned against the counter.

Aki's eyes teemed with tears, sailing her fortune cookie across the table, and getting up. "Chicken, fire-baked potatoes, and corn-on-the-cob for supper," she said, making no eye contact. "I'm cooking. Come if you want." She jerked on her jacket and hood.

"Aki," Carsyn responded, her voice softening as she touched her arm, "wait. I didn't mean it the way it sounded."

"Sure you did," Aki said, meeting her gaze directly. She traversed both campsites without a glance over her shoulder.

Carsyn lifted the rectangular bottle from the shelf, sighed, and returned it unopened. *Not the answer*, she told herself.

* * *

"Well, I suppose it's about time for me to shuck some corn," Courtney announced, nodding in the direction of Carsyn's trailer.

"That didn't take long," Aki commented, watching Carsyn come out, palm two apples to her horses, and turn toward her. Truth was, she'd been hoping that it wouldn't.

"Didn't think it would," Courtney said, "not when you told me what happened. If Jack gets back with the kids before you finish talking, we'll go for a walk to give you some additional time alone."

"Thanks," Aki responded. She shook her head, tossing a pebble into the fire. "I could feel myself overreacting," she said quietly, "but I couldn't seem to stop myself. I think it was her tone more than her words, but I don't know."

"Just talk to her," Courtney responded. "I'm not sure what happened, but she's usually as easy going as they come. You two should be able to work this out."

"And you're sure she's not in a relationship or something?" Aki asked softly.

"One-hundred-percent," Courtney responded.

* * *

"You forgot your fortune cookie," Carsyn greeted, holding it out as an offering.

"So, I did," Aki answered, her facial muscles tightening. "Keep it," she said, "it's yours."

"No, it's not," Carsyn said quietly. "I'll save it for you," she added, slipping it into her pocket. She swallowed, meeting her eye. "I was hoping that we could talk for a few minutes," she continued, "hoping that maybe you'd come back to my place for a little while."

"Courtney would have to watch my chicken," Aki responded, frowning.

"Look, I know you're angry," Carsyn continued, "but I can explain if you'll just hear me out."

"I'm hurt, more than angry," Aki corrected, locking gazes. "Sit tight," she added, her tone softening, "I'll go get her."

They traversed the campsites in silence.

"So, what time do we need to be back?" Carsyn asked, holding the door open.

"By five if we want to eat as a family," Aki responded, stepping inside. She dropped her jacket on a hook on the way to the sofa.

Carsyn took a soft breath, sitting beside her. "So, when I said that there was no us," she began, "I didn't mean that there wasn't."

Aki tilted her head, looking up.

"What I meant," Carsyn continued, swallowing hard, "was that what we have can never be more."

Aki caught her breath, looking off.

"I'm too old for you, Aki," Carsyn said softly, laying her hand on her thigh.

"People age differently," Aki responded, "eight years is nothing, not in the grand scheme of things, it's not."

"It's not nothing," Carsyn insisted. "Now, granted, it's not as bad as twenty, but it's definitely not nothing. You're only thirty-five," she added, "beautiful and in your prime." She brushed Aki's cheek with the back of her hand, peering into her eyes. "And I'm almost forty-four." She tipped her head down. "Look, my hair's already starting to turn grey, and I've got wrinkles around my eyes. It won't be that long before my sex drive dries up and I'm checking out retirement homes.

You don't want someone old like me," she added, "I'd just end up holding you back, and ruining your life."

"Did you just hear yourself?" Aki asked, her mouth falling open. "Where in the world is this idea that you're so old coming from?" She wrinkled her brow, speechless for a long moment. "Once again," she added, "I have no idea where to begin, I guess with a bit of thirty-five-year-old wisdom." She shook her head slowly, her voice softening. "I've never experienced anything like this," she said, "and I can hardly believe that it came out of nowhere." She cupped Carsyn's cheek, peering into her eyes. "Love is a gift, Carsyn," she continued, "it's a gift that should never be squandered." She looked off, shaking her head, and chuckling.

"What?" Carsyn asked quietly. "What's so funny?"

"That it took me all this time to find someone," Aki said, rolling her eyes, "and then I did, but she turned out to be a woman, and I had to go out and buy all these books to know what to do with her. And then, when I think I've got that part figured out, she has this hang-up about our tiny little bit of age difference." She exhaled, continuing. "And she rambles on and on and on about grey hair and wrinkles and retirement homes and low sex drive and ruining my life. And here I am, still trying to figure out what to do with her." She licked her lips. "I mean, I haven't even finished chapter one in my book about first lesbian experiences."

"You bought books," Carsyn said, a slow smile building, "well, I'll be darned."

"I certainly did," Aki answered, her eyes widening. "And I'll have you know that it was one of the bravest things I've ever done in my life. That, and I think the clerk may have been flirting with me."

"I'm not surprised," Carsyn said. "Guys sometimes find lesbian sex to be a turn on."

"This wasn't a guy," Aki responded, wiggling her eyebrows. "It was an attractive older woman."

"I'm not sure I like the sound of that," Carsyn said, arching an eyebrow.

"Is that right?" Aki murmured, her lips parting.

"It is," Carsyn said, moving to kiss her forehead, the tip of her nose, and her mouth.

Both jumped to their feet at the sound of a child's voice.

"Aunt Aki," Lizzy screamed, thundering up the steps. "Aunt Aki, come quick. It's Charlie."

CHAPTER 22

"Charlie? What's wrong with him?" Aki asked, moving swiftly to the door, and down the steps with no thought of her ankle.

"He's hurt," Lizzy answered. "I think he poked his eye. And my mommy's crying and I think my mama wants to." She sprinted off, leaving Aki far behind.

"Here, take my keys," Aki said, tossing them to Carsyn. "My medical bag's in the trunk." With that, she picked up her pace to a painful jog.

"The fire popped," Courtney greeted breathlessly. "Hot embers, they flew into his eye. I was turning the potatoes. It happened so fast. I couldn't do anything about it."

Aki touched her shoulder, making gentle eye contact. "Accidents happen," she said softly. "Let's see what we've got."

"Thank God you're here," Jack said, looking up, wide-eyed. "I knew we needed to do something before we took him to the ER, but I couldn't think what."

"You knew not to let him rub his eyes," Aki responded, noticing Jack's gentle restraint of her son's arms. "Now, tell me what else you've done."

"I irrigated with a little water," Jack said, "but I don't think I got it out."

"What you did was spot on," Aki responded, dropping to her knee beside Charlie. With his eye shut tightly, all she was able to assess was the burn on his eyelid. "I'll bet that hurts a little bit, huh?" she said softly.

"Uh-huh," Charlie whimpered, nodding.

"I have some medicine that'll make it feel better," Aki said, "but I'm gonna need you to open your eye really wide and hold super still for me. Can you do that, sweet boy?"

Charlie nodded, meeting her gaze with his one good eye.

"Here you go," Carsyn panted, skidding to a halt, and handing over the bag. "I hope I got the right one," she added.

"You did," Aki responded, pausing for an extra moment of eye contact. She unfastened the buckle and reached into the end pocket. Constructed of nylon, the bag had a spacious compartment and a gusseted front pouch. She liked it for its color, carnation pink, and for the way it organized her instruments and supplies. Examining young children often presented challenges under the best of circumstances. By their very nature, they were moving targets, prone to squirm and cry whenever someone messed with their eyes. She leaned in, stroking Charlie's forehead. "I'll move quickly," she promised, assuring him that in a split second the first part would be all over. He was scared and in pain which could cause him to become uncooperative with little notice. She applied a topical anesthetic, allowed time for it to take effect, irrigated with a sterile saline solution, and administered an antibiotic. "Good job," she said softly.

"So, what do you think? Courtney asked, clutching her stomach, and stepping closer.

Jack moved to stand by her side. "Yeah, what do you think?" she echoed, swallowing.

Aki looked at Carsyn. "Would you sit with him for a minute while I talk with Jack and Courtney?" she asked quietly.

"Of course, I will," Carsyn answered, smiling, and settling next to her Godson.

"Let's sit at the picnic table," Aki suggested, making a mental note to check with Courtney about her stomach. "So," she began, taking a soft breath, "the injury appears to be relatively minor. I doubt he'll require surgical intervention."

"Thank God," Jack sighed, kissing Courtney's forehead.

"He'll still need a thorough ophthalmologic exam," Aki continued, "and possibly a night of hospitalization."

"We'll just leave everything," Jack said, looking to Courtney. "I'll come back at some point to pack up."

"I'll break camp for you," Carsyn called out. "Leave the dogs too if you want," she added, stroking Charlie's hair and smiling at him. "I can drop them by when I drop off your stuff."

"Thanks, pal," Jack responded, meeting her eye. "That really helps."

"Not a problem," Carsyn said, her gaze following Aki as she sat down to write a note.

"I want you to give this to the ER doc," Aki said, scribbling down medications administered and their dosage. With direct eye contact, she handed Jack the slip of paper. "It's very important that he not be administered additional topical anesthetic in the ER."

"Got it," Jack responded with a firm nod. "You're coming, aren't you?"

"Yes," Aki said, "but I want to talk with Carsyn for a minute before I head out. As Jack carried Charlie to the Wrangler, she walked over to her.

"You're an amazing woman," Carsyn said, peering into her eyes. "I've never seen anything like what you did, never."

"Not amazing," Aki responded, smiling thinly, "just well-trained, that's all." She took a breath, exhaling slowly. "Did you mean what you said, what you said about you being too old?" she asked, peering into her eyes. "Because I've been thinking about it," she added, "and I certainly hope not." She wrinkled her brow, shaking her head slowly.

"Yes and no," Carsyn responded, swallowing. "I know some of it is some ways off, but the part about me holding you back and maybe ruining your life, yeah, I meant all of it."

"Where in the world did that come from?" Aki asked, concern in her eyes. "You're good-looking, smart, and funny, how in the world could you possibly ruin my life?"

"I just could, that's all," Carsyn responded, looking off.

"And what do you base that on?" Aki persisted softly.

"Experience," Carsyn responded, making direct eye contact.

* * *

AKI TURNED on her signal well in advance of the parking garage. She'd known where she was going, having just been there on Friday. She collected her ticket, traveled up a series of ramps to the sixth floor, and rode the elevator to the ground level. After that, she made her way through a pair of sliding glass doors.

"May I help you?" the hospital volunteer asked, smiling warmly.

"I believe I know where I'm going," Aki responded, "but thank you." She walked a long corridor, turning left, and then right. With a hiss, glass doors allowed entry into the ER waiting room. "Sorry it took me so long," she greeted, hugging Jack. "I assume they're working on him," she added, hugging Lizzy, and sitting down.

I don't think so," Jack answered, pursing her lips. "Courtney called Charles on the way in and of course he demanded that the Director of Ophthalmology be called in." She exhaled loudly. "I don't think she's here yet."

"She is now," Aki responded, standing up, and extending her hand. "Dr. Matsumoto," she greeted, "it's good to see you again."

"And you as well," Dr. Matsumoto responded, her brow furrowed slightly. "I left you a voicemail," she added. "I had high hopes of hearing from you by now."

"Camping trip with no cell service," Aki responded.

"Ahh, I see," Dr. Matsumoto said. "Well, I'd love to talk now, but I have a patient who's been waiting well over an hour."

"My nephew," Aki responded, adding, "topical anesthetic, irrigation, and antibiotic within fifteen minutes of the injury."

"You're welcome to assist if you'd like," Dr. Matsumoto invited.

"Thank you," Aki responded, turning to Jack, and adding, "I'll see you in a little while."

CHAPTER 23

Carsyn stepped into the larger tent, collecting scattered items by the handful, and zipping them into the available luggage. She stuffed what remained into a black garbage bag. On another day, she might have taken time to sort and fold. After everything was loaded, she walked over, staring down the structure. *Now, for the hard part*, she thought. She pulled out the muddy stakes, removed the poles, and lifted the tent above her head to shake it out. "It's about time you guys got a camper," she mumbled. Then, she folded and rolled and crammed the monstrosity into a bag, made too small. "One down, one to go," she said, stooping to go inside the smaller door. "So, where's her stuff," she asked out loud. The bed was made, and she saw no sign of Aki's personal items. Her brow furrowed, trying to determine when she'd had time to pack and load her car. She crinkled her brow. Had she done it this morning? If so, this was when she'd planned to leave all along. She bit her lip, taking a shallow breath. She'd planned to leave and hadn't even bothered to tell her. She exhaled, lowering onto the air mattress. But why would she do that? Why, when she'd done nothing if not make it clear that she wanted more? Why, when they only had until Sunday? *Because you shut her down at every turn*, she told herself with a hard swallow. *She just got tired of pissing around with you.* She took another breath, laying her head on Aki's pillow, aroused by her scent. Eight years, maybe that wasn't so much. *And regardless, you won't be together that long. You'll just be her first, that's all.* She got up —disassembled, folded, rolled, and loaded. "Can you keep an eye on my horses?" she called out from the road. "I should be back by midnight."

"No problem," Ringo responded. "Hey, how's the little boy?"

"In good hands," Carsyn answered. "I think he'll be fine."

"That's good," Ringo said, nodding as she pulled off.

* * *

IT WAS an attractive two-hundred-bed facility with an adjacent parking garage. Carsyn collected a ticket at the gate, traveled up the ramp, and took the first available space. "You guys stay put," she said, giving each canine a biscuit. "And no barking. I'll be back in a bit." She locked the door, rode the elevator to the ground level, and approached the information desk.

"May I help you?" the hospital volunteer asked.

"I hope so," Carsyn answered. "I'm looking for my Godson, Charles Holloman-Camdon," she added. "He had a little accident this afternoon, and I'm not sure whether he'll still be in the ER or in a room by now."

"Ahh," the older lady responded, "the Chief's grandson." She checked her screen, adding, "He's in the ER. Do you know where you're going?"

"I do," Carsyn said, swallowing, as her last visit to that department came to mind. Maybe it hadn't been such a good idea to come this evening. Maybe she should've waited until Charlie got home. But she had to come. She'd already wasted too much of their precious time. She caught sight of Jack and Lizzy as she walked by the water fountain. "How's he doing?" she asked, sitting down beside them.

"Last update, he needed a couple more tests," Jack responded, "but Aki doesn't seem worried, so I think he's gonna be fine."

"That's good," Carsyn said. "He had us scared half to death there for a moment, huh pal?"

"Yes, he did," Jack responded, swallowing. "Thank God Aki was along."

"My brother could've lost his sight, or maybe got burned really bad," Lizzy said seriously. "That's why we're not supposed to get too close to fires."

"Yes, it is," Carsyn responded, changing the subject. "So, Aki and Courtney, they're back with Charlie?" she asked, looking around.

"Yep," Jack said, "Aki's assisting and Courtney flat refused to leave his side."

Carsyn wrinkled her brow. "Aki's treating him?" she asked. "I thought doctors had to have privileges or something."

"They do," Jack said with a quiet chuckle. "I think the Director of Ophthalmology gave them to her as she walked by."

"Guess she knows a fine doctor when she sees one," Carsyn responded, feeling lighter as if a weight had just been lifted from her shoulders. "Let's hope that she has the sense to offer her a job."

"She already has," Jack said, lifting both eyebrows. "But Aki's not gonna take it," she added, "because LA's home, you know."

"Yeah, I know," Carsyn responded with a soft sigh. "But that children's hospital hasn't made her an offer, so there's still hope."

"That we know of," Jack said. "It could be sitting on her voicemail along with this one for all we know. And if it is, trust me, she's gonna snap it up."

Carsyn's stomach rolled with a hard swallow.

"Oh my God," Jack said softly, "you really like her, don't you?"

"Yeah," Carsyn responded, her lips pressed tightly together, "but I'm too old for her."

"You're not too old for her," Jack said, wrinkling her nose. "I know plenty of couples with way more age difference than you two have and they get along just fine together."

"But that's not always the case," Carsyn countered, "and when it's not, it can have devastating consequences." She replayed the course of events leading up to the accident in her mind. "You know that I'm right," she added, meeting Jack's eye. "I shouldn't even be considering the possibility."

"No, I'm afraid I don't," Jack responded quietly. "What happened with Sylvia was a totally different situation. And comparing her to Aki is like comparing an apple to a tomato or something."

"I believe it's an apple to an orange," Carsyn said, almost smiling.

"Not when it comes to those two, it's not," Jack responded.

"Maybe not," Carsyn said pensively, looking up to meet Aki's gaze when the door swished open.

Aki's eyes narrowed. "I didn't think you were coming," she said, poking her tongue lightly into her cheek.

"I wasn't, but then I was," Carsyn responded. She took a breath, suddenly aware of her heartbeat.

Aki nodded, her gaze shifting to meet Jack's. "He's fine," she said, smiling softly. "Another hour or so and he'll be ready to go home."

"He doesn't have to stay?" Jack asked, her eyes widening.

"No, I don't believe so," Aki responded. "That was dependent on his pain tolerance, and so far he's maintaining on just the one dose." With a hug, she added, "Dr. Matsumoto should be out shortly to discuss his follow-up."

*　*　*

"So, what changed your mind," Aki asked, stepping aside.

"I had a clarifying moment when I was breaking camp," Carsyn responded. "I figured out that I was being a piss-ant and needed to talk with you."

"A piss-ant, huh?" Aki responded, breaking a smile. "Nice analogy." She nodded toward two seats in the far corner. "You want to sit down?"

"No," Carsyn said, "what I want is for you to come with me to drop off their stuff, leave your car in their driveway, and ride back to the campground."

"To stay the night?" Aki asked, her eyes narrowing.

"To stay the rest of the week," Carsyn responded, biting her lower lip. "Come back with me, Aki," she said softly, "stay with me and let's see where this goes."

"And this change of heart," Aki asked with a swallow, "it came about because of your clarifying moment?"

"Yeah, mostly," Carsyn said, furrowing her brow, "that and something Jack said a while ago." She moistened her lips, holding Aki's eye. "You're so beautiful," she said softly. "I should've told you by now."

"You did tell me," Aki whispered, her breath catching in her throat. "And even if you hadn't," she added, "it was easy enough to tell that you thought I was." She felt a warm surge tingle from her center to her toes. "I still haven't had a chance to finish chapter one," she blurted out.

"That's okay," Carsyn responded. "Bring it along if you want." She squeezed her hand, holding her eye. "But I don't really think you'll need it," she said softly.

"Okay," Aki said, nodding, and releasing the breath she'd been holding. "We'll have to wait until they're finished talking with Dr. Matsumoto," she added. "I wouldn't want just to leave, you know?"

"Of course not," Carsyn responded, smiling softly. "We're not in any hurry," she added, "for tonight and the rest of this week, we have all the time in the world." She cocked her head, lifting an eyebrow. "If you want, I could go unload the truck and just hang out at the house until you get home."

"That might be better," Aki responded, her breath bursting in and out.

"Hey, what's going on with you?" Carsyn asked quietly. "Look, if you don't want to do this, it's okay." She threaded their fingers together, adding, "You just need to tell me."

"I want to," Aki responded, swallowing. "And I'll be fine once these crazy butterflies settle down. You just caught me by surprise and it's taking me a minute to process that fantasy could become reality. It's nothing you need to worry about."

"And it's nothing you need to worry about," Carsyn answered, peering deeply into her eyes, "because your fantasy can remain a fantasy for as long as you like."

Aki's lips parted, murmuring, "I'd kiss you if we weren't in public."

"And I'd kiss you back," Carsyn responded, "public or not."

CHAPTER 24

"Thank you, Doctor," Jack said, pausing to shake hands with Dr. Matsumoto once they were outside the consultation room.

"Yes, thank you," Courtney echoed, standing beside her.

"You're quite welcome," Dr. Matsumoto answered. "Be sure to call my service if you have concerns before tomorrow's appointment."

"We will and thanks again," Jack responded.

"May I have a word?" Dr. Matsumoto asked, looking to Courtney's father.

"Certainly," Charles responded, turning to his daughter. "Don't leave before I have a chance to say goodbye to Charlie."

"We won't," Courtney promised.

"You think we should go on down to pick up his prescription," Jack asked. "It should be ready by now." The nurse had called it in over an hour ago.

"I'll go," Courtney responded. "Come on, Lizzy," she added, extending her hand. "Come with Mommy."

Jack smiled, watching them step off. Then, she turned to Aki. "Thanks," she said. "I know you had him squared away before we ever got to the hospital. God, thank you so much."

"You're welcome," Aki answered, pressing her lips together, and lifting an eyebrow. "You're welcome for the umpteenth time."

"I'm sorry," Jack said with a shake of her head. "It's just that I feel like I can't say it enough. We're so appreciative of all you did for our son."

"He's my nephew," Aki responded, her voice rich with emotion, "and I'd move heaven and earth to help him." She looked over her glasses. "And the same goes for my niece, and my sister, and my sister-in-law." Since she'd found them, her heart was full.

"Family," Jack said.

"Family," Aki echoed.

"I get it now," Jack added. "No thanks required."

"That's right," Aki responded, holding her gaze softly. She took a breath and let it go. "Hey, before they get back, can we talk for a minute?"

Jack patted the seat beside her. "You bet we can," she said. "What's on your mind?"

"Carsyn wants me to stay with her at the campground for the rest of the week," Aki said, forming a steeple with her hands, and raising it to her mouth. "And I told her that I would, but now I'm having second thoughts."

"And these second thoughts," Jack responded, "what's their source?"

Aki wrinkled her brow. "Their source?" she asked.

"Yes," Jack answered, nodding, "their source."

"I'm not sure," Aki answered. Her eyes narrowed, pondering for a moment. "Fear and doubt, I guess. I was good with my decision while she was still here. But as soon as she left, all I could think is what if this and what if that."

"The mind," Jack said softly, "she speaks with a thunderous voice, doesn't she?" She smiled, shaking her head, and adding, "And the heart, she speaks only in whispers."

Aki squished her eyebrows together. "So, what are you telling me here?" she asked.

Jack turned, resting her hand on Aki's thigh. "What I'm telling you, little sister, is that you should quiet your mind so that you can hear the soft whispers of your heart. Listen as you might for a light raindrop to fall on your window. Your path will always be straight ahead of you, but not always visible. If you listen when your mind is quiet, your heart will give you direction."

"How did you become so wise?" Aki asked, putting her arms around her neck, and hugging her tightly.

Jack touched her bear claw. "Whatever wisdom I have," she said quietly, "I draw from the spirit realm." She smiled gently, saying, "So, I can see by your expression that you have your answer."

"Yes," Aki said softly. "When I listen to my heart, I know that I have to see if there's an us."

"I'm glad," Jack whispered. "It'd be hard to do much better than Carsyn." She pursed her lips, shaking her head. "She's suffered more than anyone should ever have to suffer and she's got a heart of gold."

Aki tilted her head to one side. "Suffered how?" she asked quietly.

"It's not for me to tell," Jack responded, "but when the time is right, she'll talk to you about it."

"I understand," Aki said, standing to go. "We'll be back by mid-afternoon on Friday," she added. "Maybe we could have dinner together or something?"

"You bet," Jack responded, grinning. "If it's a nice evening, I'll fire up the grill."

"Sounds good," Aki answered, smiling as she stepped off. "Oh, I almost forgot," she said, turning around, "Carsyn said to tell you she'll let the dogs out before she puts them downstairs."

"Thank her for me," Jack responded, nodding. "And remind her to take it easy on Deadman's Needle."

"I will," Aki responded.

* * *

CARSYN LIFTED Aki's suitcase from her trunk, pausing to ask if she wanted to bring the books too.

"Maybe a couple," Aki said. "Oh, what the heck, bring all of them."

When Carsyn peeked into the bag, her eyes twinkled.

"Don't say anything," Aki responded, her cheeks flushing. "Not one word, Carsyn Lyndon."

Carsyn winked. "Not one," she responded, chuckling as she hefted the suitcase into the bed of her truck. She set Aki's books on the backseat and opened the passenger door. "After you, my dear," she said, smiling.

"Thanks," Aki answered, her gaze lingering as she climbed up to fasten her seat belt.

"My pleasure," Carsyn responded, shutting the door, and walking around to get in the other side. "And you're doing okay?" she asked softly.

"I can't promise that I won't have a moment or two as we go along," Aki responded, "but I'm good for now."

"Good," Carsyn said, pulling onto the road. She drove across the bridge, following her route to the campground. "So, you've got choices," she said, looking over, "the sleeper sofa, it's a queen with a decent mattress; the bunk bed, it's a twin that sleeps about as good as a sheet of plywood; the booth, it makes into a pretty decent little bed; or mine." She glanced over, adding, "It's a king with a top of the line mattress, one that you can have with or without me lying beside you." She swallowed, returning her eyes to the road.

"The king," Aki said, licking her lips, "with you lying beside me." She caught her breath as a shiver traversed her spine. "But I'm not sure how this'll go, Carsyn," she added, biting her lip. "I may end up being quite the disappointment."

"Oh, sweetie," Carsyn responded, smiling softly as she reached over to clasp her hand, "that's not even possible, so you may as well stop worrying about it."

Aki's gaze became watery, tapping her foot on the floorboard.

"Are you having second thoughts?" Carsyn asked softly, "because if you are, I can take you back right now." She laid her hand on Aki's thigh. "You won't hurt my feelings if you decide not to go. No pressure here, none at all."

"I'm not used to being in a situation where everything feels out of my control," Aki responded quietly, her voice cracking with emotion. "And I'm not used to not knowing what comes next…or how…" Her tone was shrill when her words broke off.

"So, do you want to go back," Carsyn asked. "We can turn around. It's not a problem."

"No," Aki responded, shaking her head slowly. "I just wanted you to understand what was going on with me, that's all."

"I do," Carsyn said softly, falling silent for a little while. Then, she cocked her head, asking if Aki liked to play Scrabble.

"I was the Scrabble Queen of my sorority," Aki responded, smiling as tension released from her shoulders. "I haven't played much since I was an undergrad, but I used to enjoy it."

"Good," Carsyn said, smiling from her cheeks to her eyes. "I need to take a shower," she added, "but after that, we'll get it out, and you can show me what you've got."

"I used to be pretty good," Aki responded. "I may just be more than you can handle."

"Maybe so," Carsyn said, "but I'll have you know that I have plans to beat the socks off of you."

"Do you, now?" Aki murmured, their gazes locking.

"Yeah, I do," Carsyn said softly.

CHAPTER 25

"Be out in a few minutes," Carsyn said, pausing to meet Aki's gaze before clicking the bathroom door shut.

Aki wondered if she'd paused, considering whether or not to leave the door ajar? Had the extended eye contact been an invitation to join her? *Possibly,* she thought. Her stomach fluttered, thinking about her, thinking about how if they came together it might go. She sucked in a breath, her heart pounding—ratatat-tat like a drum. Where had this come from, this desire for a woman? Would she have given serious consideration to sleeping with one before now? She shook her head, making her way into the bedroom. She didn't think so. *How about Carsyn, would you have slept with her?* she asked herself. *If you'd met her in college? Or even in high school?* Her skin tingled, nodding. *How about in medical school? Would you have made time for her when you made time for no one?* Aki pressed her lips together, pushing back tears, and swallowing hard. She unloaded her suitcase into the three empty drawers, sliding her fingers along the edge of each one. *Probably Sylvia's,* she thought. She inhaled, trying to catch the scent of Carsyn's late wife's cologne. She wondered what she'd been like and how she'd come to die so young. *Probably just slightly younger than Carsyn is now,* she told herself. *Maybe that's why she thinks of herself as old; she became a widow when she was still young.* She thought about Carsyn's family, wondered why she never mentioned anyone. She envisioned her stepping out of the shower when the water turned off, scurried to the sofa, and looked up when the bathroom door opened.

"Hi," Carsyn said, smiling, "I hope this is okay." She glanced down at her attire. She wore a white sleeveless ribbed undershirt and a pair of scotch-plaid pajama bottoms—men's clothing with an exquisite feminine flair. The bottoms had a drawstring above the fly.

"Of course it is," Aki answered, feeling warmth ooze throughout her body. She licked her lips, examining Carsyn's nipples from afar.

"Watch it," Carsyn said, smiling that slow sexy smile, "you're gonna make me blush."

"Well, that'll make two of us," Aki responded, clearing her throat. "I'm sorry," she added, covering her face with her hands, "I didn't mean to stare." She closed her eyes, taking a soft breath when they opened. "It's just that you're beautiful in those." She furrowed her brow, watching Carsyn's reaction. "Wrong word?" she asked. "Of course it was," she answered, "Courtney says you're like Jack."

Carsyn chuckled, responding, "In some ways, in other ways, not." She smiled, moving closer. "Beautiful is fine, sweetie," she added. "You can call me whatever you want."

"But attractive or handsome would've been a better choice, right?" Aki responded.

"Yeah, probably," Carsyn whispered, stroking a lock of hair from her eyes before kissing her slowly.

"Mmm," Aki moaned, bringing her fingers into Carsyn's hair. Her head was tilted, and her mouth was open. "What a good kisser you are," she murmured.

"Mmm," Carsyn responded, low and long. She planted gentle kisses around her lips. "You are too," she whispered, kissing her again with a little tongue.

Aki slid her fingertips up Carsyn's abdomen, pausing just shy of her breast, and moaning.

Carsyn tipped back, meeting her gaze softly. "It's okay, you can touch me."

Aki trembled, responding, "I think we'd better stick to a game of Scrabble for now." She took a breath, straightening her posture.

"That's good too," Carsyn said softly, kissing her temple. "But before we do," she added, "I believe we have old business to tend to."

"Old business?" Aki asked, furrowing her brow.

"Yes, old business," Carsyn responded, lifting an eyebrow. "I believe you have something you need to open." She collected Aki's fortune cookie from the drawer, placed it before her on the table, and added, "There you go."

"You saved it," Aki said, touching her lips with her fingers.

"Of course I saved it," Carsyn responded, scooting in beside her. "Go on," she said, grinning, "let's see what your fortune is."

Aki ripped the transparent wrapping, broke the cookie in half, and removed the thin slip of white paper from its center. She swallowed hard, reading it silently.

"Go on, read it out loud," Carsyn urged, her eyes widening.

Aki held her gaze, sitting quietly.

"Go on," Carsyn repeated, cocking her head to one side, "read it."

"Your tongue is your ambassador," Aki read as her stomach turned over.

"In bed," Carsyn added. "It was your rule. Come on; you have to say it."

Aki bit her lip, her eyes teeming with tears.

"Hey, I didn't mean anything by it," Carsyn said, gently squeezing her hand. "I was just teasing, sweetie." She cocked her head, grimacing. "Oh God, Aki, I'm so sorry. I'd never upset you intentionally. You have to know that."

"I do," Aki answered. "It's just that I'm anxious, especially about that." She smiled thinly, adding, "You didn't do anything wrong."

"Yes, I did," Carsyn responded. "I should've known better than to tease you," she added, her jaw taut. "This is serious stuff." She moved closer, slipping her arm around her shoulders. "I should've been more sensitive, and I'm sorry."

"I don't know why that part scares me the most," Aki continued, her voice quiet as she looked off, "maybe because I've never done it before." She shook her head. "But there are other things that I've not done that I'd try without a second thought." She met her gaze, curling her upper lip. "Do you know that all I have to do is look at the cover of that book, the one the clerk picked out for me, to become nauseous? Ridiculous, huh?"

"Not at all," Carsyn whispered. "Everyone has things that suit them, and things that don't." She peered into her eyes. "There are many ways to make love," she added, "and that's just one of them."

"But if we do," Aki responded, "I want to do it right."

Carsyn peered into her eyes. "This isn't a test question where you have to know the right answer or how to do something," Carsyn said quietly. "It's not something that you need to study for or worry about." She brushed her cheek with the back of her hand. "If we make love, Aki, and I very much hope that we do, we're gonna have our own style. It'll just be you and me doing what works for us."

Aki released a breath, tension leaving her body. "Thank you," she said, touching her arm.

"No thanks required," Carsyn responded. "So, are you ready to lose your socks?" she asked, smiling.

"I'm ready for you to give it your best shot," Aki answered, rubbing her hands together. She turned, watching Carsyn stretch to retrieve the Scrabble game from the top shelf of a nearby closet.

"There you go again," Carsyn said, catching her eye, "always making me blush." Their gazes locked for a long moment before she opened the board and shook the tiles. "First seven are yours," she announced with a wide smile.

Aki's eyes narrowed, studying them before placing six on the board.

"S-C-L-E-R-A, is that even a word?" Carsyn asked, raising an eyebrow.

"It's the white of the eye, Einstein," Aki responded. "Eight points, doubled," she said smiling.

"Not bad for someone who hasn't played for a while," Carsyn commented, "but not as good as mine." She grinned, spelling out S-P-I-C-Y.

"Twelve points," Aki responded, looking over her glasses, "you're already behind." It went on like that for some time. "Okay," she said, "I can't use this last one. I'll deduct one point from my score." She nodded toward the board. "Go on, give it your best shot. It'll take a miracle to beat me now."

Carsyn smiled, placing C-L-I-M-A-X on the board.

"Did you just draw that X?" Aki asked, "because if you didn't, you should've used it on your triple word a while ago."

"No, I had it since the first draw," Carsyn answered, holding her eye. "I was saving it for the right word."

"I thought so," Aki responded, her eyes sparkling. "I mean, what's the chance that with one exception, all of your words would be sexy in one way or another?"

"There was no exception," Carsyn answered, arching an eyebrow.

"Sure there was," Aki countered. "See, right here," she added, pointing to the board, "S-P-I-C-Y."

Carsyn laughed, nuzzling her neck with a soft inhale. "That's your scent, baby," she murmured, locking gazes, "the sexiest word of all."

CHAPTER 26

First sexual experiences didn't always turn out like they did in romance novels or the movies. But the magic that occurred between the pages and on the screen was what Carsyn wanted for Aki. She wanted their first voyage, possibly their only voyage, to be so magical that the stars aligned when their lips came together. She wanted their passion to culminate with an orgasm so exquisite that it would be forever etched in Aki's memory. She wanted that and so much more for Aki.

"What are you doing?" Aki asked, stepping out of the bathroom. "It's almost midnight; you don't need to change the sheets. If they were good enough for you last night, they'll be good enough for me." She wore flannel pajamas, playfully printed with Christmas puppies.

Carsyn suppressed a smile, thinking, *so cute and sexy.* "But I do," she responded, grasping the fitted sheet over the top right corner of the mattress, and pulling it under.

"I'll get the other side," Aki said, her brow furrowing when she touched the sheet. "Are these silk?" she asked incredulously. "Surely not," she answered. "I mean, who puts silk sheets on their bed when they're camping in an equestrian campground?"

"Me," Carsyn answered, smiling as she tugged the burgundy fabric toward the lower right corner. She looked up, winking. "Well, I didn't used to, but I do now," she added. "I picked them up on my way to Jack's place."

"Oh God, you are so sweet," Aki said tenderly.

"The tricky part's gonna be to get the candles lit if you don't give me much notice," Carsyn continued, coming around to collect the flat sheet. She didn't mention that she'd also picked up a dozen roses. They were stored in the bottom drawer of the refrigerator.

"Come here," Aki beckoned softly. "I think you need to kiss me."

"Yes, I do," Carsyn whispered. She gathered her into her arms, peering into her eyes, and swaying their bodies gently. "I need to kiss you here… and here… and here," she said, planting soft kisses all over her face.

Aki swished her hair when she gently palmed her cheek.

"And here," Carsyn murmured, lightly licking the outside of Aki's lips before kissing her deeply. She longed to touch her intimately but didn't.

Aki sucked in a breath, her lower lip trembling.

"You okay?" Carsyn asked.

"I'm fine," Aki answered, leaning in for a light kiss. "And you are so sweet."

Carsyn smiled, feeling content like she hadn't for a very long time. "Come on," she said, "I think it's time for bed."

"Oh, that's right," Aki responded, "you have to get up early to teach."

"Not to teach as much as feed the horses," Carsyn corrected. "They'll want their breakfast by daybreak." She crawled into bed, extending her arm across Aki's pillow. "Hold you for a little bit?" she asked softly.

"I'd like that," Aki responded, sliding in, and nestling close. "Can we talk for a few minutes?" she asked, tilting her head up to meet her eye.

"Sure," Carsyn answered, closing her eyes as she kissed her forehead. "What do you want to talk about?"

"Oh, I don't know," Aki said with a sidelong glance and hesitation in her tone, "maybe Sylvia?"

Carsyn sucked in a breath as her mind whipped through a series of images and worst case scenarios. "What do you want to know about her?" she asked, locking her jaw, and swallowing hard.

"I'm sorry," Aki said kindly. "It's a recent wound," she added, brushing her cheek with her fingertips, "you must miss her a lot."

"I don't miss her at all," Carsyn said, her body temperature on the rise. She dropped her legs over the side of the bed and got up.

After a moment, Aki followed her to the sofa. "I'm sorry," she said softly, sitting down beside her. "It's not my business. I shouldn't have asked about her."

"It is your business," Carsyn responded, inhaling deeply with a roll of her neck and shoulders. "It's just that I don't talk about it very—" As her words broke off another wave of irrational panic took hold. Her heart ached, pained like a racehorse on drugs. She felt the burn of the flashback, heard screams, and choked on non-existent smoke. "I can't lose control," she said, storming out.

*　*　*

Carsyn was down the steps and out of sight before Aki fully processed what had just occurred. She reached for her jacket, put on her athletic shoes, and stepped outside, shivering in the chill of the night. She paused at the sound of a nicker, decided to check the truck, and climbed in on the passenger side. "Does it happen often?" she asked quietly, "the panic attacks?"

"No," Carsyn responded, her jaw still taut, "not if I stay away from my triggers." She glanced over. "Just hearing or saying her name doesn't usually set me off. I think it did tonight because I was trying to figure out how to tell you about her." She took a breath, staring out her window. "They don't usually last long," she added, "only a few minutes, but I'm vulnerable afterward." She looked over, pleading with her eyes. "Please, Aki, not now, I won't be able to maintain composure."

Aki touched her arm, responding, "You don't always have to be strong, you know. You don't always have to be in control." Her voice softened, peering into her eyes. "Not with me you don't."

"Butches don't cry," Carsyn said, swallowing, "butch characteristics, one-oh-one."

"Don't they, now?" Aki responded, holding her gaze with a thin smile. She squeezed her hand, pulling her door handle. "Come on," she invited, "come inside, and I'll give you a back rub."

* * *

AKI VARIED THE PRESSURE, feeling Carsyn's neck and shoulder muscles move beneath her skin.

"Oh God," Carsyn moaned, the memory of her recent panic attack fading fast. "Mmm, right there." She rolled one shoulder and then the other. "Oh God," she groaned, "where'd you learn to do that?"

"If I say medical school," Aki answered, smiling, "it'll give you the wrong idea about the quality of my education." She applied circular pressure with her palms. "Did you know that a massage can help you regulate blood pressure and boost your immune system?" she added.

"No, I didn't," Carsyn moaned. "Ohhh God, that feels good, right there." She turned her head from one side to the other. "Mmm, hands of an angel," she murmured.

Aki chuckled, saying, "Take off your shirt."

"Really?" Carsyn responded, a slow smile building with intense eye contact.

"Really," Aki answered with a wink. "Go on, take it off, and lay face down on the bed."

"Mmm, my pleasure," Carsyn responded, locking gazes as she peeled the garment over her head, revealing her breasts.

"Could you move any slower?" Aki asked, flushing as her tongue darted out to moisten her lips.

"I believe you're blushing, Doctor," Carsyn commented, grinning as she assumed a face-down position on the bed.

Aki shook her head. "I'm sure I am," she said, crawling over to straddle her. "Now, be quiet," she added, palming evenly down her back, "I want you to relax."

"I am relaxed," Carsyn moaned, melting into a puddle.

"That's good," Aki murmured, massaging a while longer before changing position. "Lay still for a minute," she said, trailing a finger down her spine, "I'll be right back."

"Not going anywhere," Carsyn responded without moving a muscle.

"That's good," Aki said, smiling warmly. She returned with a bottle of lotion, rubbing it in, and settling beside her.

CHAPTER 27

Aki scooted closer, not wanting to wake Carsyn. She'd fallen asleep on her stomach, minutes after she'd screwed the cap on the lotion. Aki felt tightness in her throat, remembering her reaction when she'd asked her about Sylvia, feeling bad about upsetting her but wanting them to talk about her. *You need to sleep,* she told herself, struggling to keep her eyes open. She moved her hand, nearly touching Carsyn's sculpted upper back. "You're so handsome," she mouthed inaudibly, moving within an inch of her body. She closed her eyes, inhaling her masculine, cool, fresh scent. As she nestled into her pillow, her muscles relaxed, her brain slowed, and the material world disappeared—*And the white eagle swooped down from his high branch, landing before her. He hung his head, the black tips of his wings on the ground.*

Aki's eyes narrowed. "Why am I here?" *she asked.*

The eagle screeched, flapping his wings. "You don't know, Little Deer?" *he answered. It felt as if they'd had this conversation many times in the past.*

"My name is Aki," *Aki responded.* "I'm a doctor, not a deer." *She turned her head so slowly that it seemed unnatural.* "Why did you call me by that name?" *she asked.*

"Because it's who you are, Doctor," the bird screeched, flying above her, his powerful claws pulling her hair. "Wake up, Little Deer!"

Aki yelped, watching him fly into the eastern pre-dawn sky. "What's that light," she called out from slumber, "the one over there?"

"You don't know, Little Deer?" the white eagle asked. "You don't recognize the light that appears in the eastern sky before sunrise?"

"No," Aki responded, her voice becoming childlike, "but I want to because she's so beautiful."

"Then, you must offer her what you have to give," the eagle answered, "because without your help she'll be darkened." With a flap of his wings, he allowed her to peer into the not so distant future.

"No," Aki screamed, "her light can't be extinguished, it'll kill her."

"Then, you must hurry, Doctor," the bird screeched. "You must help her, Little Deer."

"But I don't know what to do," Aki called out. "I don't know how to help her."

"Then, I'll show you," the Black Bear growled.

* * *

"Don't know how to help her," Aki mumbled, thrashing beneath her cover, "don't know how…"

"Shhh…Shhh…Shhh…," Carsyn cooed, "it's just a dream."

"I'm sorry I woke you," Aki said, reorienting to her surroundings. "I should've had the sense to sleep in the other bed." She hadn't slept with another person in the same room since her residency.

"No," Carsyn responded, kissing her temple, "not when you belong right here." She repositioned onto her back. "Everyone has bad dreams," she added, pulling her close.

"Not every night, they don't." Aki countered, swallowing. "Not unless they have a problem."

"I have nightmares too," Carsyn admitted quietly, "sometimes night after night."

Aki kissed her breast. "There are medications," she said, meeting her gaze tenderly, "one, in particular, that's been shown to be effective in the treatment of nightmares associated with Post Traumatic Stress Disorder."

"I know," Carsyn said, "but I don't like to take drugs."

"No one does," Aki said softly.

"You take anything for yours?" Carsyn asked.

"No," Aki answered, "but if they continue much longer, I probably should. Restful sleep is an important component of good health." It felt as if their souls had just connected on a whole new level.

"Your dreams," Carsyn asked, "do you want to talk about them?"

"No," Aki answered, shaking her head slowly. "They're not much more than nonsensical storylines and vivid imagery. I can't see how talking about them would help." She smiled thinly, meeting her eye. "How about you," she asked softly, "you want to talk?"

Carsyn bit her lip, taking a breath, and looking off. "Mine are different," she said quietly, "painfully vivid and completely based in reality." She kissed Aki's forehead. "Maybe tomorrow I'll have a couple of drinks and tell you about them."

Aki pressed her lips together, tensing.

"It's the only way I know how to tell you about Sylvia and what happened without falling apart," Carsyn added. "I won't get drunk, I promise. I'll just have a couple to take the edge off."

Aki lifted her head, making direct eye contact.

"I know, I know," Carsyn responded, "there's a host of medications that could help me with that."

"Yes, there are," Aki said quietly, "but I guess a couple of drinks now and then won't kill you."

"I don't have to do it that often," Carsyn continued, "just when I'm triggered."

"I understand," Aki responded quietly.

* * *

CARSYN LOWERED THE GAS FLAME, stirring maple syrup into the bubbling pot. At six in the morning, her horses had already been calling for their breakfast for more than half an hour. They'd have to wait a bit longer because, like it or not, Aki's breakfast came first. She padded to the bedroom door, peeking in soundlessly. It'd been ages since Carsyn had tiptoed out of her bedroom to make breakfast for a gorgeous woman. She smiled, watching her breathe steadily for a couple of minutes before returning to the kitchen. Using both hands, she opened and shut the oven door quietly.

"What are you cooking out there?" Aki called out. Her voice sounded sleepy and her words were interspersed with stretching sounds. "Whatever it is, it smells amazing."

"Old-fashioned maple-pecan oatmeal," Carsyn called back, turning off the burner, "and pumpkin muffins." She crawled over the end of the bed, lying beside her, and kissing her lips tenderly. "Did you sleep well?" she asked, brushing a lock of hair from her eyes.

"Like a baby after we talked," Aki responded, clasping her fingers above her head with more stretching sounds.

"That's good," Carsyn said, smiling. "I was worried that you might've been disappointed in me when we rolled over."

"No, not at all," Aki responded. "Our conversation just anchored back to something that happened a long time ago." She stroked her cheek, peering into her eyes. "You have to do what feels right," she added. "My only concern is that you're okay."

"I am most of the time," Carsyn responded. She kissed her again, saying, "I need to check on the muffins."

Within minutes, Aki emerged from the bathroom wearing faded jeans and a UCLA sweatshirt. "What can I do to help?" she asked, slipping her arms around her from behind.

Carsyn turned her head, kissing her lips as she stirred. "Not a thing," she responded, arching back into her touch with a soft moan. "Just keep me company while I dish up breakfast."

"You've got it," Aki said, lightly brushing Carsyn's breasts as she stepped off to slide into the booth.

Intentional or not? Carsyn wondered, deciding that the jury was still out. When she looked over, noticing that Aki's neck and cheeks were flushed, she changed her opinion to intentional. *Well, aren't we getting bold,* she thought. She scooped their oatmeal into stoneware bowls, sprinkled pecan halves on top, and buttered their muffins. "You want to go for a ride this afternoon?" she asked. "I thought maybe we could pack a picnic, ride out for an hour or so, and stop for lunch."

Aki took a breath, releasing it slowly. "It's been a long time since I've ridden," she answered with a swallow, "I'm not sure how well I'd handle a horse."

"Well, you wouldn't actually be handling one," Carsyn said, lifting her eyebrows. "Lily hasn't been ridden for over three years," she added, shaking her head, "and I wouldn't want to take a chance on you getting hurt." She met her gaze, loading a spoon full of oatmeal. "I was just gonna have you swing on behind me on Relic."

"Now, that I can handle," Aki responded, her eyes taking on a sparkle.

CHAPTER 28

Aki tucked her legs underneath her body, taking a sip of coffee as she cracked the spine on her second book. "*Lesbian Sex Positions: Let's Get Naked,*" she read out loud. She'd been disappointed in *Your First Lesbian Experience* because it was more about feelings than process. What she needed was a good old-fashioned technical manual, a step-by-step, this is how you do it kind of book. Facing her fear, *The Lesbian Tongue: Wild and Free* would be up next, followed by, *Lesbian Sex: The Complete Reference*. "Oh my," she murmured, turning her hardcover ninety and then one-hundred-eighty degrees. "Doesn't that position look interesting?" She took another sip of coffee, licking her lips. *"The Ridin' Cowgirl,"* she read, smiling. She thought through how the position might work with Carsyn, thinking that she seemed like more of a straddling kind of woman than one who'd put her bottom on two pillows. She tabbed the page for future reference, moving on to what she thought might become her personal favorite. "*Dinner Is Served, Ma'am,*" she read, tingling in her center as she studied the graphic. "Mmm, now that looks interesting," she murmured, feeling wet, envisioning her legs draped over Carsyn's shoulders as she tongued her clitoris. Her pulse sped up at the sound of Carsyn's footsteps and nickers. "You're home early," she said, shoving her bag of books into her suitcase, and clicking the latch. "I didn't expect you for another hour," she added, feeling like a school girl who'd almost been caught thumbing through the pictures in a Playboy magazine. *Uh-huh,* she thought, *your crush on* Sister Mary Kathleen *wasn't the only clue. There were also the Playboy magazines. How in creation did you miss this?*

"I gave 'em an extra reading assignment," Carsyn answered.

"I'm sorry," Aki said, looking up, distracted, "you did what?"

"I gave my students an extra reading assignment," Carsyn repeated, lifting an eyebrow. "You know, so that we could call it a day early," she added.

"Oh, okay," Aki responded, folding into her arms.

"Who wants to be digging when they could be taking their girl for a ride and having a picnic?" Carsyn asked, kissing her.

Not you," Aki responded, warming as her thoughts returned to *The Ridin' Cowgirl.* "I made tuna salad," she blurted out.

"That's perfect," Carsyn answered, smiling, "I love tuna salad." She cocked her head, furrowing her brow. "Are you okay?" she asked. "You look a little flushed."

"I'm fine," Aki answered, pushing, *Dinner Is Served, Ma'am,* out of mind. "I'll make the sandwiches," she added, "while you saddle Relic."

"Sounds like a plan," Carsyn said with a gentle squeeze of her behind.

* * *

"WE WON'T RIDE TOO FAR," Carsyn said, helping Aki mount behind her. "Riding double is okay, but not that comfortable." She put pressure on the side of Relic's neck, turning him to the right. "Get up," she said with a firm voice. "I thought we'd ride along the river by the mounds," she continued, turning her head to catch Aki's eye, "have our picnic, and circle back."

"Whatever you want to do is fine," Aki responded, slipping her hands around Carsyn's flat belly. As they rode, she brushed her lower breasts with her fingertips.

Carsyn took a breath, shifting in the saddle. "There's a picnic table by that tree over there," she said, "the one right before you get to the mounds."

"I see it," Aki responded, laying her cheek against her back. "That's a beautiful spot," she added with another caress of Carsyn's breasts.

Carsyn squirmed in the saddle, before lifting her leg over the horn, and lowering to the ground. She asked Relic to stand squarely and dropped his reins.

"That's impressive," Aki commented.

"What?" Carsyn asked, "the way I dismounted or the way Relic stands?"

"Both actually," Aki responded.

"Turn this way," Carsyn said, reaching up to hold her on both sides of her abdomen, "and I'll help you down." When she did, she backed her against the tree, grazing the swell of Aki's breasts with her hands, and kissing her deeply and slowly. She cocked her head, locking gazes. "I didn't want you to think that I didn't notice," she said, pressing her leg between Aki's, and kissing her again. All the while, Relic stood quietly.

Aki touched her throat, catching her breath as their bodies parted. "I can't promise that I won't do it again," she responded.

Carsyn smiled a slow smile, saying, "And I can't promise that I won't let you know that I noticed."

* * *

CARSYN LIFTED her head at the sound of a click. "Mmm, I'll bet I know what you're thinking," she murmured, rolling over.

"I thought you might be awake," Aki said, laying the lighter on the nightstand, and folding into her arms. They'd watched a movie in bed, turning in early. "We don't have much time before I leave," she said, swallowing, "I thought we should make the most of it."

"Yeah," Carsyn said, taking a breath, "we probably should." She bit her lip, adding, "God, am I ever dreading Sunday."

"I am too," Aki responded, looking off for a second. "I guess I could cancel the interview in Chicago," she added, "I already know that I don't want the job." She tilted her head, lifting her eyebrows. "That'd at least give us a few more days before I have to fly back."

"That'd help," Carsyn responded, forcing the heartbreak from her voice. They'd been saying goodbye since the start.

"We'll still see each other," Aki promised.

"I know we will," Carsyn said with a hard swallow. "It's what, only a three-hour flight?"

"About that," Aki said quietly. "I don't know why I wasted so much of our time," she added. "I don't usually let fear hold me back."

"Because our moving forward would be a life changing event," Carsyn answered.

"The life-changing event occurred on Friday," Aki countered, meeting her gaze directly. "It happened when I looked into your eyes and knew that I wanted you." She touched her cheek. "And you wanted me too," she added softly, "I could tell."

"I did," Carsyn murmured, trailing her fingertips down her arm, "but like you, I was afraid to move forward. I was afraid that I was about to repeat the mistake that nearly destroyed me."

"So, what changed your mind?" Aki asked softly.

"It just hit me that this is a totally different situation," Carsyn answered. "I know it sounds stupid, but I had to figure out that you weren't Sylvia."

"Nothing you say sounds stupid," Aki said, meeting her gaze gently. "You want to talk about it?" she asked hopefully.

"No," Carsyn answered, "but we need to." She shook her head, adding, "God, talk about a mood spoiler."

"We've been hot for each other since Friday," Aki said, "there's always tomorrow."

"Yeah, right," Carsyn responded. She sucked in a breath, holding it as if it might be her last. "I'm gonna stop if I can't hold it together," she added, "I just want you to know that."

"Okay," Aki said, gently meeting her eye. "But don't do that for me," she added, "because I already know butches cry." She cupped her cheek. "I also know keeping things bottled up isn't healthy."

Carsyn nodded, swallowing as Aki laid her arm across her belly, and held her tightly. She took a breath, before speaking in a monotone voice. "Sylvia's phone rang," she began with a heavy sigh. "She'd just gotten in the shower, so I answered. If I'd just let it ring, everything would've probably gone on as it was."

Aki rested her head on her shoulder, stroking her abdomen softly.

"It wasn't like I didn't know," Carsyn continued, beads of sweat visible on her temple and forehead. "I mean, women called her all the time. I'd watch her answer, giggle like she did when we first got together, and step off." She shook her head, curling her upper lip, and pausing for a crack in her voice. "I knew what was going on. I'd known for a long time, maybe eighteen months of our two years of marriage."

"I'm so sorry," Aki whispered, lightly stroking her forearm.

"So, I answered," Carsyn went on, "and this woman, probably all of eighteen, thought I was Sylvia." Her mouth opened, shaking her head slowly. "I mean, what do you do when that happens? I didn't know what to do, so I listened. I listened and became more enraged by the minute—*Mmm, I never knew anyone who tasted as good as you do. Mmm, I can't wait to see you again. What time did you say your old woman has class on Thursday night?*" She clenched her jaw. "They were sleeping together, and she didn't even recognize her voice. So, I hung up and let Sylvia have it when she came out. I told her I wanted a divorce."

"I'm so sorry," Aki repeated, stroking her softly.

"And she freaked, screaming and crying," Carsyn continued, "not because she loved me, but because she knew that she'd have to get a job." She shivered, feeling impending doom and death on her doorstep. "My actions set off a chain reaction," she added, gulping a breath, "a falling row of dominoes that resulted in the death of her and my parents."

"Sylvia's actions," Aki corrected, nestling against her breast.

"What was I thinking?" Carsyn went on, the past gripping her by the neck. "I knew my mom and dad were on their way over to go pick up pumpkins. My mom used to carve a whole bunch, all with different faces, and line them up in front of their house—my house now." When her breath hitched, she paused again.

"You're doing great," Aki whispered, kissing her gently.

"So, when they got there," Carsyn said, shaking her head, "Sylvia and I, we just agreed to finish the argument later, and put on our happy faces. My dad moved over, Sylvia slid under his wheel, and I followed in my truck." Her breathing was deep and rapid as she finished the sentence. For a millisecond, she thought she was having a heart attack.

"Easy," Aki whispered, her eyes narrowing.

Carsyn nodded, making eye contact, and squeezing her hand. She'd almost made it and needed to push through to the end. "I saw it happen," she choked, "I saw them die right before my eyes. The signal was flashing. I was two cars back, stopped at a red light." Her eyes bulged, unable to blink as she watched her nightmare unfold in memory. "Sylvia drove right through the gate. I don't think she'd have done it on purpose. She wasn't a bad person, just young. My best guess is that she was distracted by how she was gonna pay her bills without my income. She liked nice things and had no qualms about putting them on plastic." Her breath came hard, tears streaming down her cheeks. "The gate snapped," she whimpered, "and in the next second, a locomotive barreled into them. I heard his horn as my dad's car burst into flames. I tried to get to 'em, but I couldn't."

"That's how you got the burns on your hands," Aki said quietly.

Carsyn nodded, falling silent.

CHAPTER 29

Aki's eyes opened before Carsyn stirred beside her. She'd held and stroked her through the night, trying to wrap her mind around what she'd witnessed, and marveling at how she'd managed to survive. To watch your family, die a violent death, right before your eyes, was unimaginable. Inner strength was one of the many things that she loved about her.

"Hi," Carsyn said, her eyes fluttering open. "Sorry about last night."

"Hi," Aki responded, planting a gentle kiss on her lips, "and there's nothing to be sorry about."

"Sure there is," Carsyn countered. "I kept you awake half of the night." She shook her head, muttering, "God, I don't know what got into me. It took forever to get a grip on myself."

"Release is what you needed," Aki said softly, stroking her hair at the temple. "How are you doing this morning?"

"I'm okay," Carsyn answered, "other than being embarrassed, I guess."

"Well, you certainly don't need to be," Aki responded, propping onto her elbow to meet her eye. "Because I'll tell you a little secret," she added, "those tears, the ones you work so hard to contain, are a sign of strength, not weakness." She nestled against her breast. "And last night," she whispered, "I saw just how strong you really are, and I love you even more this morning."

"I love you too," Carsyn responded, rolling to top her, their tongues dancing a slow waltz.

Aki caught her breath, warm and flushed, saying, "How about I fix our breakfast this morning? Maybe something like poached eggs on toast?"

"Mmm, sounds good," Carsyn murmured, stroking her cheek, and trailing her fingers slightly lower. Then, she glanced at the clock. "Crap," she blurted out, "I've gotta get going." She dropped her legs over the side of the bed, pulling on her jeans, and promising more tonight.

"Is it okay if I help feed the horses?" Aki asked, getting up.

"Of course it's okay," Carsyn responded. "But you've gotta watch 'em when there's a chill in the air," she added. "They're pretty frisky in the morning."

"I'll be careful," Aki promised, unbuttoning her nightshirt, and smiling when Carsyn noticed her breasts.

***

Relic stretched his neck toward Lily with his chin elevated and his ears pinned back. Before Lily could move, he lunged at her with his mouth open. He snapped his teeth together, missing her hindquarter by only a few inches.

"Carsyn," Aki screamed. "Carsyn! Come quickly!"

"What?" Carsyn called out, running to the rear of the campsite full-tilt, "what's wrong?" she asked, skidding to a stop.

"He went after her when she wasn't doing anything wrong," Aki responded. Her eyes were wide, and her mouth was hanging open. "He tried to bite her, then kicked at her with both hooves." She took a breath, adding, "He almost got her too."

"He dominates," Carsyn explained. "He probably told her to move and she didn't." She smiled, kissing her temple. "Don't worry, honey," she added, "they're tied far enough apart that he can't get to her."

Aki glared at the gelding. "That was mean," she said, "you leave her alone."

"He's hungry," Carsyn defended.

"Well, she is too," Aki responded, her gaze still fixed on Relic, "so that's no excuse to be mean to her."

Carsyn kissed her again, saying, "I'll get their hay bags and that'll put an end to it."

* * *

"THESE ARE GREAT," Carsyn said, forking a double sized bite of egg and toast. She leaned over, lightly kissing Aki's lips, and adding, "She's sharp as a whip, beautiful, and she can cook too."

"It's not that difficult to poach two eggs and set them in the center of two slices of toast," Aki responded, "but thank you." She took a breath. "Lily," she asked, "she was Sylvia's?"

"Yeah," Carsyn responded, nodding slowly. "She wanted her, but hardly ever rode her."

"But you don't ride her either," Aki observed, furrowing her brow.

"No," Carsyn said, pressing her lips together. "That's why when we're camping I have to lunge her," she added. "Relic gets his exercise on rides, but she needs it too."

"So, why don't you ride her sometimes?" Aki asked, taking a sip of coffee. "Is it that she's not trained well enough?"

"No, her training was top-notch," Carsyn responded. She shook her head, curling her upper lip, and adding, "Only the best for Sylvia."

"Then why don't you ride her?" Aki persisted. "She seems like a really nice horse."

"She is," Carsyn said, meeting her gaze directly. "I don't ride her because she was Sylvia's." For some reason, it seemed easier to talk about her this morning. "She wanted things without loving them—got bored and moved on."

"I'm sorry," Aki said, gently squeezing her forearm.

"Her mother tried to talk me out of marrying her," Carsyn continued, "but I didn't pay any attention. I just thought she had a problem with our age difference and moved forward." She shook her head. "Turns out, she cared about me. She was just trying to save me from a lot of hurt down the road." She took a breath, blowing it out slowly. "God, if only I'd listened to her."

"You were fond of her too," Aki said softly, "I can hear it in your tone."

"Yeah, I was," Carsyn responded, smiling thinly, "my mother-in-law was the best part of my marriage to Sylvia." She swallowed hard, glancing out the window.

"Do you still have contact?" Aki asked, rubbing her shoulder.

"No," Carsyn answered, pursing her lips, and clearing the dishes from the table.

* * *

"Oh my goodness," Aki exclaimed, "you're grilling lobster tails."

Carsyn looked up with a soft smile. "I am," she said, peering into her eyes, "because tonight's the night." She licked her lips, adding, "Kind of goes along with silk sheets."

Aki brushed against her, murmuring, "I'm ready."

"Thought maybe you were," Carsyn said, kissing her deeply. They ate by candlelight and held hands as they watched the most vivid orange sunset. From their lawn chairs, they moved to the sofa, and then to the bedroom.

Aki's breathing quickened when Carsyn closed the distance between their bodies, kissing her with unrestrained passion. "I've never felt like this before," she panted, "didn't think it was possible." She traced the sculpting of Carsyn's arms, murmuring, "How is that I've just come to notice handsome women?"

"I don't know," Carsyn whispered, kissing her again, "but I'm certainly glad that you did." She twirled a lock of hair, peering into her eyes. "Maybe it's that you were meant to be mine," she added, unbuttoning Aki's shirt, and unclasping her bra, allowing the items to fall to the floor.

"I think I was," Aki responded, breathless.

"Mmm, you are so beautiful," Carsyn murmured, caressing her breasts, and suckling her nipples. She peeled off her hoodie, holding her, skin on skin. "So, what do you think about that?" she whispered, nibbling her earlobe.

"It's like nothing I've ever experienced," Aki whispered back. She caught her breath as Carsyn backed her to the bed.

"I think we need to get rid of these," Carsyn said, helping her out of her jeans and panties. She moaned, licking and kissing her neck, her navel, and her abdomen.

Aki closed her eyes, whimpering as gentle waves of pleasure rippled through her body. When Carsyn nibbled where her inner thighs met her groin, she oozed natural lubricant onto the silk.

"You're so wet," Carsyn murmured, pushing inside her, and taking her with her mouth.

"Ohhhh, God," Aki whimpered, "Oh, God, Carsyn…"

"Mmm, you taste so good," Carsyn moaned, syncing with the movement of Aki's hips as she might a boat on turbulent waters.

"Ohhhh, God…Ohhhh….Ohhhh, God," Aki panted, pain and pleasure swirling inside her as her vaginal muscles contracted and relaxed with the intensity of a rolling thunderstorm. "Carsyn…"

"I've got you," Carsyn murmured, moving to hold her, and brushing a tear from her cheek with her thumb. She kissed her forehead, whispering, "I've got you, beautiful woman." As they snuggled, Aki fell asleep in her arms.

CHAPTER 30

Aki opened her eyes as a stock trailer bounced through the campground. A chorus of whinnies followed it down the road. She smiled, believing Lily's voice to be one of them. Then, she stretched, drawing a deep breath into her lungs, and yawning. As she pulled her cover over her breasts, she slid her palm across Carsyn's side of the bed. The sun was up, the sheet was cool, and she was gone. She bit her lower lip, calling sweet memories of last night's lovemaking to mind. "You're so sweet," she murmured, glancing at the nightstand. In a crystal vase, next to the digital clock, sat a dozen long-stemmed roses. Propped against it, was an envelope. She reached over, touching the velvety red petals with her fingertips, and dabbing a tear as she read the card.

Dearest Aki,
My heart is bursting this morning.
Last night was beautiful, sweetheart.
Your breakfast is warm in the oven.
Love, Carsyn

Aki buried her face in Carsyn's pillow, aroused, and wishing she'd been brave enough to make love to her during the night. She slipped on a snug pair of jeans, a hoodie, and a jacket. Then, she poked an apple into each pocket and went out the door. "One for you," she said, palming the squishy delicacy into Lily's mouth, "and one for you," she told Relic. She patted his neck before returning to gently rub Lily's ears and stroke her muzzle. "You're a good girl," she whispered as the bay with the white star on her forehead checked her pockets. "I'll give you another one when I get back," she said softly. She walked across the campground, over the footbridge, and through the trees to the dig site. Then, she spread her jacket onto the ground, sitting in a location where she hoped she'd be able to see and hear without being noticed.

"Listen," Carsyn said, meeting the eyes of her students. "Can you hear them? Can you hear the voices of our ancestors whispering your name? Can you hear them ask that you carry their flame onward? If you can't, then this is not where you belong." As if sensing Aki's presence, she looked over to catch her eye, smiled, and returned her attention to the group. "Dig carefully," she instructed, "I believe we're getting close to something." With that, she stepped off, saying, "I'll be back in a few minutes."

"I love hearing you speak," Aki greeted, aching to throw her arms around her neck, and kiss her slowly. She smiled tenderly, adding, "And I loved my breakfast and my card and my roses."

"I'm glad," Carsyn said, holding her gaze softly. "Last night was beautiful, sweetheart."

Aki took a savoring breath, moving closer. "Yes, it was," she responded, feeling warm in her innermost parts.

"I'm glad you came over," Carsyn said, touching her hand. "It was gonna be a long haul, not seeing you until one o'clock."

"You care if I stick around for a while?" Aki asked. "I won't get in the way; I'll just sit over here at the edge and watch."

"You can join us if you want," Carsyn said, "I'll be a tad distracted, but I can handle it."

"No, I'd better just stay here," Aki responded, "I don't want to embarrass you."

"You won't," Carsyn answered with direct eye contact.

"Maybe next time," Aki said, seeing a lanky young man move toward them.

"Dr. Lyndon," he called out. "I think we found it."

"On my way," Carsyn said, her voice lowering as she looked back to Aki. "Come on," she urged quietly. "Come watch; this is the fun part."

"Are you sure?" Aki asked, pursing her lips. "I don't want to embarrass you."

"You're not gonna embarrass me," Carsyn responded directly, "because there's nothing to be embarrassed about." She held out her hand to pull her up. "Come on," she said, "join us."

"Okay, if you insist," Aki responded, brushing off her jacket, and slipping it on.

"I can introduce you as Dr. Williams, Aki, or my girlfriend," Carsyn said as they walked toward the find, "your choice."

Aki's stomach fluttered. "I think I like the sound of your girlfriend," she responded, feeling as if she'd just grown an inch taller.

Carsyn held her hand as she made introductions. "So, what have you discovered?" she asked her students as she squatted near the excavation site.

"Some kind of tool," her graduate assistant answered, turning it over in his hand. "Made out of stone," he added.

Carsyn nodded, taking a closer look. "What kind?" she asked.

"Looks kind of like an ax," another student piped up.

"Yes, it does," Carsyn responded, smiling as the find was carefully brushed off. "And a very nice one, I might add." She brushed along its once sharp edge, saying, "This one was painstakingly created by repeated pecks with a harder stone." She cocked her head, lifting an eyebrow. "So, what's an ax doing near burial mounds?" she asked.

"Didn't they put, like treasured possessions and useful stuff, in with a deceased person?" the lanky kid asked. "Maybe an axe was his favorite tool or something."

"Or her favorite tool," Carsyn responded. "In the Ojibwe culture, and in many others, you'll find a third gender known as two-spirit. Presumed to have power, they were often your visionaries, interpreters of dreams, and healers."

"So, these women," one asked, "they were the ones our book referred to as Iron Women?"

"Yes," Carsyn responded, "because they assumed a man's role and did his work." She glanced at Aki, smiling. "And sometimes," she continued in a quiet tone, "they even rose to the respected position of Shaman." She smiled, adding, "I just happen to be good friends with one. Maybe one day next week, we'll invite her to stop by and talk with us."

* * *

AKI FOLLOWED Carsyn into the bedroom. "That was fascinating," she said, sitting on the edge of the bed. "What you said gave me a better understanding of Jack."

"I'm glad," Carsyn responded. "I thought you might be interested," she added, unbuttoning her shirt, and putting it into the dirty clothes bag.

Aki smiled shaking her head.

"What?" Carsyn asked.

"Oh, nothing," Aki responded. "I was just thinking that your students didn't even blink when you introduced me as your girlfriend."

"It's not that big a deal anymore," Carsyn said, sliding her sports bra over her head. "More and more, people are recognizing bigotry for what it is." She looked over with a cock of her head, adding, "Don't you think that's the case?"

"I'm sorry, what?" Aki answered, her gaze fixed on Carsyn's chest.

"That there's a lot of tea in China," Carsyn answered, smiling with a slow shake of her head. "I think you're becoming a small boob woman," she added with a wink.

"Not without significant breast reduction," Aki responded, taking her comment completely out of context.

"What a horrible thought," Carsyn said, grimacing.

"Don't worry," Aki answered, her slow smile building, "it's definitely not in my plan."

"That's good," Carsyn said, "because, from my perspective, they're perfect just the way they are." Her gaze lingered, stepping out of her mud-splattered jeans.

"God, you're sexy in those," Aki murmured, taking a deep, savory breath.

"What, these old things?" Carsyn asked, grinning as she snapped the elastic of her boxers. "I've had 'em forever."

"Not those in particular," Aki responded, "just that you wear them." She bit her lower lip, adding, "And the ribbed undershirts without a bra, and the boots, and the flannel, and the men's cologne."

"Hmm," Carsyn said, moving toward her. "I think what you're trying to tell me is that you're attracted to butch women."

"Just one," Aki murmured, her lips parting as she leaned back to prop herself up with her hands.

"I hope it's me," Carsyn whispered, kissing her.

"You know it's you," Aki answered, massaging her neck and shoulders.

"Mmm, that feels good," Carsyn said. "I love your touch," she added with eye contact.

"Show me what you like," Aki murmured, gently caressing her breasts.

"I like that," Carsyn answered, taking a breath.

Aki licked inside her ear, sliding her hand down her abdomen.

"I'm filthy," Carsyn said, feeling Aki's fingers slip inside her elastic. "I need to take a shower before we do anything."

"You want company?" Aki asked, moistening her lips.

"Mmm, I'd love it," Carsyn murmured, holding out her hand. She adjusted the water temperature to just beyond warm, washing her hair under the spray as Aki stepped in. "It's been a long time," she said, turning to kiss and hold her, "I mean, since a woman made love to me."

Aki's body tingled. "I have mixed feelings about that," she whispered, soaping her hands, and pressing into her. "I hate that you were alone," she added, skating soapy hands over Carsyn's breasts and abdomen, "but I'm glad you waited for me."

"I am too," Carsyn responded, arching into her touch.

"So sexy," Aki murmured, teasing her nipples between her fingers, palming down her abdomen, and caressing between her legs. "Mmm, you're so aroused," she added, stroking with a light circular motion.

"What'd you expect?" Carsyn asked, her breath quickening.

"That you'd be hard," Aki answered, nibbling her earlobe. "Show me," she whispered, encouraging Carsyn to place her hand over hers.

Carsyn opened her stance, saying, "Like this," demonstrating a firm side-to-side motion. She caught her breath when Aki took over, taking a nipple into her mouth, and stroking harder with each of her moans. "Oh, God, baby… Oh, God, Aki… Oh, God… Oh, God…Oh, God, I'm coming."

CHAPTER 31

"That's it," Carsyn announced, securing the wheelbarrow.

"That was impressive," Aki commented.

"What was?" Carsyn asked, "that I got everything on?"

"That, and how you maneuvered to get it done," Aki responded. "I felt like I was watching a chimp move through the trees there for a moment."

Carsyn arched an eyebrow. "I'm not sure I like that analogy," she responded, jumping to the ground.

"Trust me," Aki said, "it was a compliment." Carsyn tossed the web cargo cover over the load, having Aki help her buckle it down.

"It was a beautiful week," Aki said softly, melting into her arms, "I had so much fun."

"Me too," Carsyn responded, kissing her lips, and holding her. "Too bad it's all coming to an end," she added with a hard swallow. It was as if her soul had been awakened only to be returned to slumber.

"It's not all coming to an end," Aki answered.

"I know," Carsyn said, "but once you go back, it won't be the same, trust me."

"No, it won't," Aki agreed, "but long-distance relationships are doable. They just take a little more effort."

"And we'll do what it takes," Carsyn responded, meeting her eye. She loaded the horses, said goodbye to Ringo, and opened Aki's door for her. "Hop in," she said with a thin smile, "I think we're ready to go."

"I can't wait to see your house," Aki said as she clicked her seatbelt.

"It's not fancy like Jack's," Carsyn said, creeping toward Deadman's Needle, "but I couldn't stand the thought of selling it." She swallowed, adding, "I moved in after—"

Aki reached over, laying her hand on her thigh. "Of course, you couldn't sell it," she said softly, "it was where you were raised." She shook her head slowly. "It was different for me," she continued, "probably because we moved around so much." Her dad had been career military. She took a breath, looking over. "I still live where we lived when I was in high school, but I wouldn't have qualms about selling." She startled when the load shifted. "What was that?" she asked.

"Probably Relic being his restless self," Carsyn responded, handing over her smartphone. "Click right there," she said, pointing to the camera application, "and you'll be able to see what's going on."

"He's got his head way over on her side," Aki announced, pinching her brow.

"I'm sure he does," Carsyn responded, noticing that Aki had taken quite the liking to Lily.

"He's stealing her hay," Aki added, sucking air through her open mouth.

"That's because he's probably already finished his own," Carsyn responded.

"Well, I'll fix him," Aki said with a firm nod, "I'll just give Lily his apple when we get home." Home, was that how she thought of where they were going? Carsyn hoped so.

"Sounds like a just punishment," Carsyn said, turning down her road.

"Oh, my goodness," Aki said, "Is this your house? It's gorgeous." She shook her head, squishing her eyebrows. "You had me thinking it was old and rundown." Built in nineteen-fifteen, it was a quaint two-story with a beautifully landscaped front yard.

"I didn't say that," Carsyn responded. "What I said was that it wasn't as fancy as Jack's—and it's not." She pulled to the back, bringing her rig to a halt near the barn. "I'll get the horses tucked in, and we'll go inside," she added. "Stay in the truck if you want, it won't take long."

"I'll come with you," Aki responded, pulling her door handle. "I want to see Lily's stall." She stood at a safe distance, watching Carsyn back her down the ramp to the driveway.

"Here," Carsyn said with a warm smile. "Hold onto her while I get Relic and you can lead her into the barn."

* * *

"What a beautiful home," Aki said, stepping onto the back porch, and inside through the kitchen doorway.

"My great-grandpa built it," Carsyn responded, smiling with pride, "and my grandpa was born here."

"How wonderful," Aki said, "to be living in a home designed and built by your great-grandfather." She trailed her fingers along the shiny white countertops, pausing to examine their reflective glass tile backsplash. "Someone along the way did a fabulous job of transforming the interior into a modern living space," she commented.

"My mom," Carsyn responded, tightening her jaw. "She was almost finished when—"

"When she passed away," Aki said softly.

"Yeah," Carsyn said, swallowing.

"So, you had to complete what she started," Aki added with a slight lift in her voice.

"No," Carsyn responded, looking off, "it's just like she left it."

"Oh my," Aki said, stepping through the dining room and into the living room. "I love the transition from white to bright colors and the upholstered swivel chairs with matching ottomans." She sat, adding, "I love her style."

"Yeah, I do too," Carsyn said with a slight smile. "I'm glad she decided to get the new furniture early; you know, before it was all done."

"Me too," Aki said softly. As they made their way up the stairs, it struck her that there were no pictures sitting around. "Mmm," she said, touching the double wedding ring quilt, "how striking, the master is decorated with a blend of white and bright colors too." She poked her head into the large bathroom, adding, "And look at that gigantic whirlpool." When she turned, she melted into Carsyn's arms, saying, "Your home is beautiful, sweetheart."

"Thanks," Carsyn responded, squeezing Aki's bottom, and kissing her as she backed her against the wall.

"Mmm," Aki moaned, writhing as smoldering embers burst into flames between her legs.

"We've got two hours before we have to be at Jack's," Carsyn said, nibbling her earlobe, "Do you want to test it out?"

"The bed or the whirlpool?" Aki responded, locking gazes as she unbuttoned her blouse.

"Maybe both," Carsyn murmured, slipping the garment off of her shoulders.

* * *

"So good to see you," Jack greeted, kissing Aki's cheek, and taking her coat. "Did you have a good time?"

"The best," Aki responded with a smile that twinkled in her eyes. "How's Charlie getting along?"

"He's doing great," Jack answered. "The Doc said she was pleased with how well he was healing during his last visit."

"Excellent," Aki responded, "I expected him to get along just fine."

"I set the rest of your luggage in the second bedroom on your right," Jack said. "It's the larger guest room, but if you'd rather be in the one on the end, that's fine."

"Well, about that," Aki said, lifting her eyebrows, "I believe you're gonna have to get by with just seeing me for dinner a few times."

"Ahh," Jack responded, grinning with a playful lift in her voice. "I see," she added, "you're staying with Carsyn."

"She twisted my arm," Aki responded with a slight blush.

"I couldn't help myself," Carsyn added as their gazes locked.

Aki released a breath, saying, "Where's my nephew? I want to examine that eye for myself."

"He's in his bedroom playing a board game with his sister," Jack answered. "I'm surprised they didn't come running when you rang the bell."

Aki held out her hand. "Come with me?" she invited softly.

"Of course," Carsyn responded, winking, and patting her butt as they stepped off.

Jack shook her head, joining Courtney. "Just wait until you see our lovebirds," she said quietly, pressing into her from behind, "they're so adorable."

CHAPTER 32

"Mmm...marinated portobello burgers," Aki moaned, stepping onto the deck.

"Yep," Jack said, meeting her eye before flipping the next one. "I thought you might be getting tired of meat after several days of camping."

"Not too bad," Aki responded, watching Carsyn gently toss a ball to Charlie. "Her taste for food is similar to mine," she added, "and we were in the camper, so we could pretty much cook what we wanted."

"You're lucky," Jack said, chuckling, "if Courtie had her way, we'd eat pizza, burgers, and french fries all the time."

"Not healthy," Aki responded, adding, "and speaking of Courtney, I should probably go in and see if she needs me to do something."

"Tell her these should finish up in ten minutes," Jack responded.

"Will do," Aki said, sliding the patio door open.

* * *

"So, what can I do to help?" Aki greeted, touching Courtney's shoulder.

"You can put ice in the glasses if you want," Courtney answered, looking up from her potato salad.

"I'm on it," Aki responded, dropping cubes into the first one. "I appreciate the invitation for dinner."

"It's our pleasure," Courtney said, smiling. "We're so pleased that you found us."

"No more than I am," Aki responded, holding glass number two under the ice dispenser. She fell silent for a moment and then moved forward. "So, how's your stomach?" she asked quietly.

Courtney tilted her head. "My stomach?" she asked, looking at her.

"Yes, you seemed like it was bothering you just before you took Charlie to the hospital," Aki said. "I was just concerned and wanted to check on you."

"You're very observant," Courtney responded, "and yes, it was, but I popped a couple of antacids, and it was fine by the time we got to the ER." She shook her head. "It's the price I pay for drinking like a fish before Jack and I got back together." She smiled, adding, "Don't worry, it's just related to anxiety, and I've had it checked out."

"Good," Aki responded, wanting more detail but opting not to ask for it.

"Go ahead," Jack said, grinning as she came through the door, "take a whiff of these sizzling little delicacies." She waved her platter under her wife's and then Aki's nose. "Mmm, smell good, don't they?"

"They do," Aki responded with a wide smile.

"Delicacy might be a slight exaggeration for grilled fungi," Courtney commented, lifting an eyebrow. "Lizzy, Charlie," she called out. "Wash your hands; it's time for dinner." She set her potato salad at one end of the table and the lettuce salad at the other. Jack placed her platter in the center.

"Yum, mama's mushroom burgers," Charlie exclaimed, his eyes dancing with enthusiasm.

"I like mommy's potato salad better," Lizzy said, curling her upper lip.

Courtney smiled when Jack winked at her. "Dig in, everyone," she said. As she swallowed her first bite, the doorbell rang. "Good grief," she muttered, shaking her head.

Lizzy jumped up, running to peek out the front window. "It's the lady with the tear in her coat," she announced.

"Tell her I'll be there in a minute," Jack said, sliding back from the table.

"My mama will be here in a minute," Lizzy echoed. "I'm sorry, but you have to wait out here."

"Why does she always show up when we're just sitting down to dinner?" Courtney asked, making direct eye contact.

"Because the last bus runs at seven-thirty," Jack said quietly, "and it's her only means of transportation."

Courtney took a breath, releasing it in increments. "Alright," she said, "I'll put your burger in the warmer." Her lips were pursed as she collected it onto a smaller plate.

Jack paused to meet Aki's and then Carsyn's gaze. "I'm sorry," she said, "I'll be back as soon as I can."

"Don't worry about it," Aki said softly, "you can't control when people get sick."

"She smells like she needs a bath," Lizzy blurted out, rejoining dinner.

"I'm not surprised," Courtney said, scooting her chair under the table, and resuming the conversation. "I apologize," she added, meeting Aki's gaze, "I shouldn't have put our dirty laundry on display. It just hits me sometimes, that her medicine has to permeate everything." She shook her head, smiling thinly. "Dear Lord, I never expected to see the world so clearly from my mother's perspective."

"Being married to a healer can be trying," Aki responded, her eyes darting to Carsyn for a split-second.

"Yes, it can," Courtney said, "but for the most part I'm okay with it." She released a soft sigh. "Even with this lady," she added, "I know she's mentally ill and going blind. I don't really begrudge her the care. I just want us to be able to finish our dinner for once without being interrupted."

"I understand," Aki said. "You don't need to explain." She furrowed her brow, meeting Carsyn's gaze as she put the pieces together. "This is the patient Jack spoke with me about at the campground," she said as much to herself as anyone. She shook her head, sliding back from the table. "And in all the excitement," she added, "I forgot to share my thoughts on the woman's care."

"I'll put your burger in the warmer," Courtney said, smiling thinly.

* * *

"I WISH you'd let me take you in to see an ophthalmologist," Jack said softly. "Your vision is worsening, and I'm at a loss as to what to do to help you. There are treatments that could save your eyesight, or at least some of it," she added, "if only you'd consider them."

"No blood tests and no white man's medicine," the seventy-year-old woman responded, brushing back a long lock of tangled hair. "You're a powerful Mitä'kwe," she added, her tone softening, "and I have faith in your medicine."

Jack released a breath. "Are you still drinking my tea," she asked.

"Just like you told me," the woman said.

Jack arched an eyebrow. "And you're staying away from donuts and sweet rolls?"

"Mostly," the woman answered, "except that this morning I had one for breakfast."

Jack pinched her brow gently. "No, not even one," she said firmly.

"Okay, Mitä'kwe," she answered with a thin smile, "I'll toss out the rest of the package."

Jack looked up when the door opened.

"I'm sorry to interrupt," Aki said, "but could I speak to you for a moment?"

"Sure," Jack responded, "but join us first, okay?" She smiled with pride, introducing Aki as her long-lost sister, a sister who just happened to be a brilliant ophthalmologist.

"Praise be to the Great Spirit," the old woman said. Her voice cracked with tears and she lifted her upturned palms to her face.

"Ohhhh, Kitche Manitou," she whimpered, her chest caving with each breath, "you have answered this old woman's prayers."

Jack cocked her head; her mouth slackened as she met Aki's gaze.

Aki's eyebrows squished together as Jack rested her hand on the old woman's back.

"What is it?" Jack asked softly, "why the tears?"

The old woman looked up, clasping her hand, and reaching for Aki's. "My sweet babies," she sobbed, "my heart broke when they didn't place you together." She told them about the orders of protection filed by Jack's parents and how they'd been offered Aki's placement. "They had no right to bar me from my baby," she cried softly, brushing her cheek. "I wouldn't have taken you."

"You've always known," Jack said, peering into her eyes.

"Yes, Mitä'kwe," Wabun said tearfully, "but I didn't want to disrupt your life, so I didn't say anything. I just needed to know that you were okay."

Jack clenched her jaw, unable to think as heat flushed through her body. How could her parents have kept this from her?

Wabun looked at Aki. "And you, sweet girl," she said tenderly, "I did everything the white doctor asked of me and still they ripped you from my arms and placed you in foster care." A wave of sobs escaped. "And when I checked on you," she choked, "your parents swept you away."

Aki closed her eyes, covering her mouth with her hand.

"I'm so sorry," Jack murmured, gathering her biological mother in her arms, and reaching for Aki.

"We're so sorry," Aki whimpered.

CHAPTER 33

"Come on," Jack said softly, "let's go inside."

"I'm sorry, but I can't tonight," Wabun responded, squeezing her hand. "In fact, I should be going."

"I'll take you home," Jack said, "you don't need to worry about catching the bus."

"Or we can take her," Aki added, extending her hand to help the older woman up.

"The cold air," Wabun responded, "it takes a toll on old bones." She smiled, displaying missing teeth. "Thank you, honey."

"You're welcome," Aki responded, smiling back.

"I have a rosemary and turmeric tea that'll help with that," Jack said softly. "You two go on in the living room," she said, "and I'll get it for you."

Aki led Wabun in, sitting down beside her on the sofa. "So, while we wait for Jack," she said softly, "how would you feel about your daughter, the ophthalmologist, taking a look at your eyes?"

"Proud," Wabun said, meeting her gaze, "that's how I'd feel, proud."

"That makes me very happy," Aki responded with a gentle smile. She told her that she'd interviewed locally and felt certain that she could gain access to the necessary instruments for the exam.

"It'll make the Mitä'kwe happy too," Wabun said. "She's been after me to do it for the longest time."

"Yes, it will," Aki responded, smiling, and slipping her arm around her shoulders.

* * *

"You brought her into our house?" Courtney asked. Her lips were flat, and her eyes were narrow. "I thought you weren't going to do that."

"This is different," Jack said, making direct eye contact. "You're not gonna believe what I just found out." She shook her head, frowning. "God, I'm so disappointed in my parents right now, I can hardly stand it."

"Why, what'd they do?" Courtney asked, tilting her head to one side. "Hey, sit down for a minute," she added, touching her arm, "and talk to me."

Jack dropped into the chair beside her. "Are the kids upstairs?" she asked.

"Yes," Courtney answered, "they just went up with Carsyn." She laid her glasses on the table, resting her hand on Jack's arm. "What's wrong, sweetie? What did you find out that's got you so upset?"

"That Wabun's my bio-mom," Jack answered, rubbing the back of her neck. "I don't think she was ever gonna tell me, said she didn't want to disrupt my life." She took a breath, allowing it to escape slowly. "But then when she saw Aki, she couldn't hold it in any longer." She shook her head again, swallowing. "It was pitiful," she added, "broke my heart."

"Oh my goodness," Courtney responded, her eyes widening, "that's almost unbelievable."

"I know," Jack answered, "but it's true." She exhaled loudly. "And my parents knew all along," she snarled, "but didn't tell me. They even had orders of protection against her." Her voice faded to black. "God, I just can't believe they didn't tell me."

"I'm sure they had a reason," Courtney said quietly. "They would never hurt you intentionally."

"That's what I always thought," Jack responded with a hard swallow, "but obviously I was wrong." She raked her hair back aggressively. "Oh, and they even declined Aki's placement with our family," she added, meeting her eye. "Can you believe they did that?" she asked directly. "Can you believe they said no to my baby sister being placed with our family and didn't even bother to tell me that she existed?" She released a heavy sigh. "And then," she went on, "when she turns up on our doorstep, still they don't mention that they knew about her. God, I'm so disappointed."

"You need to talk to them," Courtney said, reaching for her bottle of antacid, "hear their explanation." She pinned her arms around her stomach.

Jack cocked her head, studying her.

"Oh my God, you knew," Jack said, her mouth hanging open, "I can tell."

"Not very long," Courtney admitted, clearing her throat, "and not about the old woman being your biological mother, just that your parents had Aki's orders of protection."

"How long?" Jack asked, glaring. "How long have you known, Courtie?"

"Just since Sunday," Courtney responded, dropping her eyes.

"Since Sunday," Jack muttered, staring at her.

"After I dropped Aki off," Courtney continued, "I stopped by the office and logged on to the county website." She swallowed. "I was just curious," she said, "I wanted to see if I could turn up court records about Aki's adoption."

"And you didn't feel I deserved to know what you found?" Jack asked, clenching her jaw.

"I didn't see the point," Courtney answered. "I knew it would only upset you." She took a breath, meeting her eye. "That, and from the looks of the case, your bio-mom was as crazy as a loon. I couldn't see any good coming out of telling you."

"Here we go again," Jack said with a fiery glare, "I thought you learned your lesson about dishonesty." She was never going to get over what occurred before they got back together.

"This is different," Courtney squeaked, her lower lip beginning to quiver.

"No," Jack said curtly. "No, Courtney, it isn't." With that, she stood, shoved her chair under the table, and walked to the living room.

* * *

"What's this I hear about the Mitä'kwe being happy?" Jack asked, rejoining Aki and their mother.

"I've decided to do what you want," Wabun answered, smiling, "I've decided to see an ophthalmologist."

"You're right," Jack said, "that does make me happy." She slipped her arm around her shoulders, hugging her. "Let me guess," she added, with a cock of her head, and a lift of her eyebrow, "the one you'll see just happens to be your daughter."

"Better to keep business in the family, I think," Wabun said with mock seriousness.

"Good point," Jack responded, catching Aki's eye with a thin smile. She felt tired, asking, "So, are you running her home, or am I?"

"We'll take her home," Aki answered with a wink at Wabun. "That way I'll know where to pick her up for our appointment."

* * *

Silence—so loud it was deafening.

Jack unloaded the dishwasher.

Courtney set the breakfast dishes on the counter.

Jack walked the dogs.

Courtney filled their bowls with food and water.

Jack laid out their kid's pajamas.

Courtney supervised one bath and a shower.

Jack read Charlie a bedtime story.

Courtney read one to Lizzy.

The parents passed one another in the hall, kissing their children goodnight, and made their way to the master bedroom.

"No, surely not," Courtney commented, her hands on her hips as she watched Jack collect a flat sheet, a blanket, and her pillow, "not over this." She exhaled loudly. "There's a bed in the guest room," she added, "but you're not sleeping in there because you want me to worry about you being uncomfortable on the sofa." She sighed, meeting her gaze for a moment. "Did you call your parents?" she asked softly, knowing that she hadn't. "If you don't, they'll wonder why they didn't get their call."

"Then, let them wonder," Jack responded, stepping into the hallway.

* * *

JACK SPREAD THE SHEET, tucking it under the cushions. Then, she dropped her pillow at one end and secured her blanket at the other. Angry, she was angry at everyone except her sister, her bio-mom, and her children. She laid down, bending her knees so that her feet didn't hang over, and listened for footsteps moving toward her. Sooner or later, she felt confident that her wife would come to her. As the clock chimed on the half-hour, she drifted off—*And the black bear lumbered down the hill, catching a trout as he crossed a gurgling stream, and eating it as he sat down by the sofa.*

"Why do you always bring your smelly fish inside the house?" Jack asked, sitting up in her dream-world.

"Because it always gets your attention," the bear responded.

"Finish it quickly then," Jack said, shaking her head slowly.

"I will," the bear answered, "and then we have things to discuss."

"I'm not in the mood," Jack said, telling him of her recent betrayals.

"Mistakes are sometimes made in an effort to protect those we love," the bear said, resting his chin on her forearm. "So, you're angry with Wabun as well," he added.

"No, of course not," Jack answered, furrowing her brow. "Why would I be angry with her?"

"So smart," the bear said, getting up with a low growl, "and yet at times so slow on the uptake."

"Hey, where are you going?" Jack asked. "Since I'm awake, I thought we could talk a while longer."

"No," the bear responded, "I'm still hungry, and you have much to think about."

CHAPTER 34

Aki checked her messages, laying her phone on the dresser. "Still nothing from LA," she said, crawling under the covers.

"They'll call," Carsyn answered, extending her arm across her pillow.

"You don't know that," Aki countered. "It's a highly sought-after position," she added, "not to mention that there were many qualified candidates."

"They'll call," Carsyn repeated quietly, holding her close.

"I know you'd just as soon they didn't," Aki said, nestling against her breast, and kissing her nipple through her undershirt.

"No, that's not how I feel," Carsyn responded, stroking her hair, and twirling a lock between her fingers. "You've worked hard," she added, "I want you to have the position that you want." She swallowed. "I just wish it wasn't so far away, that's all."

"I know you do," Aki said softly, kissing her. "But you have to trust that it'll all work out."

"I do," Carsyn responded, changing the subject. "That was really something about your mom, huh?"

"Oh yeah," Aki responded, "a scary kind of something."

"What do you mean?" Carsyn asked. "I thought you two hit it off."

"We did," Aki said, "but seeing the diseases that'll one day be coming for me up close and personal—" Her words broke off with a shudder. "When you're adopted," she added, "you get to skip merrily along, not knowing."

"That's not necessarily a good thing," Carsyn responded, "and you know it."

"I know, it's better to know," Aki said, releasing a breath as she settled onto her pillow, "but still—"

Carsyn tucked her arm around her abdomen, snuggling close. "Night, sweetie," she whispered, planting a kiss between her shoulder blades.

"Night, darling," Aki mumbled, drifting off—*And the white eagle swooped low in the valley to join the gathering, a celebration of sorts.*

"So glad you could make it," the bear growled softly.

"Wouldn't miss it for the world," the eagle responded.

"What am I doing here?" Aki asked, crinkling her brow. She rode bareback on a colorful Appaloosa inside a circle of guests. A deer followed her. "And what am I doing in this beautiful dress?" she added. It was long and white with a lace bodice and white daisies on the headband.

"You're coming to terms with your priorities," the eagle responded. "Just stay with your horse, and you'll be fine."

"I will," Aki said, nodding as her reins came to life. "It's a snake," she screamed, throwing her hands in the air as the reptile slithered down the equine's mane, biting her belly. "Oh my God, it bit me," she cried out as fangs drew blood a second time.

"He got her twice," the bear growled.

"He did," the eagle screeched, flapping his wings.

"He bit me," Aki cried into her pillow, "Oh my God, he bit me. I'm going to die."

"Shhh…you're not gonna die," Carsyn cooed, gathering her into her arms.

"But he bit me," Aki sobbed.

"It was just a dream, sweetheart," Carsyn whispered, wiping her tears. She stroked her hair, adding, "Come on, baby, get fully awake, and you'll see that everything's fine."

"I can't stand it," Aki whimpered, trembling, "these dreams, they're driving me crazy."

"So, what do you need to do about them?" Carsyn asked quietly.

Aki took a breath, releasing it. "I need to see my primary doctor when I get home," she said, swallowing.

"That's a good idea," Carsyn responded, "but what can you do right now?"

"I guess I can talk to Jack," Aki said. "She offered to talk a while back, but I was too embarrassed to share the details." She pressed her cheek against Carsyn's breast, closing her eyes. "I'm scared I might be developing schizophrenia," she squeaked almost inaudibly.

"You're not," Carsyn soothed, kissing the top of her head. "You're just Jack's sister, that's all."

"I hope that's all," Aki responded.

"It is," Carsyn said softly. "Now, come on," she urged, stroking her, "it's two o'clock in the morning."

* * *

AKI LISTENED to Carsyn's heartbeat, falling asleep, and awakening in her arms. They showered, dressed, and had muffins. "I need to stop by the hospital while we're out," she said. "I doubt I'll catch Dr. Matsumoto, but I can at least leave her a note." She took a breath. "I don't feel like I have time to lose with regard to Wabun's eyes."

"Yeah," Carsyn responded, "it doesn't sound like it. Whatever you want to do is fine." She wrapped her arms around her, rocking them gently from side to side, and peering into her eyes. "I love that you're staying around," she said softly.

"For a little while," Aki answered, "at least until LA does or doesn't call." She feathered through Carsyn's hair at her collar. "And if they don't call," she continued, looking off—"

"They're gonna call," Carsyn interjected. "I don't care how many candidates they have; if the place is as top-notch as you say it is, you'll be the one that gets the job offer."

"God, where have you been all of my life?" Aki asked, kissing her.

"Waiting for you," Carsyn murmured, lifting her onto the counter.

"Carsyn," Aki objected, her eyes widening with the unbuttoning of her blouse, "we have windows all around us—and the blinds are open."

"I know," Carsyn answered, "but we're in the country, I don't get that many visitors, and it's six o'clock in the morning."

* * *

"Got it," Aki announced, smiling as she opened the door.

"Good deal," Carsyn answered, smiling back. "When is it?"

"From one to three next Friday," Aki responded, her eyes narrowing with a slight pinch of her brow. "That should be enough time," she added. "If not, I guess I'll request more."

"So, you got to see Dr. Matsumoto then?" Carsyn asked.

"I did," Aki responded, nodding. "I had no idea that the department offered a free clinic on the first and third Saturday of every month. Everyone offers their services," she added, "it's really cool."

"That is cool," Carsyn said, "tells you something about the organization, doesn't it?"

"Yes, it does," Aki responded, glancing back for another look at the main door.

"So, did you tell her that you weren't interested in the position?" Carsyn asked, swallowing.

Aki took a soft breath. "I told her," she responded.

Carsyn nodded, falling silent as she pulled out of the circle drive. "Next stop?" she asked with a sniff.

"Do you mind if we stop by to tell Wabun that we have an appointment?" Aki asked. "I don't think she has a full schedule, but still…"

"No, of course I don't mind," Carsyn said, turning the corner, and traveling to the projects.

"Looks even worse in the daylight," Aki said as they bounced into the parking lot. "I hate it that people—my mother—has to live in a place like this." She shook her head, adding, "A place so dilapidated that even rodents wouldn't want to live here."

"You don't know," Carsyn said, "it might be okay once you get inside."

"I doubt it," Aki responded, tears burning behind her eyelids as she met her eye. "I don't know why communities can't offer decent low-income housing," she continued. "Yes, I do," she muttered, "it's because those who can afford it don't want their taxes raised a few dollars." She inhaled deeply, pulling her door handle. "Come with me?" she asked quietly.

"I wouldn't send you in alone, that's for sure," Carsyn responded, locking the doors with her remote, and walking around the vehicle. "I think this is the oldest government housing in the city," she added, stepping the crumbling sidewalk to the door. "I read in the paper the other day that some of the poorest residents in the entire state live here." She pointed to the rear of Wabun's building. "There was a gang-related shooting right over there the other night."

"Please stop," Aki responded, pressing her lips together, "I don't want to know."

"Okay," Carsyn said quietly, tugging the fire door open.

"She was so stiff that she could barely get out of the chair," Aki muttered as they made their way up the dark stairwell, "and she's on the third floor." She shook her head. "I'm almost afraid to see her apartment."

"It might be okay," Carsyn said, gently touching the small of Aki's back with her fingertips.

"We'll know soon enough, won't we," Aki responded, tapping lightly on the door.

"Oh my, what a surprise," Wabun greeted, clasping Aki's hand, "it's my youngest daughter." She widened the opening in the doorway, saying "Come in." As her guests stepped inside, she looked to Carsyn, adding, "You're the Mitä'kwe's friend."

"I am," Carsyn responded, smiling.

"And my girlfriend," Aki added, slipping her arm around Carsyn.

"How wonderful," Wabun responded. "I just brewed a pot of the Mitä'kwe's tea," she said, "we can share a cup if you'd like."

Carsyn twitched her nose, forcing another smile, and saying, "We'd love some."

CHAPTER 35

Feet pattered above them before making their way down the stairs more quietly.

"Where's mommy?" Charlie whispered, his tone harboring a bit of concern. "And mama," he added.

"They're here somewhere," Lizzy responded, opening the front door to check the porch.

"We're in here," Courtney called out, making firm eye contact with her wife. "Mmm, that was nice," she murmured. "Maybe we need to fight more often."

"Oh no," Jack responded, kissing her lips. "I had quite enough of that last night." She kissed her again, saying, "I'm sorry."

"It's okay," Courtney said, lightly brushing her cheek. "I understand why you were upset." She peered into her eyes. "In trying to protect you, I hurt you, and it's me who's sorry."

"Okay, we're both sorry," Jack responded, wiggling her eyebrows. "So, you liked the new position, huh?"

"Oh God yes," Courtney responded, feeling warm as she untangled her limbs, and adjusted her nightgown. "Shhh," she said, "here they come."

"What are you guys doing in here?" Charlie asked, plopping on top of them.

"Just fell asleep," Jack responded with a bear hug, "like you do when you watch a show past your bedtime." She mussed his hair. "Okay, up you go," she added, "time for breakfast."

"Pancakes," Courtney announced, getting up.

"Yay," Lizzy answered, jumping up and down, "chocolate chip."

"Banana," Charlie countered.

"Buttermilk, frozen," Courtney responded, catching Jack's eye. "You want me to wait a couple of minutes to give you time to call your mom and dad?" she asked.

"No," Jack responded, "it won't take long for me to tell them I forgot to call last night. I don't want 'em to worry that something was wrong."

"I love you, Jack," Courtney said softly.

"And I love you, Courtie," Jack responded.

* * *

It was the fourth invitation that week. "You don't have to keep feeding us," Aki said, kissing Jack's cheek as she came through the door.

"I know," Jack responded, smiling. "But you came all the way from California, and now you're staying longer, so the least I can do is feed you a couple of meals. Where's Carsyn?" she asked, poking her head out the door.

"She dropped me off on her way to the hardware store," Aki responded.

"Let me guess," Jack said, "she needs more trowels."

"You got it," Aki answered with a smile. "She'll be back shortly."

"So, you saw Wabun today," Jack continued, hanging up her coat, "I'm afraid to ask what you thought."

"I almost called you," Aki said, "and then I just thought we'd talk tonight." She sighed. "Severe retinopathy," she added, "that'll most likely require a vitrectomy."

Jack furrowed her brow.

"It's a procedure used to treat severe bleeding," Aki added. "And even with that," she went on, "I'm afraid her best-case scenario is extremely low vision."

"Damn," Jack muttered, clenching her jaw.

"It took a lot of talking," Aki continued, "but I finally got her to let me make a referral to a retina specialist."

"That's good anyway," Jack responded, pursing her lips, and nodding. "Now, if you can just talk her into having blood work so that we can confirm that she has diabetes, and get her on medication, we'll be rolling."

"I checked her blood sugar while she was in the office," Aki said, looking up with a sigh. "It was over three-hundred."

"Damn," Jack responded, clenching her jaw, "I should've gotten her to the ER."

"You tried," Aki answered softly. "Anyway," she continued, "I started her on insulin and got her linked with in-home services. I also asked that the provider assist her with some cleaning and organization as well as diabetic management."

"That's great," Jack said, nodding slowly, "thank you."

"No thanks required," Aki responded, smiling.

* * *

"So, do you cook much?" Courtney asked, adding parsley, garlic, and oregano to her sauce.

"Some," Aki responded, "it depends on how much time I have."

"Yeah, it's the same for me," Courtney said, looking up. "If I'm trying a case, either Jack cooks, or we eat out."

"Did you learn how from watching your mom?" Aki asked, remembering special times in the kitchen with her own.

"Heavens no," Courtney responded, shaking her head. "Her idea of cooking was a takeout pizza that you heated in the oven." She glanced over, smiling. "My mother-in-law taught me everything I know," she added. "God, I love that woman. I thank Him every day that she's still in good health."

"That's sweet," Aki responded, picking up the wooden spoon, and stirring, "that you have that kind of bond with Jack's mom."

"There's my girl," Carsyn blurted out, joining them. "Ahhh, Courtney's lasagna," she added, "I love that stuff."

"Francisca's recipe," Courtney responded.

"I know, but you give it your own twist," Carsyn said, slipping her arms around Aki from behind, and squeezing. She kissed her cheek. "Miss me?" she asked, nibbling her earlobe.

"Of course, I missed you," Aki answered, fighting the urge to turn around and kiss her. "Go on, now," she said with a slow wink, "dinner'll be ready in a little while."

"Your wish is my command, my lady," Carsyn responded with a bow, "I'll be thinking about you," she added with a playful lift to her voice.

"And I'll be thinking about you," Aki responded, flush creeping up her neck.

"I never thought I'd see it," Courtney commented, shaking her head.

"See what?" Aki asked, squishing her eyebrows together.

"Carsyn in love," Courtney responded with a tender smile. "After all she's been through, I must say, it's a beautiful site."

Aki bit her lower lip, a butterfly fluttering through her stomach. "I love her too," she said softly.

* * *

"COME ON," Courtney said, "time to say goodnight." She nudged her children with a gentle touch on their shoulders.

"But we haven't finished our game," Charlie whined.

"There's always tomorrow," Courtney responded.

"But," Charlie objected, frowning.

"Charles, don't argue," Courtney added, making firm eye contact.

"I'm going," Charlie pouted, hugging Aki, Carsyn, and his mama before plodding up the stairs.

"We'll remember where we left off and finish the next time I'm here," Aki called out gently.

Charlie paused, looking back. "Or we could start over," he said.

"Yes, we could," Aki responded, smiling, "what a good idea."

"I'll see you in thirty minutes or so," Courtney said, collecting Lizzy.

* * *

CARSYN NODDED TO AKI, saying, "Go on, now's the time."

"Time for what?" Jack asked, her eyes narrowing as she refilled their coffee cups.

"To see what you think about my dreams, the ones I keep having," Aki responded, shaking her head. "I don't hold much stock in the supernatural," she added, "but at this point, I'll try just about anything."

Jack cocked her head, lifting an eyebrow.

"That wasn't personal," Aki added.

"I didn't take it that it was," Jack answered.

"She loses sleep almost every night," Carsyn said, slipping her arm around Aki's shoulders. "I encouraged her to talk with you in hopes that you'd be able to help her."

"I can try," Jack said, turning to her sister. "I wish you'd have said something."

"I was too embarrassed," Aki responded, exhaling. "I was afraid that you'd think I was mentally ill." She took a soft breath, closing her eyes, and exhaling. "And now with what we know about our bio-mom, I'm sure that you will."

"I wouldn't bank on that," Jack responded, taking her pen from her breast pocket, and collecting a piece of paper. "Okay, I'm ready," she said. "Just take me through them, one at a time."

"Will do," Aki answered, inhaling a deep breath. "So, the first is recurring," she began, her eyes narrowing. "I'm not sure exactly when it started."

"Days, months, years?" Jack asked.

"Years, maybe," Aki said, "a couple, anyway." She described her dream of the mounted brave, the deer, the exploding eagle, the hills, and the dust cloud.

"Hmm, interesting," Jack said, lifting her pen, "lots of imagery, some of it quite puzzling."

"Sounds like a description of burial mounds to me," Carsyn commented, turning to Aki. "Maybe you're dreaming of my dig site."

"Can't be that," Jack responded, "because it's been going on too long."

"Now that I think of it," Aki added, "the hills in my dream do look a lot like the ones near your excavation site."

"But those sites, don't they all look pretty similar?" Jack asked.

"Not all, but some," Carsyn answered.

"Okay," Jack said, shaking her head, "I'm stumped for the moment, so let's go on." She rested her chin in her palm, listening intently as Aki shared the details of dream number two.

"The deer could be a spirit animal," Jack said, "and the eagle, a spirit guide, maybe."

Aki relaxed, reading her sister's non-verbal language, relieved that she didn't think she was hallucinating.

"And the eagle called you Little Deer?" Jack clarified.

"More than once," Aki answered.

"So, are you fond of deer?" Jack asked, "maybe notice them here and there?"

"It's funny that you say that," Aki said, smiling, "because I've loved them since I was a little girl. They used to be my favorite animal."

"Used to be?" Jack responded, cocking her head.

"Yes, used to be," Aki said, laughing, and glancing at Carsyn.

"I think the horse may be running a tight race at the moment," Carsyn interjected, laughing with her.

"Ahh, I see," Jack said, tipping her head back. "Well, the deer could still be your spirit animal," she added. "So, basically," she summarized, "your dream is about Little Deer being called upon to help the bright star, the one that appears in the eastern sky before sunrise, and she's told to hurry before her light is extinguished."

"You've got it," Aki said.

Jack shook her head, chuckling.

"What's so funny?" Aki asked, her eyes widening. "This is serious," she added, "this dream scares me to death."

"I'm not laughing at your dream," Jack answered, her eyes sparkling, "I'm laughing because it was so easy to interpret."

"Our mother's name is Wabun Ahnung," Jack said.

"Right," Aki responded, looking at her.

"Well, in Ojibwe, her name means morning star," Jack added, "and the morning star is the brightest in the eastern sky before sunrise."

Aki's mouth opened, tilting her head. "So, the light being extinguished," she said, "it's symbolism for blindness?"

"I believe so," Jack said, glancing over her glasses. "So, Little Deer," she continued, "your help was needed to save our mother's vision—and your dreams called you here."

"That's amazing," Aki said, feeling a twinge of belief below the surface.

"And even more amazing," Jack continued, "was that you began having the dream just as I was pleading with Wabun to see an ophthalmologist." She squeezed Aki's hand, adding, "I don't think you'll have this one again."

"Why's that?" Aki asked, tilting her head.

"Because you've identified the problem and made a referral for her to get treatment," Jack responded. "You've done all you can do, Little Deer." She shimmied her shoulders, grinning. "Okay, ready for dream number three," she said.

Aki released a breath. "Well, I've only had this one once," she responded. "Thank God, because it nearly drove me to a heart attack."

"It was just the other night," Carsyn added, stroking Aki's back as she described her dress, the horse, the snake that bit her twice, and the gathering of guests.

"And the bear and the eagle," Jack clarified, "they were both in it?"

"Yes," Aki responded, "just like in the second."

"And you were told to stay with your horse," Jack said, chuckling. "How cool is that?"

"What?" Aki asked, not putting the pieces together. "Why are you laughing?" she added, "Another easy one to interpret?"

"Very easy," Jack said, meeting Carsyn's gaze for a fleeting instant.

"So, tell me what it means," Aki said.

Jack opened the mail application on her phone, typing in her interpretation."

"What are you doing?" Aki asked, leaning forward. "You're sending it in an email?"

"Yep, an email to me," Jack answered, pressing send, and laying her phone on the table. "That way it'll have a date stamp."

"So, you're not gonna tell me what it means," Aki said, looking at Carsyn in disbelief.

"Nope, not now," Jack responded, leaning back with pleasure in her eyes. "But don't worry," she added, "I highly doubt that you'll have this one again, at least not in the near future."

"How can you be so sure?" Aki asked.

"I just am," Jack responded.

"So, are you ever going to tell me?" Aki asked, her mouth hanging open.

"After it comes to pass," Jack responded.

"What?" Aki asked, "you're going to wait until a snake bites me?"

"Figuratively speaking," Jack responded with a belly laugh, "trust me, sweetie," she added, patting her leg, "you're gonna like how this one turns out."

CHAPTER 36

Aki collected Carsyn's cup and her own, setting them on the top shelf of the dishwasher. "It was a wonderful dinner and evening," she said, smiling with a sidelong glance to Jack. "Even if I did discover that my sister has a mean streak."

"I don't have a mean streak," Jack responded, "I'm just doing my part to help you expand your horizons, helping you to discover that there are things of great value which haven't yet been verified by science."

"You've got a mean streak," Aki responded, kissing her cheek, "but I still love you."

"We had a great time," Carsyn echoed, squeezing Courtney's hand, and shaking Jack's. "Next time, it needs to be at our place."

"Sounds great," Jack said, stepping off to collect their coats.

"You guys like barbecue?" Aki asked. "I could do chicken in my mom's sauce tomorrow night."

"We love barbecue," Courtney responded. "What can we bring?"

"Just yourselves," Aki said, smiling, "oh, and Charlie's game." When her cell rang out from her pocket, she muttered, "Now, who could that be?" Within seconds, she squealed, "Oh my God, it's LA." Then, she inhaled deeply, exhaled slowly, and answered, "Hello... Dr. Williams..."

Carsyn leaned back against the wall, crossing her arms tightly over her chest.

"I'm honored to have been selected," Aki said, trying her best to catch Carsyn's eye as Courtney crossed the room to stand beside her. They spoke softly—too softly to hear—as Aki tried to concentrate on the details of the job offer. She fought back nausea when Carsyn clenched her jaw, forced a thin smile, and stepped off. As the front door clicked shut, Aki experienced a life-altering moment. In that millisecond, the perfect job, the best hospital, and the highest salary were no longer what was important. "I'm sorry," she said, "your department is outstanding, and your offer way beyond fair, but I can't accept the position." She wished them luck in their search for the best candidate and terminated the call. "I have to go," she said, meeting Courtney's gaze, and then Jack's as she moved through the foyer, stepping onto the porch. She looked one way and then the other before poking her head back inside. "Her truck's here," she said, "but it's dark, and she's not in it." She took a breath, adding, "I don't see her anywhere."

"There's a bench," Jack said quietly, "right out there, by the water. Here, take a flashlight," she added, placing one in her palm, "I think that's where you'll find her." She looked over her shoulder. "Biboon," she called out, "go with her."

The white, blue-eyed, Siberian Husky fell in step on Aki's heel as she stepped off the porch. She patted his head, saying, "Let's go find Carsyn." She spotted her on the bench as they made their way down the hill. "I didn't accept it," she greeted softly, sitting down beside her.

"You didn't take the job?" Carsyn responded, her mouth open, and her eyes wide.

"No, I didn't take it," Aki said, resting her head on her shoulder as the dog laid down at their feet.

"Why not?" Carsyn asked, nudging Aki's chin upward to meet her eye. "I could tell they were offering you pretty much everything you wanted."

"And more," Aki responded, exhaling softly.

"Then, why didn't you take it, honey?" Carsyn asked, gathering her in her arms.

"Because I realized that by accepting the position," Aki whimpered, "I'd have everything and nothing." Her lips parted and they kissed slowly. "I love you, Carsyn," she said, "and I love my family." She swallowed. "Our local hospital will be good enough."

"And when they get you on staff," Carsyn said, kissing her forehead, "they'll be stepping up to a whole new level." She stroked her hair, peering into her eyes. "And before long," she went on, kissing her again and again, "they'll have the best pediatric ophthalmology department in the country."

"But before all of that," Aki responded with a slight smile, "Dr. Matsumoto will need to re-offer me the job."

"Do you have her number?" Carsyn asked, winking, "probably not too late to give her a call."

"I have it," Aki responded, her lips parting as she raked her fingers through Carsyn's hair, "but I'm busy right now."

* * *

"Thank you," Mo said with a firm nod. "We appreciate you taking a special interest in us." She looked around the waiting room. "I know you bump us to the head of the line every time we come in." The Saturday clinics were always busy with patients being served on a first-come, first-serve basis.

"Now, would I do that?" Aki asked, winking. "Come on back."

"You're Jack's sister," Mo responded with a serious crinkle of her brow, "so I think you would."

"I don't bump you ahead," Aki said, "but it is documented in Jackie's record that he should see me, and it's possible that I make sure that I'm available."

"See, I told ya she pulled some strings," Mo said, nodding to her wife.

Aki lowered to Jackie's level. "Are you ready to hop up in my big chair so that I can take a look at your eyes?" she asked, her smile and eyes widening as she helped him into position. "Okay," she said, holding his gaze, "here comes my bright light." Once she'd completed the exam, she said they were all finished and thanked him for being a good boy. The appointment was a follow-up to his recent surgery, during which she'd adjusted the tension of his eye muscles.

"So, will he need another surgery?" Jenny asked, concern creeping into her voice, "because you said he might."

"No, I don't believe so," Aki responded. "I'm pleased with his alignment." She smiled at Jackie, trading the item from her desk for a small toy. "His eyes will be red for another week or so," she added, "but he's cleared to return to preschool."

"Thank you so much," Mo said, shaking her hand, and then shaking it again before looking at her wife. "Can't believe we've got a doctor as good as this one who's just like family," she said, turning to thank Aki one more time.

"You're welcome," Aki responded with a thin smile.

"So, we're at your place for Thanksgiving this year?" Mo asked, leading her family through the waiting room.

"Yes," Aki said, holding the door open, "at noon."

* * *

"Almost done," Carsyn called out, hearing the garage door roll open, and Aki's car door shut.

"Coming your way," Aki said, pausing to see Lily at the hitching post on her way to the barn. "Decided to clean tonight, huh?" she asked, peering into the bay's stall.

"I wanted them to be clean for tomorrow," Carsyn responded, leaning on the handle of her pitchfork as she made eye contact.

"Oh yeah," Aki said, stepping carefully for a kiss, "I'm sure our company will come out right after dinner to check the condition of the stalls."

"Are you giving me a hard time?" Carsyn responded, arching an eyebrow.

"I am," Aki said flirtatiously, "and I hope it gets me in terrible trouble."

"Count on it," Carsyn responded with a slow smile. "Did you have a good day?" she asked.

"I did," Aki said. "I really like the people in my department."

"That's good," Carsyn responded, telling her that she'd received the call she'd been expecting from the moving company.

"So, we've got a few weeks," Aki said, furrowing her brow. "I hope we haven't overestimated the amount of room we'll have for my furniture."

"We'll figure it out," Carsyn responded, snapping the handle of her pitchfork into the tool holder. "Maybe if we have extra pieces," she added, "we can see if Wabun wants them."

"Good idea," Aki answered, smiling, "especially since she's got an empty room in her new apartment." She shook her head, adding, "God, I'm so relieved that we got her out of that crime ridden area."

"I have to admit that situation was bad," Carsyn said. "But you didn't just get her out of there, you found her a place in that cute little senior housing area over by Jack's parents."

"I know," Aki said, her eyes taking on a sparkle. "It was pure luck that a unit came available." She winked, heading for the door. "I'll go get Lily," she said, collecting a molasses horse cookie. As she stepped outside, she turned back. "I want you to teach me to ride," she said.

"In the spring?" Carsyn asked with a cock of her head.

"No, sooner than that," Aki responded, patting Lily's butt as she trotted into her stall. "She's waited long enough," she added, making the face that she made when she meant business. "A good horse deserves to have a rider."

"Okay," Carsyn answered, taking a soft breath, "we'll start on Sunday."

"That's good," Aki responded, smiling when Lily lipped her second cookie through the bars. "And we need to visit Sylvia's mother one of these days," she continued on their way across the yard. "It's the holidays and she's probably lonely."

"Okay," Carsyn answered, putting her arm around her, and peering into her eyes. "Have I ever told you that I love you?" she whispered, kissing her temple.

"Once or twice," Aki said with a tender smile.

CHAPTER 37

"Carsyn's mom was fearless when it came to her use of color," Aki said, leading her guests through the dining room. "I love that about her," she added, saying that she hoped to be as bold when she decorated the guest rooms. The three rooms, down from the master, were all that remained to be finished at the time of the accident.

"She was fearless," Francisca agreed, "in more ways than just that. I think she was working with an interior decorator," she added, "I'm sure Carsyn would still have the man's name if you wanted to use him."

"I'll check, thank you," Aki said, smiling broadly. "We have punch and appetizers on the hutch," she announced, speaking loudly. "Dinner should be ready in thirty minutes or so. Make yourselves comfortable."

"Can I help?" Francisca offered.

"Sure," Aki responded, "I think we have room for another pair of hands in the kitchen…Oh, and I meant to thank you for picking up Wabun this morning."

"You're welcome," Francisca answered, "but it was no trouble, especially now that she lives right around the corner from us." She took a breath and swallowed. "I'm glad we're getting a chance to know her."

"I know Jack is too," Aki said with a warm smile.

"We used to be afraid of her, you know," Francisca said, her words dropping with the weight of a lead balloon.

Aki paused, pulling two chairs from under the dining room table, and sitting down beside her.

"As a young woman," Francisca continued, "she was extremely mentally ill, and our adoption worker warned us that if we didn't watch her, she'd run off with Jack, or maybe even hurt her."

Aki made gentle eye contact. "I understand why you'd have been afraid," she said softly.

"We never told our daughter," Francisca said, falling silent for a long moment, "that we knew about Wabun—or you." She met Aki's gaze before dropping her eyes to her shoes. "We feel bad about that now," she added, "but there's nothing we can do."

"You should talk to her," Aki said quietly, "tell her how you feel."

"I know," Francisca responded, "but if we do, we might lose her."

"You won't lose her," Aki said, touching her arm. "She's your daughter. She may be upset, but you won't lose her."

"We should've said yes when they wanted to place you with us," Francisca continued with a sniffle.

Aki smiled with the gentleness of her spirit. "I believe things work out the way they're supposed to," she said softly. "I had wonderful parents whom I wouldn't have traded for the world." Tears burned behind her eyelids as she continued. "They're gone," she added, pressing her lips together, "and I miss them terribly."

"If you'll have us," Francisca responded, intertwining their fingers, "we'd be honored if you'd think of us as your parents too."

Aki wrapped her arms around her neck, saying, "I already do."

* * *

"What a stunning table," Courtney said, setting her Jell-O salad at one end. "I love how you've incorporated traditional holiday decor with family items." She touched the candle centerpiece. "Francisca's?"

Aki nodded, saying, "Her mother's actually."

"And the pictures," Courtney continued, touching a small frame. "I don't think I've seen one of Carsyn's parents since before the accident."

"It was a tough evening," Aki responded, taking a soft breath, "one that ended with a good, long cry in the attic."

"You've been so good for her," Courtney said, meeting her gaze. "We can hardly believe the difference."

"We've been good for each other," Aki said, smiling thinly.

"I've got it," Jack blurted out, carrying the turkey in from the grill, "where's Aki?" she asked.

"In here," Aki called out, dabbing a tear, "coming your way." She cleared a place on the counter for the crispy smoked bird. "Mmm... smells good," she said. "So, what have you got?" she asked.

"I was staring into the grill," Jack said, "and I figured it out."

"You figured what out?" Aki asked, tilting her head.

"Your first dream," Jack answered as if she should've known, "you know, the one you keep having."

"Oh, okay, my dream," Aki said, nodding slowly. "Now, I'm with you." She shook her head, adding, "I can't believe you're actually going to share your interpretation with me."

"Of course I am," Jack said, "there's no reason not to. It's about White Eagle," she continued, her words coming quickly, "not the bird, but Wabun's father, our grandfather." She shook her head. "God, I can't believe it took me so long to figure this out." She took a breath. "He's the brave in your dream," she said. "Oh, and the hills," she continued, "they are burial mounds. You're gonna have to describe 'em in more detail so Carsyn can figure out where they are. And the ashes," she went on, pursing her lips, "they're his remains." Her eyes widened. "And the sod," she added, "that's you, Aki."

"Me?" Aki asked, furrowing her brow.

"Yes, you, sweetie," Jack answered, kissing her forehead. "Aki means earth in Ojibwe." She looked around excitedly. "Where's Wabun? I have to ask her something."

"In the living room," Aki responded, her eyes twinkling, "listening to your dad tell a war story."

"It can wait, I guess," Jack said, plugging in the electric knife, and carving. "Dinner is served," she announced, setting a platter of white and dark meat on the table. "You're right here, next to my mom," she added, pulling out a chair for Wabun. She'd introduced her to her parents without mentioning the orders of protection or Aki's placement, confident that Wabun would never say a word. If they ever mentioned them, she'd assure them that she understood.

"I've never seen such a feast," Wabun exclaimed, holding her hand over her heart.

"Get used to it," Jack said with a grin, "because in this family, when it comes to holidays, we pour it on thick." She glanced down the table. "Speaking of pouring," she added, "hey, Dad, would you pass me the gravy?"

"On its way," Mick answered, sending along the mashed potatoes.

"So, I know my mom isn't gonna think this is a table topic," Jack continued, scooping a mound of dressing onto her fork, "but I have to ask Wabun something." She shoveled in the dressing and forked a chunk of turkey. "So, White Eagle's remains," she went on, "what happened to them?"

Wabun took a breath, releasing air through pursed lips. "Well, he wanted to be wrapped in birch bark and buried on sacred ground according to tradition," she said, "but we don't always get what we want."

"I know that you had him cremated," Jack said softly.

"That's all I could afford," Wabun responded.

"I know," Jack said softly.

"I know he was angry," Wabun continued, "because he invaded my dreams night after night." She gave a curt nod. "But I fixed him," she added with a satisfied smile. "I made a snake out of birch and hung it by the front door just like you told me." She touched her daughter's hand, peering proudly into her eyes. "You're very wise, Mitä'kwe."

"Spirits are fearful of snakes," Jack explained, glancing down the table, "so by displaying the snake on her door, Wabun told White Eagle that he had to journey to the spirit world alone." She shook her head, smiling. "Well, I'll be darned," she added, meeting Aki's gaze, "that's about when your dream started."

Aki's eyes widened. "I'm seriously considering borrowing the pattern for the snake," she whispered, leaning toward Carsyn.

"I don't blame you," Carsyn whispered back, squeezing her knee under the table.

"So, where is he?" Jack continued, looking at Wabun. "Where's White Eagle's physical body right now?"

"In my big suitcase," Wabun responded, "at the back of my closet."

CHAPTER 38

They moved through the house, pausing in the doorway of each room. "If we scoot everything to the left," Carsyn said, "we can make room for your grandmother's secretary in here." It was taller than Carsyn, mahogany, with three drawers, and three shelves. She looked over, meeting Aki's gaze. "Or," she continued with a soft sigh, "we could move that piece to the attic and put it there."

Aki furrowed her brow, inhaling, and exhaling—twice.

"They're gonna be here in the morning," Carsyn said with a stare, "we have to make some decisions."

"I know," Aki responded, frowning, "it's just that I hate to change your mom's arrangement."

"Ahh, I should've guessed," Carsyn answered with a slow nod. "Trust me, honey," she continued, gathering her into her arms, "she used to move furniture around just for the fun of it, she won't care." She shook her head, adding, "God, it feels good to be able to talk about my parents without knots in my gut."

"I know, sweetie," Aki said, hugging her tightly, and pressing her cheek to her chest. "And I love getting to know them through your memories." She took a breath, looking around the room again. "Okay," she said, "if we scoot everything to the left, we can put the secretary there, and the loveseat over there."

"Great plan," Carsyn responded with a nod, "I like it." She kissed her forehead, meeting her gaze. "Of course," she added, "at this point, I'd go along with just about whatever you wanted."

"Unsuspecting of my ulterior motives," Aki answered with a wiggle of her eyebrows.

"You don't have ulterior motives," Carsyn answered, peering into her eyes, and kissing her slowly. Then, she smiled, saying, "Secretary, check; loveseat, check…Upstairs, we go…" They discussed using her mom's interior decorator in the guest rooms as they moved down the hall, found places for all of Aki's furniture, and decided to give a large flat screen, two upholstered chairs, and a table to Wabun.

* * *

SOME LOVE WINTER, some hate it, and some shift from hate to love around the holidays. As a Los Angeles girl, Aki fell into the last category. Bundled in a bright red parka with fur around the hood, she crunched down the back stairs and across the yard wearing fleece-lined boots and insulated gloves. "Such a cold baby," she whispered, kissing Lily's frosted muzzle. The horse nickered, watching intently as she removed her glove, prepared to present her with the choice apple. Relic's apple was good too, but Lily's was juicier and slightly larger. As the bay lipped it gently out of her palm, Aki told her that it was Christmas Eve, and promised an even better treat tomorrow.

"Want me to saddle her for you?" Carsyn offered.

"I can do it," Aki responded. She'd practiced every day, catching on in no time at all.

"I know," Carsyn said, smiling, "you can do almost everything now, but I thought you might be cold."

"I am," Aki admitted, "but not so much that I can't saddle my horse." She turned her attention to Lily. "We're gonna ride in the snow this morning," she said, kissing her muzzle. "Won't that be fun?" Her horse moved her head up and down as if responding.

"I was thinking that we might grab dinner at that new Asian restaurant tonight," Carsyn said, tightening her cinch with an extra tug. "What do you think? Does that sound good?"

Aki looked over. "It does," she said, bearing weight on her saddle to assure that it was secured tightly. "But are you sure they'll be open?"

"Yeah, I'm sure," Carsyn said, mounting Relic, "because I called them."

"Mmm, a new sushi chef to try," Aki responded, settling on her saddle, "I love it." She gave Lily a gentle kick, asking for a trot. "Want to ride around the section?" she called out.

"Or through the cemetery," Carsyn suggested. "It's a gorgeous ride after a newly fallen snow."

"Lead the way," Aki responded.

* * *

"Oh my, sophisticated and sensual," Aki commented as they made their way back to their reserved table.

"I'm glad you like it," Carsyn said. "I poked my head in a few days ago and thought it looked pretty nice."

"May I take your order?" the waiter asked.

"Yes, you may," Carsyn responded. "We'll both have a bowl of your spicy lobster soup to start," she said, glancing at Aki. "How about a Sushi Boat?" she asked, meeting her eye. It offered an assortment of their favorite varieties.

"Mmm, that sounds wonderful," Aki said, smiling.

"And, let's see," Carsyn continued, glancing at the menu, "I think we'll also split an orange miso salmon entree…and I guess that'll be it."

"Excellent choices," the waiter responded, winking as he stepped off.

"Mmm," Aki moaned, "am I ever getting the royal treatment tonight."

"Yes, you are," Carsyn answered, peering into her eyes, and adding, "the kind of treatment that you deserve every day for the rest of your life." When their food was delivered, they used chopsticks.

"Would you care for dessert?" the waiter asked, clearing the table.

Carsyn's eyes darted to Aki before saying, "No, I think the fortune cookies will be all we have room for tonight."

"Very well," the waiter responded, nodding as he set one before Aki and the other before Carsyn.

"So, I guess we don't get a choice?" Aki said, chuckling quietly.

"I guess not," Carsyn responded, arching an eyebrow. "Maybe fate's intervening tonight," she added with a playful lift to her voice.

"Maybe so," Aki said, unwrapping, and breaking her cookie into two parts, a diamond ring rolling onto the table. "Oh Carsyn," she murmured, picking it up, and sliding it on her ring finger.

"Read your fortune," Carsyn said softly, reaching across to clasp her hand.

"I can't without crying," Aki responded, "and I think the entire wait staff is watching me."

"Then, I guess I'll have to read it to you," Carsyn said, locking gazes. *"My dearest Aki, when I first looked into your eyes, my heart whispered, 'she's the one.' Marry me, sweetheart."*

Aki's lower lip quivered, saying, "Oh Carsyn..."

"I take it that's a yes," Carsyn responded, scooting in beside her, and holding her.

"You know it is," Aki murmured. "God, I love you. I love you so much."

"And I love you," Carsyn responded, kissing her softly.

CHAPTER 39

With notes in hand, the interior designer made his initial set of recommendations.

"No," Aki said, shaking her head, "no new furniture, not one piece."

Carsyn rested her hand on Aki's upper back. "We're fond of what we have," she added kindly. "Now, what can you do, working within that parameter; you know, to spice things up a bit?"

The sharply dressed man in his fifties raised two fingers to his chin. His eyes narrowed as he stepped back to once again study the room. "What about adding a few pieces of art?" he asked, removing his stylish glasses. "You know, the kind that beckons you to take a second look."

"Now, you're talking," Carsyn said, her smile widening. "Bold colors with flashy pieces of art, that oughta do it." She turned to Aki. "What do you think, honey?"

"I like it," Aki responded, her eyes narrowing, "as long as it's a good fit with your mom's overall theme."

"I'll work up another plan and get back to you," the interior designer promised, closing his binder. "If all goes well, I should have it to you by the end of next week."

"Good," Carsyn said, nodding, "because time is of an essence. We're getting married on May sixth and want the work to be completed prior to that date."

"Should be no problem," the man promised, smiling, and saying, "congratulations."

"Thanks," the couple said in unison.

* * *

The trip had been scheduled, cancelled, and re-scheduled. Aki enjoyed spending time with her sister-in-law, but not enough to devote an entire evening to shopping, let alone for intimate apparel. Carsyn would take one look and have it off of her within minutes anyway. There was no missing that her preference was au naturel. "I don't know," she said, making a face as she examined the skimpy garment. "I'm not sure that I'd even be able to work up the nerve to come out of the bathroom in this."

"You would," Courtney responded, meeting her gaze directly. "Trust me," she added, "you'd open that door, see the hunger in your wife's eyes, and you'd come out." She took a soft breath, looking off, most likely remembering her wedding night. "You'd come out, honey," she continued more softly, "and from that moment on, you'd be done with flannel pajamas."

Aki took a breath through her teeth, holding the virtually transparent piece of clothing against her body as she stared into the department store mirror. "Ewww, I don't know," she said. "The whole thing's made of net and spandex." She curled her upper lip, adding, "And…ewww, it's got a 'V' that'll drop way below my navel."

"That's the idea, honey," Courtney answered. She stepped behind her to see the look. "Mmm, sexy," she murmured.

"Oh, and matching handcuffs," Aki continued, grimacing, "aren't those delightful?" She lifted them, dropping them as if they were a piece of slimy garbage. "Oh, I just can't," she groaned, closing her eyes. "I just can't, Courtie."

"Okay," Courtney responded, smiling a thin smile, "modest it is then." She tipped her head toward a rack of clothing to her right, saying, "I think you'll find what you're looking for over there." It was as if she'd felt an obligation to nudge Aki toward the edge, knowing that she wouldn't go there.

"Now, this is more like it," Aki said, holding a short ivory-colored nightgown to her body as she checked the look in a full-length mirror.

"It's beautiful," Courtney said, touching the silky fabric as she placed it in her basket.

"It is," Aki agreed, "and Carsyn won't laugh when she sees me in it."

"No, she definitely won't," Courtney said. "You two are a perfect match."

"We are," Aki responded, smiling warmly, "and to think I wouldn't have met her had I not come to meet Jack."

"I don't believe that's true," Courtney answered. "If she's your soul mate, and I think she is, you'd have run into her in an airport, a coffee shop, somewhere." As they waited in line to check out, she asked if they'd met with their minister.

"We just did," Aki answered, "and thank God she didn't have a problem with crossing Deadman's Needle to get to our ceremony." She chuckled, adding, "She told us that you guys had an outdoor wedding in the dead of winter, and said that Deadman's Needle was nothing compared to that."

"I'll bet she did," Courtney said, laughing.

* * *

"So, that should do it," Carsyn announced, stacking the last split log on top of a pile that she hoped would last a couple of days. "The dirty work's done, with plenty of time before we have to put on our dress clothes." She wrapped her arms around Aki. "Want to take a walk over to the pavilion?" she asked. It was a short distance from the mounds and the location of their ceremony.

"I do," Aki responded. "I think we're all set, but one last check is probably a good idea." She glanced at the picket line. "You think they'll be okay?"

"Sure," Carsyn said, "why wouldn't they be? We won't be gone more than thirty minutes."

"No reason," Aki answered, "other than anxiety." She took a breath, releasing it slowly. "I'll be fine once we get through our vows and the guests leave." They'd decided that there was no place on earth they'd rather spend their honeymoon than the equestrian campground where they'd first made love, and she was eager to get it underway. "We should do something special tomorrow morning," she said, "you know, like Jack and Courtney did on the first morning of their marriage."

"We should," Carsyn agreed, falling behind her as they stepped across the foot bridge. "What'd you have in mind?" she asked.

"Oh, I don't know," Aki answered quietly. "They got tattoos," she added, her eyes widening with a curl of her lip, "but that's not us."

"Nope, definitely not," Carsyn agreed.

"It needs to be something memorable," Aki continued pensively, "something we'll mention to one another through the years."

"So, we'll think about it then," Carsyn said, threading their fingers together. "Maybe something'll come to us as we go through the day."

Aki paused beside the river, taking in the mounds. "I can see why White Eagle wanted to be laid to rest in this place," she said quietly. "And I'm so glad I was able to describe it well enough for you to be sure that this was where he wanted to be."

"It wasn't difficult," Carsyn answered, "your description of the characteristics that are unique to these mounds was excellent." She slipped her arm around her. "I think he'd like that we're including him in our wedding."

"I do too," Aki said softly.

CHAPTER 40

Majestic oaks provided a backdrop for the ceremony. Sixty chairs were arranged in a half circle, thirty on each side of a wide aisle. Carsyn's guests sat on the right and Aki's sat on the left. Immediate family, a blend of biological and adoptive, sat in the front row. The usher was a friend of the couple. Cheerful wildflowers, embroidered by Carsyn's mother in pastels, accented the hem of the fine linen tablecloth that covered the altar. In the center, sat a beautiful vase of wildflowers gathered by Wabun and Francisca. A blazing fire crackled in the grand outdoor hearth as a string quartet played a variety of love songs. The sun was high in the bright blue sky as the couple prepared to say their vows.

Carsyn straightened her bow tie, turning to Jack. "Do I look okay?" she asked, taking a breath.

Jack nodded, adjusting the daisy on her lapel. "You look great, pal," she said, smiling. "You're one handsome devil."

"I don't know about that," Carsyn responded, tugging at her suit jacket. "God," she groaned, "my stomach's jumping around so bad that I'm afraid I'm gonna throw up." She met Jack's eye, saying, "I don't understand why I'm so nervous." She wrung her hands as she paced back and forth. "It's not like I haven't done this before," she added, shaking her head with her mouth hanging open. "God, I was fine right up until a few minutes ago."

"Yes, you've done it before," Jack said softly, "but this time's different and your body knows it." She straightened her friend's bow tie. "This is the real deal, pal," she added with a tender smile, "so I'd expect you to be a little nervous." She patted her shoulder, adding, "You know, I was just thinking about something."

"What?" Carsyn asked with another tug on her jacket.

"That from the beginning, we've always been just like family," Jack responded, "but pretty soon it's gonna be for real. You'll be my sister-in-law by the time we take a bite out of a barbecue sandwich, and I think that's pretty darned cool."

"Me too," Carsyn said, taking a breath, and releasing the tension in her shoulders. When the minister nodded, she stepped near the altar, looking up as the first notes of *The Wedding March* sounded, and watching Aki walk down the aisle on Mick's arm. Her white wedding gown had lace sleeves, a sweep train, and she was the most beautiful woman in the world. They smiled to one another as she took her place at Carsyn's side.

The minister wore a black robe with a white clerical collar that was visible at the neckline. Draped around her neck was a white stole embroidered with intertwined wedding rings and a cross, symbols of the joining of two before God in marriage. She raised her arms above her head, saying, "Good afternoon, brothers and sisters, I am the Reverend Doctor Zane Winslow and it is with great pleasure that I've come to celebrate the union of Aki Noodin Williams and Carsyn Ellery Lyndon." She smiled to the guests and then the couple. "Getting married is an everlasting promise of love," she continued, "the most significant commitment that one person can make to another. And, it's important that it's made using the right words." With a nod to Carsyn, she added, "The vows are their own."

"That night," Carsyn began, locking gazes with her bride, "when I looked into your eyes, I knew you, I knew that you were the one true love of my life." She swallowed. "I vow to carry you and be carried by you as we journey on one path. I promise to be true and to cherish you until I take my last breath. Today, I take you to be my wife."

"Do you have a ring symbolizing your commitment?" Zane asked. "If so, please place it on Aki's finger as you say her name and these words: with this ring, I thee wed."

"I do," Carsyn responded, placing a golden band on Aki's finger next to her diamond. "With this ring, Aki, I thee wed," she murmured.

Zane nodded to Aki, whispering, "Go ahead."

"My sister told me that I needed to quiet my mind so that I could hear the soft whispers of my heart," Aki said. "She told me to listen as I might for light raindrops on the window, promising that my heart would set me on the right path. She's a wise woman, my sister, and your good friend, Jack Camdon."

Carsyn nodded, meeting her gaze with tenderness.

"So, I did as she told me," Aki continued. "I listened with a quiet mind." She brushed Carsyn's cheek with her thumb. "And do you know what I discovered?" she asked, her tone softening. "I discovered that my heart only speaks one word—your name." She took a soft breath, her lower lip trembling. "I vow to love you always, until the end of our days. I promise to laugh with you, to cry with you, and to always be faithful. Today, I take you to be my wife."

"Do you have a ring symbolizing your commitment to Carsyn?" Zane asked. If so, please place it on her finger as you say her name and these words: with this ring, I thee wed."

"I do," Aki responded, slipping a matching golden band on Carsyn's finger. "With this ring, Carsyn, I thee wed," she murmured, dabbing a tear as it trickled down her cheek.

Zane raised her arms in proclamation, saying, "This afternoon, brothers and sisters, we have witnessed Aki and Carsyn pledge their lives to one another before God, friends, and family." She nodded, smiling. "And by the power vested in me through ordination and the State of Illinois, I now pronounce Aki and Carsyn, wife and wife. What God has joined together, let no one put asunder." She met one and then the other pair of eyes, saying, "You may each kiss your bride."

Carsyn gathered Aki into her arms, kissing her with a fiery passion often reserved for the wedding night.

"The couple invites you to stay for refreshments," Zane announced. "Afterward, they'd be pleased to have you stay for the brief memorial service of Aki's grandfather, White Eagle."

*　*　*

Drums played softly as Jack stepped out in shaman's armor, clothing suitable for the burial ritual. Her rawhide suit was decorated with beads and she wore a full ceremonial mask. "The Ojibwe people believe that to understand death," she began, "we must understand life. Each of us carries our spirit inside us and upon our death it journeys to the spirit world." She offered a prayer and spoke to White Eagle as she released his ashes at the foot of the largest burial mound. Then, she passed a pipe of tobacco, saying that those who didn't smoke could offer it in the fire. As was the custom, her children wore a smudge of charcoal on their foreheads, a signal that they would not follow a spirit back to its world.

Zane read John 14, verses 1-3, and offered a traditional prayer at the conclusion of the ceremony.

"That was beautiful," Aki said, shaking Jack's and the minister's hand. "As was our wedding ceremony," she added, smiling.

"Congratulations, again," Zane said. "I wish you many happy years together."

"Thank you," Aki responded, reaching for Carsyn's hand.

"Jaina and the kids," Courtney asked, "are they okay? They generally come with you when you do a wedding, don't they?"

"Yes, they do," Zane responded, "but they're in Florida for a few days." She went on to explain that their dear friend, Miss Bonnie, had fallen ill, and that they'd flown down to take care of her. "I believe she's on the mend now," she added.

"I'm glad," Courtney said, walking her to her car, and adding, "I know she's just like family."

"Yes, she is," Zane responded.

"Thanks for coming," Carsyn interjected, extending her hand, "and take it easy going over Deadman's Needle."

"You're welcome," Zane responded with a firm handshake, "and you can be assured that I will."

Carsyn slipped her arm around Aki, watching Zane drive off. Then, she kissed her, deeply and slowly.

* * *

"Until our ceremony," Carsyn said, "it didn't hit me that your middle name was Ojibwe too."

"It is," Aki responded, smiling warmly. "Wabun named me before the child protection worker took me from the hospital. My parents opted to honor her wishes, wanting me to have a connection with my Ojibwe heritage. Jack says it means wind."

"That's nice," Carsyn said softly, "Aki Noobin, earth wind." She poked at the fire. "So, I was thinking about tomorrow," she added, "you know, about doing something special."

"You have an idea?" Aki asked, resting her head on her shoulder, peaceful now that the day was their own.

"I do," Carsyn said, pushing a lock of hair out of her wife's eyes. "I was thinking, maybe we shouldn't put off having a baby. When I watch you around little kids, especially babies, I can see how much you want to be a mom." They'd talked about having children, but she'd let fear get the best of her, and wanted them to hold off. "Anyway," she went on, "I was thinking that taking a first step toward becoming parents, maybe calling for an appointment with your gynecologist or checking with the sperm bank or something, might be a special activity for us to do tomorrow morning." She touched her cheek, peering into her eyes. "We don't have to if you don't want to."

"Oh, but I do," Aki responded softly.

EPILOGUE

ABOUT ONE YEAR LATER

"You about ready?" Jack asked, poking her head through Wabun's bedroom doorway. "I let myself in, I hope that's okay."

"It's your key to use as you please, Mitä'kwe," Wabun responded, her eyes twinkling.

"I know," Jack said, "but you deserve your privacy."

"I keep no secrets from my children," Wabun answered. "That's why I gave them both a key to my apartment."

"Okay, okay, you made your point," Jack said, a gentle smile crossing her face. She handed Wabun her purse and lifted her lightweight jacket off of a hanger. Even in July, her bio-mom complained that she was chilly. She shut the rear door after Wabun had clicked her seatbelt.

"Grandma Wabun," Charlie said, holding a colorful drawing between his fingers, "look what I made for you."

"Oh my," Wabun responded, "I've never seen such a beautiful tulip. I'll put it smack-dab in the middle of my refrigerator." She kissed the top of his head, saying, "Thank you, sweetie."

"My mama brought you some tea," Lizzy piped in, "but it tastes nasty."

The corners of Courtney's lips turned up slightly, but she didn't say anything.

"Oh my little one," Wabun responded, "I think you'll find as you grow older that taste and looks aren't everything." She caught Jack's eye in the rearview mirror. "The Mitä'kwe, she's always made wonderful teas." As many times as Jack had told her that she could call her by her name, she always insisted on referring to her as Mitä'kwe.

"You think Aunt Aki will let us ride Lily?" Lizzy asked hopefully.

"I doubt that she will today," Courtney responded, "because she'll be busy with our picnic. If you ask her nicely though, I'll bet she will on Saturday." When Lizzy's lip jutted out, she added, "Besides, after dinner you'll be busy playing games."

"I know," Lizzy said, running to greet the horses the moment their car stopped in Aki's driveway.

Carsyn grilled burgers, veggie and beef.

Aki cooked corn-on-the-cob and made potato salad.

Courtney brought store-bought coleslaw and chocolate cake.

Charles and Elizabeth showed up late.

When the feast was over, the family prepared for what was to become an annual family tradition—a summer softball game.

"I set up a chair for you," Mick said, nodding to Wabun, "Over there by ours."

"Thank you," Wabun responded, scooping up enough sugar-free caramel corn for the three of them. "I'll be over in a minute," she said, collecting three drinks. As she settled into her lawn chair, Jack positioned home plate and the bases.

"She always could strike 'em out," Wabun said, watching her oldest daughter pitch.

"Yep, she had quite the arm, even in grade school," Mick agreed. "Still does, it seems, because striking out Carsyn was no easy feat." He reached for his drink as the inning changed.

"Look at Courtney go," Francisca screamed. "Oh, and there goes Mo. She's got the ball. Come on, come on, come on…"

"And it's the ninth inning," Wabun announced. "Oh look, look, look," she squealed, "Charlie just stole second base."

"Well, I'll be darned," Mick said, "his mama must be slower than she used to be." They cheered for both teams because both rosters were family. "Well, it looks like that's it for today," he said, collecting their chairs as his daughter picked up the bases. "It was a good game!"

"Yes, it was," Wabun agreed, "a good game, and a good day."

"It's not over yet," Francisca said, glancing toward the picnic tables. "Look, they're getting ready to dish up the sugar-free lemon sorbet."

"So, before we serve dessert," Aki said, smiling as she met Carsyn's gaze, "we have something to show you." She passed around an ultrasound taken on the previous day.

"Oh my goodness," Courtney said, "you're pregnant." She hugged her, still looking at the picture. "Aww, and look at those sweet little babies," she added, her eyes twinkling.

"Pregnant with twins," Jack responded, shaking her head, "well, I'll be darned." She reached into her back pocket for her cell as everybody was hugging everyone.

"Two more grandbabies," Wabun cried softly, touching the image.

"Hey Sis," Jack called out, "check your email."

Aki's eyes narrowed, looking her way.

"The snake," Jack continued, "it's a symbol of sexuality and the cycle of life. In your dream, you were sitting on Carsyn's spirit animal when it bit you twice. Interpretation of this one was a no-brainer." She got up, hugging her, and shaking Carsyn's hand. "Congratulations, you two," she said with a wide grin, "you're mamas."

* * *

"That was a fun day," Aki said, slipping into her nightgown. To date, Courtney had proven to be right about the pajamas.

"It was," Carsyn said, smiling, "and everyone was excited about the babies."

"Yeah, only eight weeks along," Aki said, touching her stomach, "and already they're bringing joy to our family." She turned back the sheet, pleased that her dreams had ended on their wedding day, and feeling differently about the one with the snake. "I'm exhausted," she added, kissing Carsyn, and climbing in.

"Me too," Carsyn agreed, scooting close, and spooning her rear. "Night, baby," she whispered, planting a kiss between her shoulder blades.

"Night, sweetheart," Aki responded, drifting off the moment her head hit the pillow—*And the white eagle swooped low in the valley to join the gathering, a celebration of sorts.*

"So glad you could make it," the bear growled.

"Wouldn't have missed it for the world," the eagle responded.

"What am I doing here?" Aki asked, crinkling her brow. "I'm sure I was sleeping." She rode bareback on a colorful Appaloosa inside a circle of guests, carrying two babies, one on each breast. A deer and two fawns frolicked nearby.

"You know why you're here," the white eagle responded as Aki's reins became a snake, slithering down, and biting her belly.

"Oh my God, it bit me," Aki cried out as fangs drew blood.

"Just once," the bear growled.

"That'll make three," the eagle screeched happily.

"Three's a good number," the bear responded.

ABOUT THE AUTHOR

K.A. Moll / Cade Brogan is a best-selling author of lesbian fiction. She writes stories about lesbians, burdened by past trauma, who find healing in the love of a soul mate. K.A. holds a bachelor's degree in psychology and a master's degree in social work from the University of Illinois. She also holds a master's degree in counseling from Eastern Illinois University. Her professional background is in mental health and child welfare. She enjoys golf, bridge, and of course, reading and writing lesbian fiction. She is the author of eight novels (*Soul Mates, Coming to Terms, Haunting Love, Change of Heart, For A Moment's Indiscretion, Blue Ice Landing, Whispers of the Heart,* and *Twice Upon A Train*) writing as K.A. Moll. In addition, she is the author of two novels (*Close Enough to Touch and Deadly Deception*) writing as Cade Brogan. All of her books are available in print, digital, and audio formats at www.kamoll.com. She resides in central Illinois with her teacup Maltipoo and her lovely wife of thirty-three years.

ALSO BY THE AUTHOR

Writing as K.A. Moll

Soul Mates
Coming to Terms
Haunting Love
Change of Heart
For A Moment's Indiscretion
Blue Ice Landing
Twice Upon A Train

Writing as Cade Brogan

Close Enough to Touch (Book 1)
Deadly Deception (Book 2)